To.

The Enchanted Reader

By

Molly F. Law

impspired@gmail.com

Cover designed by Steve Cawte

ISBN: 978-1-915819-84-0

For my mother
and the memories we hold dear

OTHER TITLES BY IMPSPIRED

Maybury –
by Mary Farrell

Polygon -
by Domonique

Leviathan –
by Jae Jenkins Scott

Hyperbola -
by Shelly Norris

Spun Tales and Woven Words –
by North Coast Writers

The Mining Muse –
by Marc Darnell

Apartmentalized –
by Dan Flore III

"Reading is the sole means by which we slip, involuntarily, often helplessly, into another's skin, another's voice, another's soul."

~Joyce Carol Oates

"There are a few places in my life that I've found more ruggedly beautiful than the Highlands of Scotland. The place is magical—it's so far north, so remote, that sometimes it feels like you've left this world and gone to another."

~Julia London

Part I

Chapter 1

Eoin

In the water's reflection, Eoin saw a young and virile king of Scotland staring back at him, even though he was centuries old, according to his rough calculations—and he certainly felt it. He never asked to be king, he never felt good enough, even though that *was* apparently his destiny from the very beginning.

Sometimes he felt, as he sat by his favorite waterfall in Caledonia, therefore, the most secluded place in the kingdom, that he was slowly losing himself—part of his soul that no one could see. He leaned back, hoping to feel the cool, refreshing mist of the waterfall on his face, but it was just a foolish wish. He felt utterly lost and could not contemplate a way to feel otherwise.

Eoin buried his musings deep within himself as he stripped down. He gave himself a running start so he could jump off the nearest cliff by the waterfall. The earth crumbled under the balls of his feet as he dove without a second thought into the dark, torrent water below.

He allowed his body to sink as deep as it could go

before swimming up for air. Through the distorted lines of the water, he saw someone waiting for him, not just anyone, but *her.* Even though his lungs burned in protest, begging to inhale, he was reluctant to surface. If only he had the ability to breathe underwater, becoming one of the mythical creatures that, as legend had it, existed in the Mealt Falls. But he could no longer avoid this conversation.

He didn't bother concealing himself as he surfaced, didn't even notice if she feigned embarrassment—she was a lady only in title.

"How long do you plan to stay out here?" Adalind adjusted her jewel-encrusted crown atop her auburn hair.

He pointedly avoided her gaze as he dressed and took a small amount of delight in her passive frustration. He shook his head to dispel the excess water from his golden-brown curls to exacerbate her further. She wiped away the beads of water that landed on her porcelain skin and emerald velvet gown.

"Forever, I suspect. And you?" He sat by the water's edge waiting for her prepared speech that he had heard countless times, contemplating what to say differently that would make her understand, to leave the fantasy she had built in her head. He briefly wondered if he had embellished anything that, in turn, created or reinforced the absurd notions she had.

When he was out here, he spent hours, if not days, camped out in the trees behind the falls—showering, fishing, swimming—without having to spare a single thought of his purpose of who or, more aptly, what he was, but with her around, he was forced to face that existential question.

"You can't." She bit the consonant at the end hard. "You must come back, you're the king, for God's sake." She came to sit by him, and he turned his head away. "And I am your gorgeous queen, poised to aid you in power, and so much more…"

"I'm the king of nothing, Adda, and you're certainly not my queen, nor my lover." He removed her sliding fingers from his arm. Maybe it was the use of a familiar name that gave her some sense of affection, he thought, but he had known her for ages, affection had nothing to do with it.

Eoin never fully comprehended how Adalind so easily molded herself to a life that was forced upon them. How she never even tried to understand him in how he felt about the burdensome positions fate had so cruelly dealt them.

"Please, Adda, just leave me here for my soul to rest in peace."

There was agony in almost feeling—on the precipice of having feelings, in which lay the acute pain and frustration. The land around him, the one they all called home was perceived as dull and lifeless and it could no longer fulfill him.

All he wanted to do was run away…run through the shaded glen, with bountiful woods described to perfection, yet without its vibrant color he knew to exist in another world. So, instead, he attempted risky jumps and climbs that in any other world would be fatal—just as he did today and every day before Adalind's intrusion.

"The court is in absolute chaos, as *you* well know." She said ignoring his plea, unable or unwilling to see his inner turmoil. "Nobody knows what to do with themselves, some have gone further on the fringes of our dimensions than even you! If we were to have a visitor—"

"It's been years, no one is coming, you don't have to worry about that." A loud clattering suddenly filled his ears, bright stars on a pointed structure blinded his vision until golden blonde hair wisped across his face, and he saw a young woman tossing and turning in her bed.

The vivid sensations left as quickly as they came. He leaped to his feet away from the bank of the loch unsure of what he was trying to find. It was like trying to capture a dream once sleep had fully departed.

The last tendrils of his vision dissipated as he heard Adalind's sharp voice from over his shoulder, "Even though you don't see yourself as the king, Eoin of Accolon, you're still our leader. You were made to be one, and I know you're finding it hard to ignore it out here." She came around to stand alongside him, observing his makeshift camp.

He felt self-conscious of what his new choice of home would reveal about himself the longer she stood next to him and walked into the clearing with the view of the castle on the hill.

A ray of sunshine, perfectly positioned to accentuate the dark stone of a foreboding Scottish fortress, indicated the lateness of the afternoon. Adalind followed just as he designed and placed a soft hand on his shoulder. He needed her to go back to that prison, that enclosure, that tomb.

"Go home, Adalind. You belong there, not me. Come to think of it, I entrust you with any and all leadership responsibilities. I bequeath it all to you, as my lawfully *written* wife." He dropped to his knee in the most dramatic fashion and took her hand. She yanked it out with a huff that amused him beyond words.

"Eoin, I cannot hold that position by myself! You know I can't convince everyone to return when the time comes…"

That's all it took, the very lie she came to believe, for him to lose every ounce of his composure. "We are in a *book*!"

He let the weight of it, the echo of his firm utterance sit there for her to comprehend. When tears began to brim at the edges of her eyes, he exhaled and whispered, "We're a story, Adalind, that's it, we're characters someone created. We won't have a visitor, *a reader*, any time soon. It's not real…none of it is real."

Bitterness hardened his heart as he heard his words spoken aloud for the very first time—seemingly cementing their fate. Yet, he felt a hint of warmth spread across his chest, reminiscent of his vision. It faded along with Adalind as he watched her walk back to the castle.

Alone. He felt alone for the first time in his life—like he no longer belonged in his own skin.

Chapter 2

Catriona

I smelled the misty mountains of Scotland before they came into view. I felt the familiar terrain of the craggy hills under the soles of my white trainers as I ran until I heard thunderous footsteps coming up behind me. I saw a pair of strong calves, those of a man from my peripheral vision. I heard my heartbeat thunder in my ears. It was not fear of this man's presence alongside me but a keen sense of belonging that I had never felt in my entire life. The blood drained from my head as my gaze traveled up his legs. He was wearing nothing. He sprinted ahead and jumped from a cliff before I could see his face or utter a scream.

The loud persistence of my mobile's alarm, on top of the clattering of pans from the café below my flat in Paris, jolted me awake. I dreamed of my home in Scotland often, but this dream felt different. It felt like another world—ancient and forgotten. I felt heat bloom in my face as I recalled the man running beside me. The warmth of his presence dwindled, and an unexplained emptiness soon took its place.

After a few minutes of staring at the popcorn ceiling, I eventually shifted in my narrow bed and heard the crinkling of papers. I had fallen asleep reading again, which would explain my dream, but the weight of my book felt oddly comforting. *What if the spell that books put us under made its way into reality? And could the reader have the same effect on the characters just as the characters affect the reader?*

I glared at my reflection, as my bleary vision finally adjusted to the light above the bathroom mirror and considered what look I should go for today. I decided to let my hair, which was not bright enough to call blonde, nor dark enough to call brown, fall past my shoulders in its natural waves. I felt lucky that all it took was a shower the night before with a small dab of set-in conditioner to form semi-symmetrical waves.

I pulled on a feather gray pencil skirt with a pale pink blouse, a navy blue blazer, and my nude pumps, for today was an important day. My boss scheduled a meeting with just me two weeks prior, which only meant one thing:

a promotion.

After I graduated from university, I waited a whole year to go from intern to editorial assistant and another two years to be now considered for an assistant editor position. To many, this wouldn't seem like much of a difference, but in the publishing world, this was a big deal, especially for someone only aged twenty-five. I also needed this promotion to prove my father wrong. To prove that my dreams could fit into the practicality of making a decent living.

I crossed the flat, trying not to let my heels click on the hardwood too loudly. I mostly wore a wide variety of colored ballet flats that I could saunter every which way without even a second thought of waking one of my flatmates. I swooped up my taupe laptop bag from the counter that contained a granola bar for breakfast and my thermal coffee mug.

As I clamored out into the Parisian streets, I tried to focus on the trees that lined the pavement, which consisted of leaves with the faintest shades of red, yellow, and orange, slightly muted against the green that still dominated—still clinging to the warm memories of summer. Yet nothing could dispel my nerves at the promise of a promotion at B&P Livre Publishers. I breathed in and out the crisp autumn air.

I still wasn't used to wearing heels as my ankles wobbled all the way to the nearest metro, avoiding the eyes of the people who quietly sat on benches and read the morning paper or a novel at their leisure under the multi-colored trees that protected them from the streams of the morning's sun with the shade they still provided.

That bright view that could be captured by any competent painter, like my boyfriend, Henri, was quickly replaced by the dull, dark, and monochromatic colors of the metro.

My time of romantic observations was over, and I automatically converted into the mindless commuter—only focused on getting to work with as little to no contact with the world around me. Just like the prior morning. And the one before that. The misty mountains of Scotland were slowly fading away.

I finally caught my breath as the black revolving

doors of the office came into view. Today, I was entering them for the last time as an editorial assistant. I would ride the lifts down as an assistant editor of fiction.

Around mid-morning, in the middle of sorting the manuscripts on my desk, I heard, "Catriona, let's grab a cuppa." Teatime was an established and acceptable excuse for a break as an editor, especially for the only two British assistants in fiction. Gemma was in PR and was expecting a promotion of her own any week now.

I hurried behind her, admiring her brilliant outfit of the day—a bright orange top with puff sleeves and matching orange, yellow, and brown plaid trousers. I always marveled at how she looked. She had dark brown hair with two proportionally placed braids that had gold leaf-like bands strategically placed, and she wore peach eyeshadow and red lipstick that complemented her dark skin tone.

"Good call, Gem. I really needed it." I said as I caught up to her with a company mug in hand.

"Oh, I could tell. You made that same face on our very first day. I looked over and saw a fresh-out-of-school nervous wreck, almost convulsin' tryin' to create the world's best poker face—and you have the exact same look today."

"Hey! I can keep a poker face." She looked sidelong at me, skeptical. "I always beat my brother." I couldn't help but laugh then. She was right as that argument had so many holes, we could have Swiss cheese with our tea—*odd combination, though.*

"I needed to get ya outta there. You're a shoo-in for that promotion, but confidence is everythin' and you need that right now." Of course, I knew that tea wouldn't magically boost my confidence, though it did have other medicinal and magical qualities; it was Gemma who would do that. She always had.

"Thanks. I guess I just wanted to dial back my guaranteed expectation in case I don't get it, so I'll only want to sob for an hour instead of all night." I laughed at my own joke, knowing it was one hundred percent accurate, and Gemma knew it as well.

"You're gonna get it." She stated matter-of-factly. "I'm so sorry I can't join yous tonight, especially leaving you to celebrate with your vapid flatmates and that what-you-call a boyfriend of yours."

I grabbed a tea towel and softly snapped her arm, "Rude."

"You know I call it like I see it." She gave me a lopsided grin. "Anyway, I'm meeting Gabriel's family for dinner, and rescheduling is the one thing to absolutely guarantee a boyfriend's family to not like you. You save that move for after you're married." She gave me a coy smile as she popped the kettle on.

"Oh, so you're thinking about marriage, huh? Why Gemma-need-to-find-out-your-middle-name-Bell, are you thinking about marrying Gabriel?" I wriggled my eyebrows as I plopped my bag of English Breakfast into my mug.

"First of all, it's Rosalee, and second of all, shut up."

"I'm loving this! Gemma Rosalee Bell is contemplating a white gown and domestic life with wine entrepreneur, Gabriel Segal. I think the world might just end. What about all your talk about not being like your parents back in York?" I held out my mug as she poured in the piping hot water.

"I'm about to change the subject, so the aforementioned heat is back on you, but in my defense, we all become like our parents, don't we? Besides, Gabriel hasn't met my folks yet, and…" she paused to contemplate something I doubt she had even admitted to herself, "maybe I do want that life." I gasped as I fixed my tea with two sugars and a splash of milk. "It makes sense, doesn't it?" Gemma gave me a wry smile. "I mean, I became friends with the whitest, most goody-two-shoes to ever live in Paris."

"*Moi*?" I said with mock humor, placing my hand on my chest.

"*Oui, vous.*" She paused to chuckle with me. "I don't know why we're talkin' about it. I'm just meetin' his mum and little sister, and just like you, with your unconvincing strategy about your promotion, I'm not expectin' anything other than what's in the present." She dinged her spoon on top of her mug, indicating that line of conversation was over. "Don't worry, lady, you've got this.

Now breathe in the healing vapors and calm down."

"I didn't get chamomile."

"I know it's English Breakfast like you always get, but it might make you even more of a jitterin' mess." I stuck out my tongue as we split off.

My tea didn't even last me to lunch. As Gemma said, it did seem like I was a shoo-in, but there was a tiny voice in my head saying I wasn't good enough—I wasn't enough compared to everyone around me.

The voice in my head grew increasingly louder until it was the unmistakable thick Scottish mumbling of my father, *"You know if you take this job in Paris and fail, your mother and I can't bail you out—with rent, grocery money, none of it. What do editorial assistants even make? Penance I believe to what it costs to live in Paris, let alone save for your future!"*

I physically shook my head to dispel the memory—to erase this conditioned line of thinking that threatened to cripple me if I would let it. Instead, I thought of my mother and little brother, which instantly soothed the sharp pang in my heart.

Five minutes before my meeting, I walked down

the gray-carpeted halls that had a red geometrical pattern every two steps. I counted each one to control my breathing. I flipped over my wrist to check the time on my watch before I ascended the only staircase that led to Ludo's office: I was four minutes early. I'd give it another minute.

Before I lifted my hand to knock, my boss Ludo Dupont ushered me in. He looked amused. "You didn't have to do that little dance; you could have just come on up."

"How did you?" I stopped and remembered that there was a line of windows in his office that overlooked the office. "Of course, I just figured the managing editor of fiction and nonfiction would be on the phone or have a previous meeting that would keep him from noticing me calculating the exact time to enter his office."

Our light-hearted laughter made me realize how foolish I had been to be so nervous. We had a great rapport, and I knew he wouldn't call me for such a formalized meeting to give me bad news.

"Catriona, please have a seat." I set my supplies

down and tucked my skirt under as he pushed the chair in. He went around and sat opposite. He was wearing his navy-blue tie with white sailboats on it that matched his snow-white coiffed hair—he was in a good mood. He only wore this tie on the Fridays he was to take his boat out with his husband and two children.

"Now, I'm sure it will come as no surprise to you that we are promoting you to assistant editor." A tiny smile appeared on my face even though butterflies were rattling in my stomach, winged with joy. "I'm glad to see you're pleased." His small smile confirmed my internal delight.

"Thank you, Ludo for this opportunity. I know I will do this job well and to the best of my ability."

"Of course, you will, that is why I am offering you the position." He said as he slid a piece of paper over to me. "Here is the official letter with your new salary. You just need to read it over and sign." He took a pen out of his suit pocket. I took it unceremoniously and tried not to overtly stare at the 2,000-euro jump. I read over the acceptance letter and signed my name with an overstated whip on the "t" at the end of Lamont.

"*Bien*, now first thing Monday morning, I want you in here a half hour early so we can go over your new list of responsibilities, although I'm sure you'll be familiar with most. We'll get your office set-up and introduce you to the handful of authors and agents you'll be working with directly." He nodded as if this was all he wanted to discuss today.

I stood and grabbed all my unnecessary folders. "Thank you again, Ludo." We shook hands and as I made my way down, I calmed every nerve ending in my body, knowing he was watching me from those windows again.

As I made it back to my desk, I smiled to myself at my total professionalism. All I wanted to do was run as fast as I could to Gemma's desk and scream. I had successfully made it without any faux pas until she saw my widening smile and screamed herself and hugged me. I dropped all my papers and looked up to see a humorous smile plastered on Ludo's face.

After enduring a whole commute with a jazz musician on the metro, I finally reached the ninth spiral of concrete stairs of my flat. My flatmates, Madeline and

Estelle, were already getting ready together for my celebratory drinks, as I wrenched my key from the lock.

I averted my gaze as Estelle was completely naked. She was not the least bit shy when it came to her body and nor should she be, but it was still very French of her—and hard to get used to. Madeline had only a purple bra and a pink thong on.

Estelle was from a small countryside town in France. She lamented, more often than not, that she couldn't properly bake in our tiny attic space as she could in her parents' previous seven-bedroom estate in Lorraine.

In vague bits and pieces, she told us that her parents went bankrupt because of bad investments on her father's part and were now head-to-head in a nasty divorce that left Estelle to fend for herself in the "dirty, squalled streets of Paris with two passably nice flatmates." Luckily, Estelle's previous, leisurely dabbling in French cooking led her to a three-star restaurant as a sous-chef a block from our flat.

Madeline was a bubbly American photographer who lived and saw life to its absolute fullest. She had little to complain about and gave out hugs like they were pieces of gum. I only gave her half of a British disapproval of American confidence as I was technically half-American on my mother's side. Because of that, I could partially embrace Madeline's buoyant, albeit abrasive personality more than others.

As they continued to dress, I was glad Henri wasn't coming. He had only met my flatmates once, but I hadn't appreciated the way he leered at Madeline and the way she seemed to have welcomed it with her shiny and flirty personality that drew anyone she had ever met to her. She had that classic girl-next-door look with long, thin brown hair and bright blue eyes that were all but a beck and call.

"So? Are we having happy drinks tonight or sad?" Madeline said as she pulled up her black, slinky sized-two dress. She turned without a word and Estelle zipped her up.

"Oh, definitely happy!" I held up my hands in a failed attempt at jazz hands with my laptop bag and mail barely hanging from grasped fingers.

"*Magnifique!*" Estelle exclaimed. "Now, letz go get… how do you say, Madeline?"

Madeline turned around and belted out her trademark laugh, "Lit?"

"*Oui,* letz go and get lit!" I had to laugh as well. Madeline was Americanizing Estelle more than I could ever make her Scottish. Both our accents were hard to distinguish, as they had a certain harshness to them, but in completely different ways. Madeline acted as a translator most of the time with her straightforward lilt.

"Two seconds," I said as I dashed across the flat. Even though it was my celebratory night, I had an overwhelming feeling that if I didn't hurry, they'd leave without me. I had always gotten the feeling that Estelle and Madeline were the popular girls at their schools—that their worlds revolved around cute boys, makeup, and the latest gossip. Whereas in school, I tended to fade into the background—and my world revolved around the works of William Shakespeare, Jane Austen, and Robert Burns.

I pulled on my gold sequin mini-dress and looked at myself in the mirror, turning side and front ways on my tip toes to determine if this would pass not only for my effortlessly gorgeous flatmates, but for my boyfriend later.

After two or three turns, I decided to put on a three-quarter-sleeve black cardigan—I never liked my arms enough to leave them completely bare.

I darkened my eyeliner, put on shimmering gold eyeshadow on top of my day's existing makeup, tried to do my lips as red as Gemma's, then puffed up the existing waves of my hair and sprayed a spritz of my perfume that was aptly called, "Mon Paris."

Madeline and Estelle were apparently ready to go as they had migrated toward the door. Estelle had one hand on the handle as I bent down to put on my black pumps. When I came back up and grabbed my clutch, she had opened the door, tapping her heel and giving me a tight smile.

Estelle was wearing a light pink silk chiffon dress, obviously designer, that covered her five-foot-eleven, slim body perfectly. I came over and stood with them, waiting for either to make a move to leave, but an awkward silence fell over us instead.

"Let's get turnt, bitches." Madeline finally yelled and slapped my ass—I yelped in surprise. I blushed out of embarrassment but smiled at the gesture of inclusion.

***

After a night full of shots, selfies, dancing, and falling off a stool—and after no deep conversation passed between the three of us, which, even when sober, never really happened either—all I really wanted was for the real party to start at Henri's.

I figured I had gotten a taxi back to his place at some point during the night but wasn't entirely positive when. His door was open, and I stumbled through the threshold.

"Hi, Basby," he slurred. He was just as wasted as I was, and I liked it. He put out his cigarette on his tin ash tray as wafts of smoke billowed around him. He swaggered over to me, beer in hand. He handed it to me, and I took a long swig then embraced his mouth fully on mine. He tasted of tobacco and oranges.

He broke free for just a second to remove his white under shirt and he tried to concentrate on my face. "Your eyes are like blueberries on a," *hiccup*, "sunny day in the gardens of Versailles." That's all it took—I was his—and then the darkness consumed us both.

I woke up to the morning light streaming in through Henri's white-sheered curtains. My head was bursting from the previous night's celebrations and what was normally a romantic way to wake up, I found the bright morning sun unbearably intrusive. I was also completely naked—I assumed Henri and I came back to further those celebrations, but my mind was having trouble grasping the full memory.

When we had first made love, I couldn't believe it was happening. For the first time in my life, I got the guy I wanted, and our love lived up to every fantasy I never dared to dream—making love in Paris with a genuine Parisian artist.

Candles were lit, soft music lolled in the background, and the evening breeze blew softly through his window, causing those sheered curtains to sway softly as he stroked every part of my body like he did a canvas with his brush. Terribly cliché, but when you've lived it, it's nothing but pure bliss. Though that bliss started to wane pretty early on, I began to find it in the little things. Just the look of him—that he was mine.

Henri was lying on his stomach with his raven black hair covering his face. I gently stroked it back to see his eyes. They were fluttering so lightly that I couldn't help but wonder what dream world he must happily be in. I inwardly hoped he was dreaming of me.

I grabbed the tartan robe from the bedpost, the one I had given him for Christmas that was of my family tartan. Although I was the one who wore it more often than he did, I reminded myself that was what a girlfriend did with their boyfriend's clothes. I quickly ignored the otherwise nagging feeling of disappointment and rejection and walked around the flat trying not to wake him.

My first mission was coffee and aspirin, but my pace immediately slowed as I walked by the paintings that littered his living area, rendering my hangover void. I scanned each canvas that bore every female form with their corresponding ethereal faces staring back at me, yet there was never mine.

Every week, I would look to see if I had quenched his artistic inspiration, to see my face reflected back at me in some array of color and texture, but not yet. No matter how passionate I thought our lovemaking had been the night before—that might have possibly ignited his imagination—the morning's harsh light extinguished it.

A sob welled in my throat. I tried several times to work up the courage to finally ask why he never painted me, his lover for all intents and purposes. And who were all these women? Were they painted from still life? Were naked models in my boyfriend's flat while I was buried in manuscripts at the office all day?

Professionally, I knew it was perfectly legitimate—*if everyone remained professional that is*. That thought didn't help the swelling in my throat or the slight burning that accompanied it from forcefully holding back tears.

I stared at one painting in particular: a young woman with porcelain skin, hair golden like the sun, bright blue eyes, a pouty mouth, and a perfectly smooth body—impossibly skinny as well.

She almost looked like me, a me if all my flaws

were gone, if I lost fifteen or twenty pounds—a me if I was divinely enhanced. If I tilted my head just so, she could almost be me, *a me he desired.* The swelling began to dissipate as I chose to see this painting in a more positive light.

At that moment, I felt Henri's arms snake across my waist, his head bowed to rest on my shoulder. "Claudia," he whispered in my ear and kissed my neck. He was still naked from what I felt on my back.

I ignored the creeping thought: was it a reaction to me or to "Claudia?" I realized; she wasn't me at all. He must have felt me tense because he said she was just an imagination that just came to him, "a figment of the Greek goddesses—the only real beauty man was able to create."

He squeezed me once then headed for the kitchen. I turned to see his lean backside, stumbling to walk in a straight line, he was still hungover, as was I, but I felt horribly sober.

I wanted to confront him once and for all, to receive some sort of closure, but he turned back to me and gave me his signature smile—a mixture of playfulness and seduction—and just like that, my protest died in my throat, along with the uneasiness of never belonging, even to him.

Chapter 3

Eoin

"We are in a Book!" He still heard his own words echo in his mind long after Adalind's crestfallen form had left him. Her intrusion caused in him what he feared it would, why he wanted to stay in the deep below. He began to remember who, or more accurately what he was, a character, the main character of this *book*. Just the word—that reality—made him recoil.

His world seemed to darken as he trudged along, a world that others deemed as exciting and revolutionary—a novel that philosophers and historians asserted, since its conception, "is not just about a clan, a culture, or nationality, but a state of mind in which Scots can find their place in the world and thrive."

His book opened to a variety of readers for centuries; he felt the touch and tempo of every individual reader, but none reciprocated the magic he and the other characters created with each new page. He may have been the leader of his fellow characters or "actors," but that was all, and that, to him, was nothing.

He knew that he was just a struggled creation of his author—yet his book hadn't been read in years, decades even—to his absolute bewilderment and, somehow, utter relief. What he could gather was that they were sitting on a shelf collecting dust. He was a bit embarrassed that he felt quite content with this arrangement as he grew tired of the façade that came with his fellow characters and even a reader.

Those around him longed to have another reader, to feel purpose once again—*one I can no longer give to them on my own.* He stooped down to pick up a smooth rock, reveling in the feel of its cool, smooth surface as he gazed out over the dark loch before him.

When he was first created and the world around him constructed itself bit by bit, he thought this was everything he ever wanted, but the author had finished writing, and as each reader approached, the newness and surprise became redundant and obsolete.

Years in the book started to wane on him and there were days he wanted to explode with frustration, but they were all obligated to follow their paths when the book opened.

He let out a sigh of relief, expelling every frustration he had kept bound and hidden deep inside the day their last reader took them to a new place—a place where the chance of a new reader was practically non-existent.

As the days and what he expected were years passed, he felt the burden that was always on his shoulders lift, and a new sense of freedom wash over him—a sudden excitement of a future unknown.

He had been fascinated with the world outside the book, where his readers lived. This was enough to keep him going through the repetitive nature of being read. In its novelty, he would mark what year it was in his reader's reality, noting items that were not described in his world, listening for their names, for their functions. Mrs. Sessford was their last reader in 1985. As his most uninspired reader ever, with her advanced age and senility, she never made it to the end—he was glad to be out of her hands.

He surmised, after some time, that she had taken them to another location, but the book was only opened for a split second and he wasn't present for it, so there was no telling where they were or what year it was. And he couldn't care less.

He slowly came to realize that he would never make it out into the fascinating world of reality. He was stuck in his book as if it were his own personal tomb—*The Adventures of Accolon*—so it might as well be.

The only similarity Eoin seemed to possess with his written character was his stubbornness, which now manifested in hostility and a deepening depression. Everything he felt seemed to reverberate out into the world around him—pushing everyone else away. *That's their problem. I am their leader, after all. This is my story. Isn't it?*

He ran the stone through his fingers once more before perfectly lining it up to skip it across the water's surface in rapid succession. He lost count of its skips, but his lips ticked up in satisfaction at his seemingly one-acquired talent.

The sound of a twig snapping interrupted his ruminations, and he turned around slowly—no one seemed to be there—but he knew well enough that it was no mere forest animal. He chuckled, "You've lost your touch, Valez."

A dark figure appeared from behind the cleft of the rock. His smile seemed to reach all the way to his ears, one that felt sinister, one of mischief. True, he was written as the villain of Eoin's story, an evil sorcerer who craved power and recognition, but when the book was closed, Valez was his closest confidant.

Valez was the only one with whom he felt entirely himself. There was no need to explain his contemplations and Valez, in turn, shared with him his innermost thoughts. Eoin was always open to Valez's observations, advice, and sometimes, even his criticism.

"You're absolutely right, I'll need to hone my skills once a reader cracks open our book and reads of my dirty subterfuge at your unwitting expense." He laughed heartily as did Eoin, yet he often found Valez's hope for a reader rather grating. Eoin would chime in ironically even though Valez was always resolute.

"You mean *if* a reader opens our book. It's been ages, my friend, no one is coming." Eoin moved to his, what he called, living section, hoping to entice Valez to a game of chess.

"That's actually what I wanted to talk to you about." Eoin tried to hide the shock on his face, but knew he failed as Valez smiled revealing his teeth.

"Well, you can save your breath, Adalind has already been here, trying her absolute best to convince me to come back, poor soul, but she failed. And I'm sure she ran to you as her next ploy to persuade me back to the castle."

"Actually, no. I have not seen her, and that's only part of what needs to happen." Valez said simultaneously smoothing down his raven black hair that barely touched his shoulders.

"What do you mean?" Eoin slowly stood, knowing the chance of a friendly game of chess was about to be out of the question.

"We need a reader, Eoin, it's no longer a question of want, but need. The pages are beginning to fade, which means our world is going to be destroyed." Valez turned and made his way to the clearing, just as Eoin had when he was trying to get Adalind to leave, where the castle was in plain sight.

"You're exaggerating, surely." He suddenly felt claustrophobic, walls closing in on his newly found freedom.

"I am not. We need a reader to thrive, to stay relevant, to have purpose. That's plain in the way you've chosen to live." He gestured dismissively at Eoin's camp. Walls began to rise around Eoin's heart, ones he had for every other character here, yet he never foresaw needing to build them for Valez.

"So, what are we to do then? It's not as if you can conjure a reader for us, your powers are fake!" Valez's face lost all of its remaining humor, a comment Eoin aimed to wound, but had little hope that it actually would.

His bright yellow eyes darkened, "Eoin, I can't convince crucial characters to come back, some have ventured farther than even you. At least you've kept the castle in view." He scoffed injuring Eoin's pride, once again, for his carefully crafted sanctuary. Maybe Valez had a point, part of him wanted to stand alone, but perhaps subconsciously he still wanted to be needed, to be easily found.

He relented, "What do you want me to do, Valez?"

"You need to become the leader you were written to be, gather the stragglers, and change your attitude. Everything you feel reverberates out, no one is reading, because the book isn't exuding light, magic, its natural appeal. It's truly all up to you, no one else can do what you can." He sighed and whispered, "Believe me, I've tried."

That caught Eoin by surprise, but the uneasiness left as quickly as it had come. He knew Valez supported him and had his best interests at heart. "It's not that. No matter how uplifted my spirits, no reader will see the difference, it's useless." He closed his eyes and tears began to prick at the edges, begging for release. "We're somewhere where there aren't people. I haven't felt the weightlessness of being picked up, have you?" He felt his throat work up and down to keep his tears at bay. "Our fate is sealed, Valez. Come back when you've woken from your delusions."

Chapter 4

Catriona

I left Henri's flat after a quick cup of coffee with the blaring sun reminding me again of my nasty hangover. I was steamin' drunk last night. Henri told me he had someone coming over today for a session, confirming my long-held suspicion. A woman named Lou-Lou was on her way over to pose half-nude in all her supposed glory.

Lou-Lou. Obviously the most made-up name if I ever heard one. The fact that it sounded so French made me think she actually wasn't French, just trying to pass for one to get this amazing gig with my brilliant boyfriend, the artiste.

My mobile rang loudly in my purse, distracting me from further thoughts of Henri and Lou-Lou. Before locating it, I dared to dream it was Henri ringing to tell me that he had canceled his appointment and all he wanted was to spend the entire day with me in bed.

When I finally retrieved it from my oversized bag, the screen read, "Mum." I sighed in disappointment but regained a happier demeanor as I answered. "Hi, Mum!" I held my free hand to my ear to drown out the street noise of a typical Saturday morning in Paris.

"Hi honey, how did your meeting go yesterday? Did you get the promotion?" My heart swelled with pride and excitement. All thoughts of Henri and Lou-Lou vanished as I remembered everything I had achieved.

"Yes! I got it! Sorry, I should have phoned you yesterday, must have got caught up in celebrating straight away."

"That's my girl! Oh, I'm so proud of you, honey. I knew you could do it! No, don't be silly, of course, you had to celebrate with your friends." I heard nothing all of a sudden, and I thought the call might have dropped.

"Mum?" I pulled my phone away to check if it was still connected. The call screen indicated it was. "Mum? You there?"

"Yeah, I was just looking for your dad. He can't come to the phone right now, but he says he's really proud of you."

My heart sank just a bit. There was always something off between me and my father. We were close in the way family had to be on the outside. Even together, there was no animosity or ill-word spoken, just an imaginary wall that had been built until "dad" was just a familial description. We loved each other; I just wasn't sure we liked one another. He certainly didn't approve of my move to Paris. Maybe that's when the wall finally cemented itself.

No wonder he wasn't overly pleased by my promotion. A promotion was final—a clear signal that my life would be here from now on. I think he secretly wished I'd fail or that the editorial assistant position would only be temporary, and I would have to come crawling back to Crieff and get a job at our local pub—just to have the inward satisfaction of being right but lamenting for everyone else's sake how horrible it was.

"Tell him thanks," I sighed. "Where's Jeremy?" My voice lifted as I said my little brother's name.

"Oh, he's off with his school mates, it's Saturday, you know, and he's a teenager, which means he's never home. Where are you now? You sound like you're in a tunnel or something."

"Is that better?" I ducked under an awning to

escape the street noise.

"Much. So, what are you doing today as newly appointed assistant editor?" Her tone carried a hint of worry, while at the same time, prying curiosity about my life—a well-honed skill exclusively branded by mothers worldwide.

"Oh, I've just left Henri's, I'm going back to the flat now to take a wee nap before going out again with Gemma to get drinks. She wasn't able to join us last night." I intentionally hurried past the mention of Henri, hoping she wouldn't comment. There was a pause, this time I didn't have to check to see if we were still connected.

"And how is he?" I ignored the slight edge in her voice.

"He's fine. He's working today." I tried to make my voice neutral, trying hard not to convey the ache in my heart that still resided there after Henri rushed me off. To be honest, I wanted to leave quickly, so I didn't have to run into Lou-Lou. My mind would just run on a never-ending reel of them together if I knew what she looked like. Futile, however, as I would find out anyway with the addition of a new canvas the next time I came 'round.

"Catriona, are you okay?" Damn, mothers can pick up on everything, and with that, my façade began to crumble, but I didn't want to break down in front of Tiffany's on the *Champs-Élysées*. This wasn't *Breakfast at Tiffany's*. No way I could get away with crying in front of total strangers like Audrey Hepburn.

"Mum, I gotta go. I'm okay, really. I love you. I'll ring tomorrow." I hung up before she made me burst into tears—before her "I love you" made me sob like a wee little girl needing her mummy. I was just knackered and hungover. It wasn't my mother or my boyfriend who was making me sad, maybe I was about to start my monthly, who knows, but it wasn't Henri—it was me.

My meant-to-be half-hour nap turned into a four-hour nap, and I awoke just under the wire before I had to leave to meet Gemma on the *Champs de Mars*. I saw that she texted with a change of plans. I smiled at my phone, knowing exactly what she was up to.

As I walked under the iron curve of the Eiffel Tower, I knew where she would be. She had taken me to a place on the green with the best view of the Tower when we first realized we were kindred spirits, and a wonderful friendship blossomed.

She waved as I approached, she had a lovely floral blanket laid out that had champagne on ice, a picnic basket with a baguette, assorted cheeses, and fruit—all arranged in a picturesque presentation. My heart swelled at the view in front of me. Gemma had prepared a celebration so elaborate for me, more than my flatmates or even my boyfriend had done. Tears pricked at the corners of my eyes.

All my life, for my family and friends, alike, I always went above and beyond, but rarely got the same in return. It never consciously bothered me, as I knew not everyone's personalities were the same, knowing their hearts were in the right place.

What Gemma did for me, I instantly realized how fortunate I was to have her in my life, and maybe it was okay to want more from those around me.

"Hiya," I said as I approached the blanket. She stood and gave me a hug.

"Alright? Here, I've already got you a glass. Cheers!" Our glasses clinked in harmony, as did the notes of citrus and honeysuckle that overtook my senses, and the fizziness left a delightful buzz on my tongue.

"Yeah, good," I said as we both lowered ourselves onto the blanket to get comfortable, while balancing our near-full glasses. Gemma was a generous pourer.

"You looked as if something was wrong. You okay?" She looked at me concerned and I swallowed hard not wanting to give anything away.

"Yeah, fine. I think I'm just a bit knackered. I had only just woken up when you messaged," I took another swig of champagne, not quite sure if it was wise to have more alcohol in such a short timeframe.

"As long as you're sure. I had the sudden urge to go and kick Estelle or Madeline's arse, or Henri's too, if I'm being honest." She downed her drink and replenished her glass. I held out mine to her for a second.

I always got the feeling that Gemma didn't like Henri, but I never pressed her—I never wanted to know how she truly felt. I don't think she quite understood, not since Gabriel was an absolute dream to her. *Such a good man. The kind of man I always dreamt of loving me.*

"No, nothing to worry about." I quickly changed the subject. "So, how did dinner go last night? Come on, tell all!"

She blushed and pushed her braids behind her ears. Before she answered, she took another sip of her champagne and tore a piece of baguette. I picked at some grapes and cheese as I waited for her to swallow. She was stalling on purpose. I let her stall so she could tell me in her own time.

"Oh, Cat, they are just as lovely and pleasant as he is! I was a little afraid that there would be, at the very least, some unconscious bias because I'm black, but there was none, not even a hint or a whisper." She spread some brie on a piece of baguette and took her time, her face became peacefully contemplative and reminiscent, as if she was back at that dinner, revealing exactly how she felt then.

She took a bite and continued, not quite finishing her mouthful, "I saw how he became such the man he is, and, um, I can't imagine doing life without him."

"That's great, Gemma! I'm so pleased for you, really! Are you going to finally take him to meet your family in York?" I made a piece of baguette just like hers and added a bit of raspberry jam on top. She smiled up at me like there was more.

"Yeah, actually we are." She paused as if she were not sure of herself.

"What is it? You know you can tell me anything."

"Catriona, we're sort of pre-engaged, or half engaged if that's a thing, don't think it is, but we're makin' it ours." She was glowing and laughing at the shared inside joke between her and Gabriel.

"Congratulations!" I embraced her, careful not to spill her drink. "What does that mean exactly, half engaged or pre-engaged…or whatever?"

"Well, Gabriel went off with his mum for a few minutes and left me and his sister, Emily, alone, which she is exactly what I pictured if I were to ever have a little sister. And when they came back, he had this cheeky grin on, one I've never seen before, his mum's eyes were moist, and he came 'round my chair, got down on one knee—it was far too conventional for my taste." She finished her second glass, but despite her best efforts, I knew Gemma loved his proposal.

She cleared her throat to continue, "I said yes, of course, but since he hasn't met my parents yet, and he was able to propose in front of his family, I want him to do it all again in front of mine next week! That's why I'm not wearing the ring. Oh gosh, Cat, I can't wait to show you, it's absolutely gorge, but I don't want to color your impression too much before you see it."

An unusual feeling passed through me, a feeling I could not quite put my finger on. "Gemma, I'm absolutely over the moon for you! No one deserves it more than you." I leaned in so our cheeks were touching and kissed the air. "You know," I leaned back, feigning nonchalance, "This is going to take a lot of planning, where do you propose to begin?"

"I know exactly where," she gave me a cheeky smile. "Catriona Lamont. Will you do me the honor of being my Maid of Honor?"

"Yes, a thousand times yes," I placed both hands

over my heart.

"Good, because I don't know two shits about weddin' plannin'." She grabbed the almost-empty champagne bottle and offered me some. I shook my head letting her have the rest.

"Well, that's why I'm here, I've given myself awards for my organizational skills."

She spurted her newly drunk champagne. "You have not!"

"Only in my head, does that count?" She rolled her eyes at me, but giggled, nevertheless. "Well, first, we'll have to come up with a guest list, I know I'll need a plus one," I said, about to continue my list of first-things-first, until I noticed the look on her face. "What?"

"Nothing, I mean the wedding might not be for another year or, at the least, six months."

"So? That sounds like plenty of time to plan."

"That's not what I mean," she said, unable to meet my eyes.

"I can't have a plus one?"

"You might not need one is all I'm sayin'."

I took a sharp breath in. The moment I had been anticipating finally arrived, I couldn't believe she chose my celebration, and now hers, to do this. "Alright, come out and say what you want to say about Henri, but then I want to hear no more of it, because he *will* be coming to your blow-out, star-studded wedding—that I'm certain of." It was my turn to take a big swig of the champagne I had largely been ignoring.

"I just…I don't think he's the one, that's all. I figured he was just a bit of fun, a Paris cliché you were going to get out of your system once you settled here, but…" She paused, her eyes searching my face—I had made it stone cold. "Cat, it's nothing you don't already know, I'm sure. He's just—"

"'Just' what, Gemma? Because, you know what? I think…I think I might actually be falling in love with him!"

She let out a sarcastic snort. "Don't be daft. And I'm sure he feels the same way, does he?"

I couldn't answer that question, and she knew it. I looked down at our picnic celebration, which was so perfect, but now it felt tainted.

"Christ, Catriona, you call me every other week weepin' your eyes out sayin' how you wish he'd treat you and that you're finally going to say somethin', but you never do, then when he's wonderful—*as you say*—you never talk about it, until he's gone and done somethin' to upset you, *again*. I just..." I looked up as her tone shifted to something more tender. "I just don't like the way he treats you, that's all. You deserve the world, Catriona, and he's not it, you know that, don't you?"

I put my glass down and wrapped the food I had opened while I listened to her unfounded criticism of my boyfriend without meeting her eye this time. She stopped me as I finished wrapping the last of the brie. "Catriona, please understand, I just love you too much to see you continue down this path with him. Believe me, I understand how you feel."

"No," I said wrenching my hands out from hers and standing up. "You don't know at all. You have the perfect fiancé in Gabriel, and I'm not entirely sure what you did to get him."

She stepped back as if I had slapped her, which I

might as well have, but I pressed on. "But I know Henri is the best I'm going to do. I'm tired of waiting for the men we read about in books. They're not real! So, what if he's not perfect…but to be here alone, with no one…" It wasn't until I tasted salt at the corners of my mouth that I realized I was crying.

Gemma was the one person I could let my guard down with and feel safe, but I never thought I'd need one to protect myself from her. "I've got to go. Congratulations again. I'm sorry."

I spun on my heel and ran without looking back, even as I heard her calling after me.

***

I ignored the pit in my stomach about what Gemma had said about Henri as he sporadically texted me on Sunday. He was clearly clueless at what my responses were truly saying—that I needed him with me, to console me. I also ignored Gemma's persistent calls and text messages. I wasn't ready to face her yet—wasn't sure who should apologize to whom.

The thought of Gemma caused too many mixed

emotions that I didn't want or need today. All I wanted was for all of that to go away so I could just go to work and set up my new office as the newest assistant editor of fiction.

My phone began to buzz in my hand as I approached the office building, it was Mum. I rejected the call, I couldn't talk to her right now, I needed to be here a half-hour early—five more minutes would make me late. As I entered the elevator alone, I saw she left me a voice message. *Good, I can check it at lunch and ring her back.*

I was tingling from head to toe as Ludo showed me to my new office—an office with walls—and a window with a view, of nothing in particular, but it was still a view, nonetheless.

"I hope this suits," Ludo said as I came around my desk and set my purse on the floor. My computer and laptop were all set up. My office phone, and things from my previous desk were already here. I had ignored Gemma as Ludo and I walked past the open desks to the corridor of offices, but to my dismay, I could still see her cubicle from this angle. As I inadvertently met her eye, I shifted my stance, so I only saw Ludo's delighted face.

"Very much, thank you, Ludo, for everything." He dodged my gratitude and indicated the sheet next to my desk.

"Here is the list of everything that now falls under your purview. Have a look. Everything should be in the shared folders, which there are more now that you have access as the assistant editor." He winked at me as I sat back in my new chair, adjusting quite nicely to my new position. My heart leapt in my chest as I glanced over the mounting list of new responsibilities. "You'll be great, Catriona. If you have any questions come find me, yes?"

"Yes, will do. Thanks, Ludo."

"*Bien*." And with that he left me to get comfortable. I dashed for my purse and removed several items I now wanted on the great expanse of my office desk. A picture of Mum, Dad, and Jeremy, and several assorted knickknacks and coasters.

I looked out the window one more time, marveling at how my life was progressing. How well-pleased I was on this average Monday morning, average to most, I should say. As I mused, it began to rain, and I turned back not wanting a reminder of Scotland and the small life my father wanted me to live.

The morning progressed into late afternoon without notice until my stomach growled so insistently, the sound reverberated off the four walls of my new office and out into the corridor. I had apparently skipped lunch all together. Normally, Gemma would swing by my work area, beckoning me to our small lunch spot and group, but we were still in the middle of a fight. Largely on my part, I realized, the longer I sat with it, but I wasn't ready to admit it.

As my inbox began to fill with new writers, other departments, and Ludo—all needing my immediate attention—I became more and more frantic. Paris faded into the background. I ignored all incoming calls and texts on my mobile, but I couldn't ignore my office phone, "*Bonjour*, Catriona Lamont."

"Ms. Lamont, your father is on line one." My father? Why was he calling? He never called. I would maybe get a text every two weeks with a brief hello, just a check-in, really, but to call me on the first day of my promotion? I wondered if Mum had put him up to it since I missed her call this morning.

I almost told Leanne to have him call back or leave a message, but something urged me to take the call. Maybe something happened to Jeremy. I was the only person who was able to talk him down from his frequent panic attacks. Maybe that's what it was.

"Uh, thanks, Leanne." I pressed one, "Dad? What is it? Is it Jeremy? If it's just a chat, I can't really stop right now."

There was no soft music playing or a camera that slowly panned away as he said the very last words that I ever imagined I would hear.

"Catriona, your mother passed away this morning." It was solid and definite, as if someone called to tell me that I needed to pay rent or the bakery was out of my favorite croissant. No words came to mind.

"No, Dad, you must be joking… you're lying!"

"Catriona." His voice was subdued. He had never used my name like that before.

"No, she… she just left me a message, sorry I haven't checked it. And I can't come home this weekend if that's what you're trying to do." I started to panic. My voice came out so loud that several people looked in as they passed by in the corridor.

The sound of Dad's soft sobs through the phone was enough to tell me this was real, it was true. Part of me needed to see her to really believe it. I never understood how people just believed their loved ones were really dead without seeing it for themselves, but the other half of me now understood.

"How?" Was all I managed to say. My mother was healthy! A woman in her early fifties. She hadn't been ill or diagnosed with anything, unless both my parents somehow kept that from me and Jeremy.

"She was in a car accident on her way to the store." He began to cry, to hyperventilate.

I started cataloging what I needed to do right there and then. "Dad? Dad? Where's Jeremy? Is he okay?"

"Yeah, yeah, he's here with me. Catriona, I know you just started your new position today. Your mum is so proud, she couldna stop talkin' about it all night." He chuckled but it was quickly absorbed by another sob. He realized he misspoke. He forgot to change the verb tense. She *was* so proud.

"Okay, tell him I'm on my way. Let me make arrangements here, and I'll text you my flight information." I hung up before my father's grief, and I imagined my brother's grief, overwhelmed my own. I looked around my office, everything stilled. Not five minutes ago, this was my new life. All was well.

I stood up, buttoned my blazer, and smoothed down the edges. Mechanical movements were all my brain would allow me to do.

"Catriona?" I looked around. I was suddenly standing in the doorway of Ludo's office. I hadn't registered walking down the corridor and up a flight of stairs. "Catriona? What's wrong?"

"My…my…my mum died." That combination of words felt odd as they tumbled out of my mouth. I almost laughed and wanted to tell him not to worry, nothing was wrong, that I'd get right back to work, but when Ludo's face fell, I reached out and grabbed the door frame to steady myself.

"S-sit down, *mon cher*." He guided me to his little conference table that sat in the corner with his grand mahogany desk just opposite. "What happened?"

"I don't know for sure. My…" I swallowed hard. "My father just called on my work phone, my *new* work phone, that she had gotten into a car accident this morning, no more details, nothing." I blinked unsure what to do. *What should I do?*

Ludo cleared his throat and hesitantly put his hand on my shoulder, uncertain of the level of comfort he should show me as my boss. "Let me call someone for you, Catriona. Hmm? They can take you home so you can get back to Scotland."

I looked up then, confused. "No, no I can't. I have so much work to finish today. Jean Claramont is waiting for feedback, for edits for his first fifty pages." I momentarily forgot I had told my dad I would book a flight home right then.

"Catriona, no, you don't have to. We'll work

everything out while you're gone. You need to go home and be with your family right now, you understand? Your job will still be yours when you feel you can return. I will clear everything with HR, yes?" I hadn't noticed that he lifted me off the chair and was now guiding me toward reception.

"I had Leanne call a taxi for you, they're here. They'll take you anywhere you want, on me." I slowly nodded, not completely processing everything.

Gemma had followed Ludo and me to reception, and I saw she was carrying my laptop bag that I left in my office. A glaze fell over my eyes. I wasn't able to process the looks everyone was giving me. I had never seen Gemma look like that, so unsure as she moved to approach me. I held up my hand to her. She didn't need to try to console me.

As I went to turn toward the elevators, she grabbed my shoulders and pulled me into her embrace. I fell on her shoulder for just a second but pushed her back, not wanting to break down here. Not yet. I took my bag from her and took the available elevator. A quiet tear escaped as the doors closed shut, and I was alone for the first time since the call.

I gave the taxi driver my address at first but changed it to Henri's. I needed to fall apart with someone I felt safe with, someone I felt connected to, someone who would realize, who would realize… I couldn't finish the thought without completely falling apart.

Memories of my mother's face blocked my vision in short spurts, all portraying her varying emotions and ages. Tears threatened the barricade that I had carefully erected.

The driver's insistent announcement of my arrival saved it from being broken. The volume in which he delivered it made me think this was not the first time he had said it. I tipped him generously for the trouble.

I braced myself, already on an emotional bridge. I didn't know if Henri would have the supports to hold me or would he let me fall? I buzzed his flat. A few seconds went by, and then, without a word over the intercom, the door gave a piercing ring, demanding a quick entrance before it automatically locked. I pulled it open without hesitation—I didn't need a lecture on how to enter his building properly right now.

As I let myself into his flat, Henri was finishing up another canvas. There was cash on the table, and the flat looked relatively sparse, indicating he had sold a few, to my relief.

"Grab a beer, babe, if you'd like, just throw a euro or two there." He motioned to the counter, implying my cash should go with the other women's money if I were so inclined to have one of *his* beers.

"No, that's…that's okay." I sat down on the couch, finally letting out the air I didn't realize I was holding. Still, he didn't look at me. "I have to go back to Scotland for a few days." I looked up to gauge his response. He just nodded. "I should be back next Monday at the latest. I know Ludo will give me the time." Another nod. "Baby, can you stop painting and come sit by me, please." At that, he looked at me, took the brush out of his mouth, and slowly sat down. Our knees lightly touched, which gave me the strength to carry on.

"What is it? What's going on?" He said a bit

exacerbated that he had to stop mid-paint.

"Umm," I swallowed the stone that was in my throat, the one holding the barricade I wanted more than anything to stay intact. I didn't want to cry before I knew how he would react. I never cried in front of Henri, although that's all I've ever wanted to do with a boyfriend—to just completely lose it, even if it was over something as simple as missing the metro or because the store was out of my favorite ice-cream—and he'd be there to listen and provide comfort. I looked back up, and he was staring at me, waiting. "My mum died this morning." It was barely a whisper, but the barricade still held.

He hugged me fast, stroking my hair, and I allowed my body to melt against his, but still, I did not cry. I felt him more than I heard him clear his throat, "I can't go with you if that's what you are getting at." He kissed the top of my head and continued to smooth my hair. "I'm sorry, *mon petite,* I just have so much work here to do, and I've never met your family, and well, under these circumstances..." He trailed off, lifting my head to hold my face between his hands. "I mean, is that alright? You can always call and text me, yes?"

I nodded just as he did moments before. He kissed my cheek and stood, offering me his hand. "I'm sure you have a lot to prepare. Let me… let me take you home on my moped, *s'il vous plaît.*" He held my hand over his heart with his hands overlapping mine, his eyes pleading, but a part of me knew he didn't mean it.

"No, you don't have to go through all that trouble," I said as he held my hand tighter and insisted in a placating manner. "Really, it's fine. I'd rather be alone anyway. I just wanted to come tell you what…what happened and that I'd be out of the country, that's all."

I grabbed my things off the floor and turned away—the Dutch boy with his finger in the dam had left, and water was slowly making its way through. I wanted to leave before it was obliterated.

He walked me to the door and kissed me. He parted my lips to deepen the kiss, even though that was the last thing I wanted. His tongue felt its way around my mouth, and when mine did not reciprocate, he finally let me go. I waved goodbye and left to find myself another taxi.

My flat was dark when I finally got it open. I presumed Estelle and Madeline were out on the drink together, and for the first time, I felt grateful to be left out. I had been holding back a wall of tears for so long that a ball of hiccups formed at the base of my chest. I dropped my bag, and my knees followed in quick succession.

My breath came in short, quick bursts, then deep moans followed. I calmed myself before I hyperventilated into unconsciousness, which wouldn't be the worst thing, but I quickly changed that course of action. I had only tonight to mourn my mother before I landed in Glasgow. After that, I would have to pull myself together again to take care of my brother and father and all the funeral preparations.

I leaned back to rest on my heels until, at long last, I gave into my tears. I stayed there, in the entryway, until I lost all feeling in my feet. The tears kept falling without any effort—they were in free fall—as I made my way over to my desk. I had to take a tiny break to book my flight back home. Then, I would allow my bed to freely take me with all I had to give.

Return flight tomorrow morning to Glasgow from Charles De Gaulle: booked, paid, done. As I closed my laptop, I thought, *What the hell? How can my mum be dead?* Reality crashed around me, and I couldn't move, I couldn't think of anything else. Most of my inner thoughts went unheard, with no one to share them with, and the one person I could was now nonexistent.

At that moment, I became lost deep inside and didn't know if anyone would be able to find me. I shut my eyes tight and held the tears in for as long as possible.

I reluctantly opened my eyes, and a flood of hot tears fell as if I had tipped over a bucket of water. I listened as my heart echoed in the silence until sleep finally conquered.

Chapter 5

Eoin

"The pages are beginning to fade, Eoin; our world will be destroyed." No matter how hard he tried to ignore the warnings Valez had delivered, Eoin could not get his friend's crisp voice out of his head. Eoin looked around his makeshift camp, hoping to go about the rudimentary routine he had crafted to keep himself busy—to keep himself blissfully unaware.

He ran his course, bounding, plummeting into the dark waters below, showering in the waterfall, hunting, and playing chess against a ghost opponent. Yet, with every distraction, he found himself confronting the form of Valez, repeating the charges he brought to Eoin's feet.

He lashed out at the figment of his imagination—so real, he thought, just maybe Valez was able to conjure the powers that were written for him. A ridiculous thought, but his own mind continued to haunt him in the shape of his closest friend.

When his distractions no longer worked, knowing exactly what would silence Valez's badgering pleas, he packed a bag for a journey, one to round up all his characters and to survey the borders of his book—to see if, in fact, the pages and its words were beginning to fade.

As he suspected, the haunting form of Valez no longer berated him, so he took his time in gathering supplies and took increasingly longer than necessary to forge the route in his head.

He might have procrastinated another fortnight if it wasn't for the sight of Adalind and her blazing red hair coming over the hill. He gathered his sack, sinking his teeth into an apple as he strode off toward the castle stables. He had no desire to look back, knowing she was smiling in satisfaction, no doubt sent by Valez to hurry his mission.

He even ignored the amusement plastered on the horse master's face as he entered, turning his back without a word and focusing his attention on the first horse in the stall. He lifted his hand in invitation for the chestnut-brown horse to eat what was left of his apple. He moved down the stalls and packed the saddlebags of his written noble steed, Arian.

"Finally finished hiding, are ye?" He heard the gruff voice over his shoulder. When they had a reader, the lowly horse master would not dare to insult his king with such audacity, but when the book was closed, they were all on the same level. Why, then, he thought, was he commissioned, even forced to gather the characters and monitor the borders?

I guess everyone can just pick and choose what character descriptions apply or not for one another when it suits best—Adalind certainly does for herself and me.

"Apparently so. You're looking good yourself, Grant. How's the wife?"

"She's fine, and yours? Sent ye on this wee errand, has she?"

Eoin ignored him as both men knew full well their wives were only in name when the book was opened, but unlike Eoin, Grant desperately wanted Beatrice to be his wife no matter the circumstance.

"Give Beatrice my love." Eoin didn't wait for what was sure to be Grant's clever rebuttal as he clicked for Arian to gallop at full speed.

He made his way to the most popular plot points in the book. Ones further in that only he, Adalind, and Valez were privy to as the rising action came to its climax, and the "extras," as he called them, were no longer needed.

Unsurprisingly, the extras that Valez had listed were all accounted for at the Black Cuillin Ridge, colloquially named Gorgon's Mount.

Gorgon was written as a fierce dragon, a creation of Valez's powers to end Eoin's life, yet the ultimate plot twist was Valez's life force was preserved in Gorgon, thereby destroying Gorgon would destroy Valez as well.

Eoin was always in awe of how much fiction differed from reality. He and Valez would break out in hysterical laughter whenever the reader closed the book as they went from mortal enemies to the best of friends in a single moment.

Gorgon, on the other hand, was nothing more than an oversized lap dog when the book was closed.

As Eoin entered the entrance of the damp cave, it suddenly had a celebratory air of a *ceilidh*—everyone singing, dancing, and retelling Scottish folklore. This reader hiatus not only suited Eoin, it would seem.

Gorgon was basking in the excitement of having almost every character there—with the attention he received along with leftovers that were given to him as a treat as well as accidental floor drops. Eoin wondered why he didn't think of coming here to escape Adalind's advances before.

The atmosphere was infectious. The royal minstrels played a festive jig, a tune they would never play confined in the walls of the throne room when they had a reader. Eoin surveyed the cave to see how others spent their furlough, for all intents and purposes. He realized he was so busy in his isolation that he had no idea what was going on in his own kingdom.

He knew without a doubt that Valez knew exactly where everyone was—only humoring Eoin; that this was his quest to find the missing extras. He fumed a bit in the corner seeing the royal chef, jesters, knights, even his royal advisor, Finnian, dancing, drinking, and laughing—all without him—without a reader.

He suddenly felt a clap on his back. "Good to see

you, my liege." Eoin rolled his eyes at the man written as his Knight Commander and best friend. He couldn't stand Samuel Ward in any state, especially inebriated as he was now. "What are you doing here?" He shouted in Eoin's ear despite it being relatively quiet in the corner Eoin sequestered himself in.

Eoin had a sneaking suspicion that he wouldn't be able to round everyone up, nor did he think he'd be able to convince them to go back to the castle to await a reader—who he was less than convinced would show up any time soon.

He plastered on the merriest smile he could muster and turned to Sam. "My friend, there's a bit of a problem that I need taken care of, one that can be handled only by what you have to offer."

"Eoin!" He belched, not noticing Eoin recoil from the stench of ale and steak and kidney pie. "I never thought you'd rely on me in this capacity without the opening of the book. What is it you need, my Lord?"

Eoin lowered his voice, taking Sam by the shoulder, giving the whole act an air of classified distinction, "I need you to gather everyone together and head back to the castle." Sam narrowed his eyes. "I need you to lead everyone back and take charge until I return, you understand? It is of the utmost importance that everyone is accounted for with what is to come." The look of pride that swelled across Sam's jubilant face let Eoin know he had him.

"Anything for you, my King." He bowed low and then stood tall. "I shall tell them the party can continue at the castle! Don't worry, I'll keep them occupied until your return." Sam offered a dramatic wink. "Incidentally, where are you returning from?"

Eoin told him he was securing the borders in case they would eventually have a reader. Something both men knew was improbable and a purely pointless campaign. However, this was enough for Sam, as he didn't have the inclination to inquire further and only ever wanted Eoin's approval.

As Eoin predicted, Sam stood on a table and stomped his foot, attracting everyone's attention. With a tankard of ale in one hand, he cleared his throat and began his resounding speech, "My friends! Too long have we wallowed in this squalor." Everyone's mouths hung agape—the only sound came from Gorgon, who growled in disapproval.

Eoin gauged everyone's reactions, afraid his plan would backfire, until he locked eyes with Sam and nodded in encouragement.

Sam inhaled, puffing out his chest, "This has been a grand party hosted by our own fantastic Gorgon the Ferocious Dragon!" Gorgon nodded, accepting the compliment, and Sam pressed on. "However, it is time for a change of scenery, a place that has not seen debauchery or infamy in ages!"

A round of "huzzahs" and tankards lifted high filled the room." Sam, clearly surprised by the enthusiasm but nevertheless chuffed, continued, "The Castle of Accolon!" Sam raised his ale toward Eoin. The air seemed to be sucked out of the cave all at once, and for the first time, everyone turned and noticed his presence. There was silence as they seemed to be waiting for his response.

The crowd moved to accommodate him as he

moved toward the table. He grabbed the tankard from Sam's hand and raised it to the ceiling, "Feel like royalty, my friends, the party is on!" After a second, the cave erupted into roars of cheers, the minstrels played once again, and the people danced.

Sam yelled above the celebrations. "Alright, you stinkin' lot! Everyone with me!" Sam jumped down, landing hard on his feet. Eoin clapped him on the back in a job well done. He was genuinely proud of his written right hand for the first time. He smiled at the image of these extras entering the castle in full fanfare.

Eoin chuckled to himself as he imagined Adalind's face contorting in shock and disgust, knowing there was nothing she could do until his return. He even liked the idea of Valez's vexation—this may have been his clever idea, but this was Eoin's quest. And he would do it in any manner he saw fit. If he had to be uprooted from his home, he would make sure everyone else felt just as displaced as he had felt for centuries—but even revenge could not dispel the fear that crept at the corners of his heart about venturing to the very end of the book alone.

A light rain began to fall over the vast horizon until a torrential downpour obscured the view. He heard a haunting cry echo over the mountains that reverberated through his bones.

A solitary tear escaped and ran down his face as he felt utter devastation in the pit of his soul. He began to shake, knowing the source of this pain was not his own, but another's. He closed his eyes so he could contrive any morsel of comfort to possibly soothe their broken heart.

Chapter 6

Catriona

"Final boarding call for flight 6884 to Glasgow," I heard my flight number and gathered my carry-on bag and purse off the floor as I detached myself from the black leather airport seat. After awkward meandering around strangers, I placed my bag in the overhead compartment and sat in my designated seat.

I had woken up early with only a couple of hours of unsatisfying sleep to catch my flight. I vaguely heard Estelle and Madeline come in. They were completely off their faces, and after a few false starts and giggles, there was finally silence. I packed a few things, sent them a group message, and then hailed my third taxi in three days.

As I sat there looking out the window and watching the repetitious movements of the men and women in bright-colored traffic vests loading the plane, a horrible realization suddenly came over me. This would be my one and only chance to mourn my mum alone.

I secretly hoped that no one had reserved the seat

beside me as each passenger walked by. I could not bear the small talk or uncomfortable physical touch that always accompanies the confinements of coach.

My whole body relaxed as the last passenger sat down behind me and the plane door was finally sealed. Rather odd for an easyJet flight, I thought, yet I wouldn't dare complain.

I closed my eyes as the pilot made the regularly scheduled announcements and the flight attendants disclosed the safety procedures in case we fell out of the sky into the abyss—which I wouldn't actually mind that alternative one bit.

The plane started its slow roll toward the runway, and I kept my eyes closed and put my head back as the plane accelerated and finally lifted. For just a moment, I felt as weightless as the plane above the clouds.

A loud crackling over the intercom caused my eyes to shoot open. We were beginning our descent into Glasgow. I searched the faces of my fellow passengers and made contact with one across the aisle. "What did he say? That can't be right, can it? We just took off!"

"You were sleeping, dear." A woman who could have been my own gran gave me a tight smile and then went back to her inflight magazine. I nodded politely and let my head rest in my hands. "I wanted to stay awake to grieve one last time." Tears slipped through my fingers until a flight attendant scolded me to be in an upright position for landing. 'Gran' wordlessly leaned over the aisle and handed me a tissue as the snippy attendant went to chide others on their improper positions. I thanked her and dried up any remaining tears.

As I waited for the others to make their way in front of me, I prayed my dad remembered to pick me up, yet a little part of me hoped that he didn't. I turned my mobile back on so I could phone him the moment I exited. I grabbed my bag from the overhead bin and waited patiently in the queue, letting 'Gran' go before me.

The flight crew thanked me for joining them—as if it was some great feat on my part. What would they say to me if they knew the only reason I had to fly with them was because of the unexpected death of my mother? I smiled obligingly and thanked them for their service.

I looked at my mobile, waiting for the avalanche of messages to come through. I wanted most of them to be from Henri, but the only message I received was from Gemma, "Phone me as soon as you get home. Love you." I wiped the tears that had escaped and swallowed the fire in my throat. Our fight seemed so insignificant now. There was nothing left to say about it, and all I wanted was to hear her voice.

Another message was flagged—the voice message my mum left right before I went to work. The one she had to leave because I couldn't be bothered to pick it up. The one she left right before she… I stared at the notification, deciding what to do with it.

I knew I was that annoying person who became a hideous obstruction to those trying their hardest to get out of the airport and quickly onto their destinations as I heard the rustle of jackets and wheely bags maneuver around me.

I was normally that person every time I came back to Paris. More than anything, I wanted to get back to the life I had built for myself. I took on that blank-slate mindset and forced my feet to move in quick succession to keep up with everyone around me.

Whenever I came back home, my mum was always there to pick me up. One year she made a placard with my name on it like I was a high-level CEO in town on important business, and every time after she would have it in her hands, sporting the cheesiest of smiles along with it.

It was the force of this memory and the knowledge that she would not be here now that almost caused me to trip mid-step.

At that moment, an impatient man lightly shoved me on the automatic walk strip as I tried my best to maneuver to the standing lane. My hyperventilating stopped me from yelling a delightfully creative string of obscenities at him.

Waiting at baggage claim was an automatic free pass to be stagnant. I could peacefully wait for my bag without thinking about the world that lay beyond those automatic doors.

I looked down at my mobile as I waited for my luggage. There were no messages from Henri and no missed calls from Dad. I didn't know what I wanted when I rang my father. I almost hung up, resolving to take several buses home, when he abruptly came on the line. "Hello? Catriona?"

"Dad? Dad? Are you here? I'm at gate B. Have you pulled around?" I saw my orange bag come around the carousel and went to retrieve it as I strained to hear his response.

"No? No, I'm at home." There was a long pause as if he couldn't quite muster an apology. One that never came.

"Umm, okay, well, I'll just come in by bus, then. Tell Jeremy that I'll be there in a couple of hours." This pause was so long that I almost didn't wait for his response.

"Jeremy isn't here, actually. Don't know where he's gotten to… not aware of much at the moment."

"God! Dad! What do you mean you don't know where he is? You've always got to know! Mum always…" I stopped short. My heart was racing from panic at Jeremy's wellbeing to sudden terror as I saw a placard with my name on it—until I saw who was holding it. I felt my smile reach my eyes as Jeremy was there—tall, lean, and more grown-up than I remembered. I immediately regretted the sentence I was about to say. "Sorry, Dad, Jeremy is here; actually, he's right in front of me." He was so close that I had to tilt my head up to look him in the eye.

"Right. Get back safe." The line went dead.

I embraced my little brother and held in tears as my face hit his shoulder. He held me for a few seconds longer than normal and made small cooing noises as I let quiet tears fall on him. When I pulled away, his eyes were glassy. He forced a smile as his throat worked to keep a sob in place.

"Got everything?" Jeremy said once he trusted his voice not to wobble.

I was about to nod when I realized… "My bag!" I had totally forgotten. I ran over to it certain this was its second lap. Jeremy walked calmly behind me and took the handle out of my hands.

"It wasn't quite that dramatic, Cat." He chuckled, and I let out a breathy laugh as well.

We walked in silence as the loud acoustic of the crowded airport didn't lend itself to deep conversation or even small talk. Even at the bus stop, we remained quiet. Not an awkward, racking your brain for something to say, like when you meet someone new, but a comfortable contentedness that was shared between dear friends. It wasn't until we were settled in our seats that we finally spoke.

"Jer, are you—"

"Don't, Cat. Please don't ask me if I'm okay. You, of all people, should know the answer to that!" His head lolled as he looked down, unable to meet my eyes. I cursed myself for being so stupid. Of course, I knew. I was definitely not okay, and I had been away from it all. He had been right there—right in front.

"I'm such an idiot. I'm so sorry, Jer." I leaned in close for him to look at me, but his stare remained fixed on the floor, so I defeatedly sat back in my seat. "Christ, that's what acquaintances fucking default to, and it's annoying as shit." That seemed to do the trick as he looked at me and laughed heartily, almost surprising himself that he still had that ability. I did, too, as I laughed right alongside him.

Our small moment that seemed to take the weight of the world off of him soon faded. "Cat, just to warn you, Dad's not… he's not there if you know what I mean? He's absolutely void of anything. Couldn't even dress himself this morning. I mean, it's bad, Catriona." He looked out the window, seeing something other than the dreary mist that covered it.

"I wouldn't expect anything less. He just lost…" My throat thickened with what felt like burnt marmalade. "Anyway, I know how to be around him, especially now."

"Good, cuz I wanted to make sure you'd go a little easy on him. Like, if he's a dick to you, I promise it's not your ongoing, 'ever-since-I've-been-born' rift." He smiled at his own cleverness but cleared his throat when he saw my face.

"Well, thanks for the heads up, but I anticipate falling into my own void with all the arrangements I'll have to make, seeing as Dad hasn't done anything." Resentment filled me and then seeped out through my voice. Jeremy and I were children yesterday—today, our roles had been prematurely reversed.

"You're not wrong. I've barely been managing Dad, let alone any decisions about Mum." That harsh reality sank in, and he began to cry, turning his body away from me. I rubbed his shoulder for a few seconds, then rested my chin there until he turned back to look at me with moist eyes.

"Don't worry, I'm here now, and I'll take care of everything."

We fell into companionable silence once more as we caught our second bus straight to Crieff. I claimed the window seat to take in the beautiful scenes of home. I always hated to admit it since I convinced myself that Paris had claimed my heart, but Scotland had a transcendent beauty beyond compare. In that moment, I recalled my dream of running through the dense forest of the Highlands with that unknown man running alongside me, who was as hauntingly beautiful as the land around us.

Deep down, I knew that Scotland, with its dark and tragic history, was the only place that could visually absorb my pain. That thought gave me such comfort that my whole body relaxed in a way I hadn't felt in days.

***

Home encompassed more than just our house. It was the entire village, it was our neighbors, and it was everywhere our mother was and had been. Seeing The Tuckie, a corner café, where we would have our standard mother-daughter date—hot chocolate and banana nut muffins were our standbys—was just the first reminder of what would never be again. Next came the downcast faces of our neighbors as we rounded the corner, the beginning of the never-ending parade of people's "deepest condolences."

Pain hit me like a stab in the chest as we entered through the kitchen door. Mum wasn't here, and she was never coming back. Our home always exuded a warmth that radiated the moment someone opened the door. It didn't matter what time of day it was; Mum was always in the kitchen. If she wasn't baking, she was cooking—if she wasn't cooking, she was canning.

The table was constantly covered with sugar, flour, spices, fruits, and vegetables—any ingredient she would ever need at her fingertips. I don't think I had ever seen the full surface of the table in my entire life.

The warm air left the room as Jeremy closed the door. It was suddenly cold and dark. Mum's things were splayed out as if she had just run to the grocery and was planning on coming back to finish dinner for us. I stood frozen in place, unwilling to press play on the mounting feelings that were threatening to erupt.

I felt Jeremy touch my shoulders as he meandered around me. "I know, Cat. Come on." He loosely grabbed my arm, leading me to my room as if I needed a tour guide in my own house, which, sadly, I did. He placed me by my bed, and I stood there looking at the clean lines of the pink and blue flower duvet with my purse and bag still clutched in my hands.

Jeremy hovered in my doorway, waiting for me to do something, but I couldn't bring myself to do anything. "I'm gonna check on Dad. Take as much time as you need." I heard the door creak but knew it was only cracked as I didn't hear it click shut as he left.

I dropped my purse and left my luggage to sit in

the middle of my room. The emotional and physical numbness I was experiencing scared me more than the grief I knew needed to be felt. *But,* if I allowed myself to succumb to my mounting grief, I would never leave the solace of my bed as, even now, it called to me.

Thankfully, the pinging of my phone caused me to lock my knees, making any kind of contact with my bed impossible.

My heart soared at the anticipation that it was Henri. It sank just a bit as I saw Gemma's smiling picture accompanied by her name on my screen. Her image stared at me until I eventually had to answer. I began to busy myself—piling my luggage on my bed and setting my purse on my dresser—as I placed my phone in the crook of my neck and shoulder to talk. "Hello?"

"Cat? Hey, how are you? Did you get home all right?" I put her on speaker and placed the phone down so I could unpack. It would be a dangerous road that would only lead to burrowing in my bed and never returning if I focused entirely on this conversation.

"Yeah, just got here; haven't had much time for

anything, really." I went back and forth between my dresser and case—unloading clothes, not wanting to nest but finding it hard not to.

"Probably best… I want to come to the funeral. I can come the day before to help in any way I can; just let me know, please."

At that, I took her off speaker. "What's today? Tuesday?" I did a mental check before she answered. "Umm, I'm making arrangements tomorrow, and I want it to be this Saturday. I'd love it if you were here with me. I'll message you to confirm tomorrow if you want to come… Friday?" I hadn't realized how much it would mean to me for her to come until I paused to let her reply.

At the same time, I found myself secretly wishing I was having this conversation with Henri instead. He should be the one to drop everything to be with me during this time. He was the one person who… I couldn't even add "loved me" because I had never actually heard him say it.

I had been tempted every time we slept together to say those three powerful words, but I always bit my tongue—somehow knowing I wouldn't receive the same in return. I wanted to stay in the world of "maybe he loved me" rather than acknowledging the possibility that he didn't. I couldn't let myself enter that world while I lived in one far worse.

Gemma wholeheartedly agreed and consoled me in a way only she could before we hung up. I sent a message to Henri that I was home, then shut off my phone. I had managed to unpack on autopilot. My gut turned sideways as I knew all that was left to do was to see my dad.

The sight of him in his recliner almost made me retch. His normal coiffed salt and pepper hair was so greasy that it stuck to the sides of his face and forehead, and his once-white V-neck was now splattered in varying colors from unidentified food stains.

Jeremy sat on the couch with his long legs stretched the length of it. Outwardly, it looked like both were happily watching the game together. Jeremy nodded as I came in. We would have to get our father out of his chair, into the bath, and then into bed.

"Hi, Dad." I held my breath and leaned in to brush a kiss on his cheek that was rough with newly grown stubble. No reaction at all. I shivered at the sudden implication of his grief. I nodded to Jeremy. He got up, and after a few seconds, I heard the bath running.

I busied myself around my dad, removing the remote control from his lap, empty crisp packages, beer cans, and newspapers. When everything was cleared, I noticed that the phone was clutched tightly in his hand. As I went to remove it, he grabbed my wrist so tightly that I yelped in surprise. It began to hurt as his face crumpled. "No, no, don't take it!"

"Dad, Dad, please let go, you're hurting me. Dad!" I began to cry and scream as he squeezed so hard it felt as if he'd break my arm. Jeremy ran in, yelling at him to let go, finally forcing his hand off me. I took a step back, moving as far away as I could, and clutched my arm—now reddened and inflamed. My father had never physically abused me, never laid a hand on me. We kept each other at arm's length emotionally, but he had never crossed that line.

Grief, I reminded myself. It wasn't about me—that much was clear as he sobbed in Jeremy's arms. Dad lifted his eyes to mine as if seeing me for the first time. I saw the shame in his eyes of what he had just done, reflecting the undeniable fear and pain in mine. His eyes flicked down to my arm as I held it with my other hand.

"Catriona, pet, I'm…I'm so sorry." He wailed. "But if… if I let go," he gestured to the phone still firmly clutched in his hand. "If I let go, she's gone—she's really gone. I want to stay frozen here. Please let me stay here. I can't, I can't." He sobbed into his hands. This was the moment I had been dreading, yet somehow, it was the exact right place and the right time to break down. With my swollen arm forgotten, I finally let go and cried.

I fell into my dad's arms, and he embraced me. The phone made a deafening sound as it hit the ground. We held each other more tightly, neither one daring to break away to face this new reality. Jeremy enveloped us both before the spell was broken, and we were forced to continue on without her.

The sudden sound of water splattering on the

bathroom floor broke the moment as Jeremy jumped up and ran for the bath. Dad and I couldn't help but laugh through our tears as we listened to Jeremy repeatedly slip and curse. It was a momentary balm—a free pass to laugh—a necessary transition to move on and be practical.

Dad's nose flared and squished up in revulsion as he sensed his own body odor. I stifled a laugh, and he joined along, but his face quickly fell when he saw my arm. I instinctively moved back as he went to touch it—he winced as if I slapped him. I grabbed his hand and guided it gently to my wrist. He tenderly rubbed it as a silent apology moved between us.

Jeremy came out of the bathroom soaking wet, but this time, Dad and I did nothing to stifle our laughter. "Ha-ha. Very funny, I know!" Jeremy scoffed, then chuckled when I snorted. Our laughter naturally waned, and we knew it was time to move forward, whether we were ready to or not.

Dad stood on wobbling, thin legs as Jeremy and I came on either side to support him. I was glad to see they had been in some use when he needed the loo, but other than that, his chair was absolutely mingin'.

Jeremy signaled that he'd take it from there, and I went back out into the living room to clean. I scrubbed Dad's recliner with a fabric cleaner and layers of Febreze until I was somewhat satisfied. I vacuumed countless crumbs and threw away at least two cases of beer cans and days' worth of old newspapers.

When that was finished, I reflexively moved to the kitchen but stopped short. I suddenly understood what Dad had meant when he said he needed time to freeze. This kitchen was its own time capsule, one where Mum was still living, breathing, and cooking. It wasn't time yet to bury it and I didn't want to be the one to do it. I hit the switch and let her be.

By the time I was done, Jeremy was just coming out of Dad's room, looking exhausted. Mine must have matched because he gave me a sympathetic smile, then made a beeline for his room. I did the same.

My first night back in my childhood room was suffocating. My breathing came in quick, short bursts. One minute, I was having a panic attack; the next, I was numb from the bottom of my soul to the prick of my finger.

After a frightful night's sleep, I knew I would have to pull it together long enough to arrange Mum's funeral, but I felt as if I had been trampled underfoot. Every move I made to get up, something came to mind and trampled me once more.

I finally gave in and just stayed in bed as the sun's light danced through the blinds. I felt weak, sore, and lifeless. After what felt like hours, the will to fight was trampled out of my soul as it took on a new emotional blow. The only thing I could think to do was turn on my phone and see if anything in it would be a possible motivator.

As I suspected, it did not. There was only one message from Henri, saying, "OK." Tears burned my eyes at such a short reply, and my heart clenched. Gemma messaged and called, all seeking the assurance of my wellbeing. That made me smile and almost gave me the power to get out of bed, but opening Facebook and Instagram squashed it.

My world had stopped when I found out about my

mum, and I was finding it exceedingly difficult not to be resentful as I watched the universe move on around me without a care.

Gemma's incoming message saved me from the spiral that was begging to burst forth. "Let me know when I should book a flight." The urgency to have Gemma by my side gave me all the strength I needed to get up and make the arrangements.

***

The next three days went by in a blur. I hardly needed to do anything as every business I called knew my family and practically bent over backward to make accommodations without me having to rack my brain too mercilessly. Even payments were deferred, and discounts were applied without any provocation.

My eyes welled up at just how well-loved my mum was to everyone and how big of a hole she was leaving behind. It was like the end to *It's a Wonderful Life* when the whole town came to bail George Bailey out of financial ruin.

Gemma was finally here, and she was the one to

bury the time capsule that was Mum's kitchen. We all clamored in the living room, ignoring what was happening as she cleaned. I was thankful for her. I thought maybe Gabriel would have come in tow, but I was secretly grateful he was not. I needed her alone the eve before Mum's funeral. All we had to do was wait in silence for the next day to come.

Time is constant and construct. Never changing. It is the human psyche that bends and seems to make time change.

Time seemed to stand still when commuting on the metro home, yet there was never enough of it when a deadline hit. But I could never have imagined the impact those early events of my mum's death had on time. Her eulogy, given by the vicar, myself, and my brother seemed to last forever. Yet the reception at The Tuckie went by like lightning.

The never-ending grief that sat on my chest didn't feel so heavy when I saw that everyone who knew and loved my mother had their own version of grief as well, but they would never know the extent of mine and I would never know theirs. It was the mourning of one shared person that was enough to help us all.

Gemma was by my side the entire time. I noticed, after a while, how she was strategically there with either food or drink to keep me going. Jeremy stayed close to Dad, sharing with him the food and drink Gemma brought over.

Dad's old uni friends and coworkers surrounded him as he sat at a small table. It looked as if time was still frozen for him, and he wasn't here. I hoped, for now, he was somewhere with her.

The thing about funerals is they don't last forever—that special space to be consoled, almost coddled ends, and people go on with their lives. But for us, it was the mark of a new life, one where Mum would cease to be. That's how it felt as we were the last to leave the café and return home.

On a normal night, the four of us used to sit in the living room—sometimes watching Telly, reading our own respective books, or listening to Dad tell one of his outlandish stories, while Mum looked adoringly on from her chair—hearing a song only she could hear. It used to slightly annoy me, but as I grew older, I wished to look at someone that way and have them look back with the same fervor and adoration.

Now, with the view of my parents' love gone, I'd gladly give up my dream to have Mum back with Dad, with us. That warm hue was now gone, and the color had faded in this room as we sat in silence, waiting for the appropriate time to sleep.

When I got to my room, Jeremy was asleep in my bed. He had graciously given up his room for Gemma. Under normal circumstances, I wouldn't hesitate to make him sleep on the floor, but tonight, I would let him sleep. He was sprawled out like a starfish. I corrected his limbs and laid down beside him. I kissed him on the head and created a space to get comfortable.

My family had always been my constant companion. I loved my brother from the moment he was born. He was a miracle for all of us. My parents had almost given up all hope of ever conceiving another child. They tried soon after I was born so I would have a sibling close in age but to no avail. Mum became pregnant with Jeremy once the pressure of ever having a baby was off her shoulders, and she thought menopause had set in motion.

I remembered how much they argued over his name until Dad finally conceded. Since my name was Gaelic in origin, Mum picked Jeremy, breaking from the Scottish origin of names, because she said, "Jeremy means 'appointed by God,' and God has certainly blessed me with him after all this time."

Jeremy may have been ten years younger than me and a change-of-life baby, but after this unimaginable week, he looked a decade older. And I wished, more than anything, for him to regain his jovial youthfulness—without any care in the world weighing him down.

The thought of me possibly helping him in this way gave me a small amount of peace, enough to drift off to sleep, to escape, even if just for this one night.

Chapter 7

Eoin

Eoin reclined his body against the cave's mouth, contemplating the hollowness that accompanied the mountains beyond. He waited there until everyone had filed out behind Sam to head back to the castle and await a supposed reader that, apparently, only Valez sensed.

Despite Eoin's casual posture, he was purposely postponing his quest—hoping he could muster enough courage to go and survey the rest of the book alone. He still couldn't get the cry from the mountains out of his mind.

Gorgon waddled past him and was about to follow his merry band of partygoers until Eoin reluctantly peeled himself from the cave's entrance to stop Gorgon's next step.

Eoin didn't care either way, but he knew Valez would not approve of Gorgon's attendance if they did have a reader. "I'm sorry, my friend, but you are to stay here." Gorgon lowered his head, and Eoin winced at his obvious disappointment.

"It's nothing personal, but we may have a reader,

and we must all be ready lest we be caught with our tails between our legs, quite literally in some cases, eh?" Eoin chuckled, but Gorgon tilted his head up, not seeming to get the joke.

Nevertheless, he bounded back into his cave with said tail wagging, back to his enormous bed of shimmering gold and dazzling jewels. Eoin rolled his eyes not believing there was any reason for all this upheaval, especially Gorgon's established way of life.

With the extras safely on their way back to the castle, Eoin mounted his noble steed, Arian, and followed the boundaries of his world that led to the end of his story. Eoin was thankful that Arian kept a safe distance from the boundary that simply cut off into nothingness, only darkness seemed to exist beyond, signifying the edge of the page.

The borders looked solid and intact to Eoin—nothing seemed to be amiss. He was almost tempted to turn back from exploring the end of the book. He never liked the feeling he got at the end. Even when the reader reached it, he always felt alone.

Eoin still recalled the early days when that feeling of loneliness was fleeting, and he was eager to get back to the beginning and meet a new reader. In those days, it seemed as if humans lined up just to read his story. He and Adalind would get to the end with one reader and then appear right back to where they started with another.

The significance of his story was not lost on him. Eoin knew that he represented the ancient uniqueness of Scotland in spite of English hostility. He overheard philosophers and historians argue that it was the role of the king, meaning him, to defend the independence of the community of Scotland.

He felt pride swell in his heart for his kingdom, for his story and what it represented—knowing that Scotland became Europe's first modern literate society—and that, perhaps, his book had much to do with that.

As time marched on and from what Eoin could gather from overheard snippets of conversations while his book was open was that Scotland had lost its freedom—it lost its princes, its parliaments, and its government. Readership began to wane after he overheard one word,

"Culloden."

The very few eyes that read his words from then on were glassy from unshed tears, reflecting defeated and mournful spirits.

On the rare occasions that they would have a reader, Eoin would dread their eventual departure as they finished and closed the book for the very last time. He and Adalind would trek back in deafening silence to the beginning—to pray and hope for a long-awaited reader to start their story all over again.

It was not until another century that he overheard a family discussing his book and its greater significance after "Culloden."

Eoin caught a gruff male voice pontificating, "The English were dead set on destroying the highland way of life, forbidding highland dress and weapons, and passing laws against the clan system until they achieved it no matter the cost."

Eoin felt a flame ignite and burn in his heart at the audacity and inhumanity of the English towards his people. Even though he was a fictional character in a fictional Scotland, he nevertheless felt a kingly responsibility to protect and defend Scotland and its people.

And he could only do that through his readers—by telling his story, but as the number of readers waned and eventually fizzled out, he knew how utterly powerless and irrelevant he had become. The day Mrs. Sessford closed his book in agonizingly slow movements with shaking hands for the very last time, Eoin felt his heart harden to stone.

As his world remained dark without the familiar touch of a reader's hands, he wondered if Scotland was even worth fighting for any longer. Time must have erased the memory, the very heart of Scottish freedom and independent spirit.

If no one cared to fight for the land his book represented, why should he care for his world and the fate of its existence at all?

Eoin was tempted to turn around and go back to his contented life of isolation and let everyone go back to their endless days of revelry with Gorgon. However, Valez would know that he hadn't gone and persuade him to return—*or haunt me forevermore if I refuse.*

The monotony of his journey, along with the endless purple of the heather blowing against the blur of darkness, allowed his mind to wander. Although his heart had hardened against what might have become of the real Scotland, he found himself wishing with every glance at the border that he could step over the edge and be catapulted out of his world and find out for himself what had happened—why they had not had a reader in ages. *What is wrong with me and my story?*

His heart quickened at the thought of catapulting himself into the dark void. If it didn't automatically whisk him to the Land O' the Leal—the land of the faithful, a land full of happiness, loyalty, and virtue—then perhaps he would just freefall before springing right back into the book.

Who knew? Either way, he thought, diving into the unknown could be the only thing to quell the unrest in his heart, even if the latter were only a temporary relief. He closed his eyes, imagining what it would feel like to be weightless, burdenless, and, just for a second, absolutely free.

He tilted his torso to the right, feeling his thighs slide from Arian's back. He stayed anchored with his hands on the reigns and his feet in the stirrups.

Before unclenching his extremities and finally letting go of every burden he had ever felt, his stomach lurched, and a sharp pang pierced his heart.

He righted himself on Arian, breathing hard through his mouth. *The unrest in my heart cannot be worth the risk of nonexistence, right*? Eoin convinced himself that the risks he took in his daily routine were enough for now, knowing his life was never truly in danger.

His hands tightened around the reigns once more as Arian perched up on his hind legs and squealed in warning—they had made it to the end. The sky darkened, and the winds picked up, swirling brown leaves and sticks in an ominous tunnel. *I don't like coming here without a reader.*

The ultimate dread that came with the ending, without the companionship of a reader or even Adalind, was too much to bear. He jumped down and stroked

Arian's ivory mane, prompting him to remain calm, to stay, to wait.

For a moment, he thought that he had caught sight of something, but his vision blurred in and out of focus. The closer he moved toward the path that signaled the end, the more he realized it wasn't his vision at all; the road was fading, leaving nothing but a dark void—a blank space.

The road that once led to his happily-ever-after with Adalind was gone. There wasn't the normal ray of sunshine above the rolling green hills that were reflected on the surface of Loch Fada. He could no longer see the Old Man of Storr—the legendary giant covered by earth with only his fingers as the shards of rock remaining. Eoin had come to think of the old giant as his protector at the end of the story.

He kicked the dirt road, and bits of rocks rolled into the black void. He no longer heard their telltale sounds, nor did he see their ultimate destination. At one moment, they were under his boot; the next, they ceased to exist.

The air in his lungs left his body without

replenishment—Valez was right. The fear that captured him replaced the irritation that might have been there with that admission.

Before Eoin could contemplate what this meant for him and his fellow characters, he felt the ground under him shake, and a sudden blast of light blinded his vision.

He was thrown off his feet and hit the side of a tree with such force that he was left disoriented until the feeling of weightlessness and peace overcame him—*we have a reader.*

Chapter 8

Catriona

It was Monday morning, a week after my first day as assistant editor, a week after *the call,* and a week without *her*. But today, I planned to take a plane back to Paris, back to my real life, even though that now felt like a past life—a fantasy.

Dad was still in a haze, the same one that came over him at the funeral. Jeremy and I didn't allow him to soil his chair as he had done before. We cleared any signs of his living there every hour. We made him use the toilet after any beverage or food consumption.

After packing the remainder of my things, the ones I needed to use last, I looked out into the living room. So quiet and empty, no clattering of pots and pans emanating from the kitchen, and the Telly wasn't turned up loud to counter-act it. It was on a normal volume for the first time, but the occupant watching was not aware of its content.

I felt an awkward sting in my heart, one that didn't sit well with jetting off to Paris, no matter how much I missed Henri, Gemma, and the faint pressure of keeping my new position. Yet the anxiety that crept into my heart about leaving my dad and, more importantly, Jeremy was greater.

I did have some wriggle room to take off another week. I rang Ludo, and he quickly agreed, and with that, my anxiety suddenly quelled—instantly confirming that I had made the right decision.

I pushed my case back into my room to unpack it later and sat in companionable silence beside my dad. He didn't acknowledge my presence, but I saw the top of his lip twitch, and I smiled as a sudden rush of peace overtook me.

That quiet peace didn't last long as I scrambled to cook dinner for the three of us, intermittently checking my phone to see if Henri had responded to my message about staying another week. I hated it when he left me hanging for so long. At times, his messages came in rapid spurts, not missing a beat, which I loved in text banter.

I ignored the probing thought that he only did that when the conversation became flirtatious, bordering sexting, but it took him lethargically long to answer normal conversation like this one.

Sometimes, I would throw in a sexy message just to get him to bite, and it would always work. This time, I had no interest in baiting him that way. The further I was away from him, the more annoyed I became with our arrangement, but I shook the thought away.

No, he's my boyfriend, and it's nice to know he's there, and we'll be back to normal once I'm in his arms.

On top of that, I was checking on my dad every other minute, making sure he was still upright, the Telly on its normal blast that made it feel like Mum was here again, but knowing it was me in her place felt hauntingly odd.

I was also worried about Jeremy. I didn't know his rules, the ones Mum and Dad had set. When was he supposed to be home after school? How late could he stay out? And who was he even hanging out with these days? Would he lie to me when I asked him what our parents had set? Dad wouldn't be able to contradict him, as he had become a functioning mute.

My anxiety grew worse as dinner was ready, and

Jeremy still wasn't home. He wasn't home after Dad and I ate together in silence, watching the game. I finally realized that Jeremy didn't know that I had chosen to stay another week. He still thought I had flown back to Paris and left him.

A wave of relief spread over me when I finally heard the front door click as I was tucking Dad into bed. He stumbled in, crashing into the coffee table. "Shit!"

I came in, leaning against the wall with my arms crossed. "And where exactly have you been? I was worried sick!"

He looked at me wide-eyed—as if I were a ghost. "You're not supposed…" *hiccup* "…to be here."

"I decided to stay another week to help out." He grunted and shoved past me. "Jeremy, you're only fifteen. You can't be out all hours, *steamin'* as well. What are Mum and Dad's rules for you?" He turned around, trying to focus his eyes, but at the mention of Mum, his face twisted in pain.

"It doesn't matter now, does… it? She's not here anymore." He shifted off balance and stuck a finger in my face. "And you're not her!" He didn't wait for my reply and slammed his bedroom door.

Shocked, I wiped the quiet tears that ran down my face. I looked back at her empty chair. *Why wasn't she here? We didn't work without her. How was this possibly going to work?*

The next morning, I started a rudimentary routine for us. I first got Dad dressed and comfortably situated in his chair with his breakfast and paper on his lap and the Telly on.

I made Jeremy breakfast and lunch for school. I had asked him after the funeral if he wanted to take more time off. I was certain that his school would understand, but he insisted on going back—that being around his friends would help—after last night, I wasn't so sure. I heard him stirring and busied myself in the kitchen, just as Mum used to do.

He was clearly hungover but was dressed and ready. When I spoke, it was at a volume louder than normal. "I made you lunch, and here's a sausage roll to go and a tea."

"Ugh, not so loud, Cat, I get it, you're pissed, but I don't deserve this." He held his head, trying to soothe the pain.

"Jer—" I paused, trying to find the right words. "I understand not knowing really how to be right now, but please, please let me know where you are and come home before dark on school nights." I came over and put my hands on his shoulders, but he didn't meet my eyes. "You know you can always talk to me. I'm here."

"Yeah, for now." He wrenched out of my grasp, grabbed his food, and left.

After the sudden pain of rejection left my heart, I knew in my mind he was right. I only planned on staying here another week, and then I'd be back to my life in Paris, leaving behind him and Dad to fend for themselves. I never fully realized how much Mum did, and I knew it was just the tip of the iceberg.

I glanced in the living room at Dad—so still and quiet that an eerie chill ran through my body. I knew everyone processed grief differently, but the way he turned inward, blocking out the world entirely, was troubling. Before she left, Gemma helped me find every medical record Mum kept for our family. I found Dad's information and rang for an appointment.

***

"And where exactly are you off to?" Jeremy asked as I was barely out the kitchen door. He was sitting at the table with his leg half crossed, biting into an apple, looking suspiciously smug.

"I don't have to account for *my* movements, you're the one skipping school." I retorted. "You know full well that I need to look for a temporary job as I'm now stuck here with the likes of you."

"Calm down, will ya? I was just teasing. God." He got up and headed to the living room. I couldn't worry about him right now. We were both on edge. Our grief went from quiet moments of weeping to sudden bursts of anger in a week's time. Dad was the only one whose grief stayed worryingly consistent, which just added a new layer to mine and Jeremy's.

Both his doctor and psychologist diagnosed him with complicated grief. A condition found in about seven percent of the bereaved who cannot cope effectively with the death of a loved one.

During his session, Doctor Gayle told us, "Patients with complicated grief are so entangled in their mourning that they subconsciously go into a silent protest to actively avoid constant reminders of the one they lost. Therefore, their grief is intense and prolonged." Thankfully, this allowed him to take paid leave from his job at the distillery, *but for how long?*

So, with the loss of my mum, Dad's diagnosis and treatment, and Jeremy's social decline, I also decided to take a leave of absence from work, which did not extend my full salary for an unforeseeable amount of time off. The decision was neither easy nor desired.

On top of everything else, Henri finally called, explaining how it might be for the best if we go on a break. Not for himself but to give *me* time to grieve and take care of my family. Once I returned, he said we could pick our relationship right back up.

"I just think, Baby, for you, this will be for the best."

"You'll barely even notice — the time will go by so fast."

"Ring me once you're back in Paris, okay?"

I agreed and hung up before he heard me cry. I would not give him more satisfaction than he already had. The truth was that freeloading amateur painter I thought I was in love with couldn't cope with my grief or a long-distance relationship, disguising it as a thoughtful gesture for my sake.

The tears I cried when we hung up dried just as fast as they had come. Part of me was surprised as just a couple of weeks ago, this would have destroyed me—but after losing my mum, nothing could destroy me more than that had, not even losing my dream career and my life in Paris.

Yet, that didn't stop a flash of Paris from crossing my mind's eye as I opened the kitchen door. I heard the busy street noises of the *Champs-Élysées* as I climbed into my dad's car. Paris was still there as I drove on the narrow streets of the Highlands that could only contain one-way traffic. I drove for miles in no particular direction, drowning my senses in melancholy music, delaying the job hunt even more.

Part of me didn't mind being lost for the time

being, anything to be away from the deafening silence of my dad and the teenage angst that came to live within my brother. There was also the thought of replacing a job that I loved with a menial one out of pure desperation—for monetary compensation and, if I was honest, a distraction from what was left of my family.

I knew I couldn't afford to be lost for long as I didn't trust either man to be left to their own devices. No doubt Jeremy would leave Dad to fend for himself so he could go off and do God knows what with his friends.

I forced myself to pay attention to the next available road sign. Finally, a small white, wooden sign appeared, "INNERPEFFRAY LIBRARY. NEXT LEFT." I pulled into the graveled parking lot that looked out of place by the surrounding woods and ancient stone wall.

The white stone building that overlooked rolling green hills and a harvest orange sky, fell into place with its natural surroundings.

The front garden was laden with white flowers in bright contrast with the dark green grass. At the very edge sat a solitary brown bench. A perfect place to get lost in a good book.

As I faced the entrance, I felt oddly unsettled, and my heart started to beat loudly. The library sign above the door was in the form of a book. The first page read, "Innerpeffray Library."

The next page included a quote by Arthur Herman that said, "The Magna Carta of the Scottish mind." My heart pounded again—one loud thump. It all but stopped when a man came out, almost barreling into me. The shock on his face revealed he was not expecting to see anyone either.

"My apologies. I didna see ya there. May I help ye with anythin, lass?" He was an older man, maybe in his early seventies, short in stature, with brown-rimmed, square glasses and a sweet disposition.

"Yes, I was wondering if you had any positions open at the moment? I have a copy of my CV here and have experience in book publishing. I was just promoted to assistant editor at B&P Livre in Paris, before, um, before..." I fumbled for the right words to describe my present circumstance as he patiently waited. "Anyway, I love books very much and the work the library does. I was actually here once before on a class trip and remember how much I loved and admired the collection of books."

"May I see your CV?" He pointed to my hands. I realized I was still clutching it as I blabbered on about my objective. "Aye, this looks verra nice. We might have something, why don't you follow me? I'm Jonathan Reid, by the way." After shaking my hand, he turned around and walked down the narrow entryway. Relieved that he didn't say no, I followed, nervous about the promise of a position.

We walked past the main room filled with a beautiful collection of ancient books, a hue of yellow and brown, and the smell of mustiness that I always loved filled my senses. He guided me to the back, past the two glass cases, all containing first and second editions, including the first edition of *A Red, Red Rose* by Robert Burns and a wall of caged books, all of equal importance.

He motioned for me to sit after he made himself comfortable in his office chair. "So," he cleared his throat, looking up at me over my CV. "We do have a position, but

I'm afraid you're terribly overqualified for it."

"What is it? I'll honestly do anything. The job prospects in Crieff haven't been promising, and staying as close to my chosen profession as I can is ideal." I smiled reassuringly, trying not to convey my unhappiness about being stuck in Scotland with my career on hold indefinitely. I needed a job, and if that job was in the vicinity of books, well, that's the most content I ever wished to be.

He furrowed his brow as he studied me but eventually smiled. "It's basically cleaning, shelving, and organizing. There is the possibility of categorizing from time to time when books are donated or if ye happen to find any during your tasks." He paused and looked up at me a bit uncomfortably. "And I can only pay ye £7.30 an hour starting at 21 hours a week." He coughed, barely able to make eye contact.

I gave him a genuine smile and stood. "I'll take it."

***

Even though I wasn't going back to Paris, my dream job was on hold, and my love life was uncertain, I was strangely excited about my new part-time job—anxious to get home and tell Jeremy and Dad. I called Gemma to give her the update.

She was happy but relentlessly told me she wished I was back in the office to have our mid-morning tea and light office gossip. I appreciated her ongoing support, as well as the constant reminders of a life I dreamed of having once more.

I let her go as I pulled up to the house and jumped out without ceremony. I ran in, expecting to find both of my guys sitting in the living room watching a game or something, but no one was there. Dad wasn't in his chair—the one he practically lived in since the funeral.

Before I let myself panic, I checked every room to find them equally empty. As I contemplated phoning the police, my phone chimed with a message from Jeremy, "Hey, took Dad out for dinner…didn't know you'd be gone so long." Releasing a breath that I hadn't realized I was holding, I rolled my eyes at the underlining passive-aggressive tone. I sent a thumbs-up emoji instead of rising to the challenge.

Half excited to have the house to myself, yet half disappointed that I would have to wait to share my news, I took this rare opportunity to order a Chinese takeaway and watch a cheesy rom-com.

I cleaned Dad's chair and even poked around Jeremy's room to clear clutter and food, partly to cover for my natural inclination to snoop—nothing out of the ordinary. I did avoid checking under his mattress as that activity of a teenage boy was none of my business and not necessarily destructive. I was mainly looking for narcotics and was relieved when I didn't find any.

I heard the front door open and quickly slipped out of his room. "Hiya, how did yous get on?" My smile faded as I saw the state our dad was in, which was not even half as bad as Jeremy's. "Fuck, Jeremy, when you messaged me that you were taking Dad out for dinner, I didn't think you were going to get shit-faced! Dad shouldn't be drinking at all on his medication, let alone be *steamin'*!"

"Get a life, Catriona. He's fine, I'm fine, so just shut up for once, please." He left Dad in the entryway and went to his room, but he came out as quickly as he went in.

"What the hell! Were you spying on me?"

"What?" I had completely forgotten about tidying his room—I was more focused on keeping Dad upright and conscious.

"Don't be stupid. You cleaned, but I'm sure that's not all you did!"

"Get a life, Jeremy." I echoed back. I slowly walked Dad to the bathroom and heard Jeremy's door slam.

After hours of staying up with my dad as he was sick in the bathroom, I cleaned him up and put him to bed. He held my arm gently as he dropped off.

How I wanted to find the silver lining in my new reality—my plan to get us back to normal failed miserably. It was a terrible reminder of exactly why I was here and what I needed to do for all of us.

***

I was a little nervous for my first day. I got up extremely early to choose the right outfit. I didn't think I needed to be as professional as an editor in Paris, but still enough to show I was serious and the right fit for this job. I wore a gray jumper with black trousers and boots.

Jeremy had been avoiding me ever since he and Dad came home *steamin'* drunk. I gathered he had overheard me telling Dad about my new job as he didn't question my preparations this morning.

My dad smiled, grabbing my hand in gratitude. We never had this kind of relationship before. Why did it have to take Mum's death for this to happen? I couldn't let myself dwell on it, or I'd be late on my very first day.

I was quite content that he was happily situated in his chair with his breakfast, a cup of tea, the paper, and the Telly blaring. I gave him his morning medicine and left a note when I'd be home to give him his afternoon ones—that I had safely stashed in my room.

There were many things about Paris I missed, but as I drove through this part of Scotland that looked completely untouched and wild, I realized how much I loved my home. Mum never wanted me to take Scotland for granted—with all its rich history, culture, and natural beauty. Since she was American, she had an outsider's view of this place and felt a deep gratitude that she fell in love with a Scot.

Almost every weekend, we would explore a new part of Scotland. I remembered being in the backseat admiring the Highlands, craning my neck to see the crags and rocks that reached far out of view, then I would settle back in my seat to the view of Dad holding Mum's hand in loving contentedness as we drove along—as a family.

I pulled in and parked next to what I guessed was Mr. Reid's red MINI Cooper. I pulled the rearview mirror down to check my face. It was a bit damp from the unknown tears that that memory caused. I wiped away any remaining tears and touched up my mascara. I carried a travel bag with makeup for unexpected tears at unexpected times since my mum's death. I gathered my things and headed in.

Mr. Reid was situated in his office but quickly rose to greet me as I came into view. "Ah, Miss Lamont, good to see ya."

At that moment, a woman wearing a tan, plaid pantsuit, who was perhaps a tad bit younger than Mr. Reid, came out. She had small wire-rimmed glasses that were perched on the end of her nose, and for good measure, she had them on a gold chain. "Shona, this is Catriona Lamont, Catriona, this is Shona McKay. She'll be showing you the ropes, as they say. If you have any questions, let her know and check in with me before your shift is over, alright?" I nodded my head. "Good, welcome aboard, lass."

Ms. McKay looked me up and down with utter indifference. "Right, well, let me give you the tour if you'd like. Jonathan told me you visited once before for a class trip or something?"

"Aye, yeah, but I'd love to get a refresher if you don't mind?"

"Not at all. Let's start in the main room." She went about the tour exactly as I remembered. I could hear a hint of pride in her voice as she spoke of the oldest editions, but it took on its normal tone as she summed up the rest. I grew excited as I pictured working alongside these esteemed books.

She showed me the second floor with another glass display in the middle and equally distinguished books on the floor-to-wall bookcases. This room was bright and airy.

The ceiling was higher than on the ground floor and more open. It was only when she led me to two back rooms that my heart sank.

The first room was in complete disarray—covered with so many books and boxes that the puce carpet they sat on was barely visible. The books I could see all looked brand new, nothing compared with the ancient books in the main rooms.

She must have sensed my disappointment. "Oh, dear, didn't Jonathan entail what you'd be doing here? I take care of the tours and restoration of historical manuscripts." She paused and looked me up and down. "He told me you were an editor in Paris. It must seem like a step-down, indeed." Her tone wasn't patronizing, nor was it sympathetic.

"No, this is what he told me I'd be doing; I just didn't realize it was to this extent or how new the books would be—that's all—but I'm here and ready to work." I did my best to convey my willingness and renewed excitement.

"Lovely, now, these books are ones that we have

acquired from other libraries. Some are donations from locals, so what you find may vary. If you do happen upon something noteworthy, bring it to me, and I'll have a look. You never know what someone has brought in, not realizing its true value."

I perked up at that thought, and so did she by the lilt in her voice as she continued. "So, our goal is to have this section as a lending library, so sort it as you see fit. You'll find a label maker in the desk there. After you have organized every single book and have set up a cataloged system, Jonathan and I will evaluate it, and then you can start creating a computer database."

"Sounds like a plan." I placed my purse on the floor to take off my coat.

"Oh, here, let me take those for you. I'll show you our employee space before you go and where you'll drop these before you start tomorrow." I handed her my things and turned to the mess behind me. "Before I forget. It pleased me to see how professional you look, but tomorrow, especially for this type of work, you're more than welcome to dress more casually." She gave me a tight smile and headed out.

I felt a bit overwhelmed but knew this was now my job, and I could take the time to organize how I deemed fit. I acquainted myself with the space—with its dated puce carpet in both rooms. I touched each box and its few contents in view, getting a brief idea of what books I'd be working with.

I was able to find a pen and notepad on the roll-top desk that sat against the far wall—nearly hidden by the number of books it had on it. I made a rudimentary checklist:

1. *Clear and dust all surfaces*
2. *Create piles by genre*
3. *Clear boxes*
4. *Vacuum carpet*

This was just a start. I knew my checklist would grow as I went on, but the first step was to clean. I made my way downstairs and asked Shona where the maintenance closet was. It was combined with the employee room, which meant that was one less thing both she and I had to do today. I thanked her as she left, and I grabbed a dust rag, polish, paper towels, trash bags, and a broom—just in case.

I barely noticed that my shift was over by the time I finished dusting the last shelf in the first room. I couldn't believe clearing the shelves of randomly placed books and boxes and making space on the floor to move around more comfortably took that amount of time.

As I looked around, I felt good about my first day's progress. This type of work almost felt therapeutic, something I could fully control, yet my mind could wander and rest freely.

I shut off the lights and shut the door. I felt better about this job, a space and project all my own. I made my way downstairs, deposited the cleaning supplies, and grabbed my things.

I didn't realize that I had completely soaked through my jumper until I heard Mr. Reid call me. I quickly put on my jacket to cover the sweat stains that had formed under my arms.

"Have a good day?" He walked around his desk, which was a bit too big for this snug office, and stood in the doorway.

"Yeah, good. I got the first room cleaned, and now I'm ready to organize the books. I'll do the same for the second room tomorrow."

"Excellent! It'll feel so good to get those rooms functional again. I'm so glad you knocked on our door, or more accurately, that I almost bumped into you about to knock on our door." He chuckled at the shared memory.

"Me too, Mr. Reid."

"Please, call me Johnathan. Now, I know we have you on a consistent schedule during the week that suits you, but from time to time, we do have special tours that, well, we'd rather not have too much scuffling going on."

He must have seen me tense. "Oh, dinna fash, you weren't too loud." I sighed in relief. "It's just for high profile tours that we like to set a certain… ambiance. So, for Friday, do you mind coming in after we close? I'll leave the keys in the post box at the end of the drive for you."

"That sounds fine. Will you have notice of these tours in advance?"

"Aye, they have to schedule at least a week out."

"Good, it's just I need to make sure my brother knows he has to be home with our father on those days, that's all."

"Your father is Walter Lamont, right? Mmm, I heard what happened to your mother, Caroline. I'm so sorry for your loss."

"You know my parents?" I didn't know why I was so shocked. We were a small community, but I had never formally met Jonathan until last week and assumed he had no association with me.

"Aye, from a long time ago—went to uni with your dad. The day he met your mother, ha, I can remember it clear as day. He bounded into the pub where we'd always meet after school and started gushin' about this beautiful American girl he had just met. Said he was going to marry her. We all scoffed and teased him—how wrong we were!"

My eyes began to fill with tears. I didn't want to cry on my very first day in front of my new boss, so I quickly turned toward the entrance but paused as I turned the handle, "Thank you for understanding my predicament, and umm, I'll make sure to tell my dad, I'm sure he'll love that memory, I know I did." I didn't wait for his response as I made a beeline for my car.

***

By the end of the week, I had cleared every box but one. Every book was organized in its genre-specific piles. Jeremy agreed to stay home with Dad Friday, promising to stay put, even though it was an "inconvenience." I gave him a few quid to get a takeaway for dinner.

When I left for my evening shift, Dad was staring at the Telly while Jeremy was on his phone, stretched out on the couch. After the week we just had, it was such a comforting sight that I wished I could sit down and join them.

But my wish would ultimately be wasted. If I didn't have to work, Jeremy would be off with his so-called friends, God knows where. At least if I had to work, he would be home safe.

It was odd going to work as the sun was setting, knowing no one would be there. Just the thought of it left me shivering, yet there was something hauntingly beautiful about the Highlands at twilight—nothing but dark hues of blue, green, and purple with the last bit of orange sun lining the horizon.

I pulled up to the post box to retrieve the key Johnathan had left—right where he said—and took advantage of his vacant spot. I turned on the flashlight on my phone to make my way down the gravel path.

The lock took me a few turns, but I suddenly felt the release and heard the click. I quickly made my way to the switches to illuminate the space with as much light as possible—I had never been fond of the dark.

I took a moment in the main room without the peering eyes of Shona or the ten-minute chit-chat with Johnathan—after seven minutes, I would slowly inch my way to the employee room to indicate I was ready to get to work, totally unbeknownst to him until I would finally open the door and say, "Well, I better get to it then, lots to do!" I ignored the thought that he was overcompensating for that first day when I had left in a hurry, trying not to cry at his memory of my mum and dad.

But being in the presence of such old books made me feel like I was in another world—an ancient Scotland that had such magic, mystery, and tradition as to fascinate authors, poets, historians, and the world over for centuries.

I knew I couldn't linger—I didn't feel comfortable leaving Jeremy alone with Dad for too long or having the library lit too late into the night. A smile tugged at the corners of my mouth. The shelves were clean, there wasn't the musty smell of boxes anymore, and I could move around more easily with each book in a designated pile, all mostly against the wall. Only one box remained until the real fun of shelving began.

As I sorted through the various books, enjoying the quiet, I thought about how much books truly mean to me. When I would find myself deep in a book—deep within a story—I didn't feel the emptiness around me—the inevitable quietness of being utterly alone.

The story would fill my ears, my mind, and my heart entirely. The minute I put a book down, reality would come rushing back. Only a good story could mask all my fears and anxieties, just as long as I kept reading.

As I only had two more books left in the box to sort, I felt an overwhelming urge to message Henri. I needed to do anything to ignore the silence that suddenly filled the room—to fill the void of loneliness in my heart. I put the first book down on the floor near my crossed legs and prodded the phone screen to bring it to life. "I miss you," I hastily typed.

As my finger hovered over the send button, the very last book in the box caught my eye. I shut off my phone and shoved it in my pocket.

The book looked old, older than most I had been handling all week. The book was leather-bound. It might have once been a vibrant crimson, but it was now faded with golden clasp detailing on each corner. It was also massive. It took both hands to carefully remove it from the depth of the box.

Once it was safely in my lap, I ran my hand over its ridged surface. I turned it over, feeling the back cover with the continued engraved geometrical pattern that bordered a symmetrical floral pattern in the center. It was its own work of art.

I moved deft hands and carefully cracked it to the first few pages. My eye caught the handwritten date, *1490.*

I sucked in a sharp breath and used delicate fingers to open it just enough to make out the title—*The Adventures of Accolon.*

Shona would definitely be excited about this. It was also a book I had been longing to find in the midst of all these modern, albeit boring, subjects. I would like to spend more time with it before handing it over to Shona.

Resolved, I opened the roll-top desk, which was now completely clear of boxes and books, and stuck it in an inner drawer. Although that seemed a tad unnecessary, as Shona would have no cause to go into what was now my work desk, I still felt better that it was in a secure place until I had a chance to peruse it for myself come Monday morning.

I cleared the last box and locked up. I felt confident with the work I completed my first week and a strange glimmer of hope that came with finding *The Adventures of Accolon.*

***

When I got home, I was pleasantly surprised to find that Jeremy had fed, bathed, and put Dad to bed. As I was about to tap on his door to thank him, I heard him crying. "Jer?" He didn't respond, just sniffed loudly.

I slowly made my way to his bed and stretched out beside him. I carefully put my hand on his shoulder. He turned over, surprising me, and burrowed his head in the crook of my neck. I smoothed down his sandy blonde hair. "Shh. Shh. It's ok. I'm here." I began to cry as well.

We both let go and found one another in our shared grief. Part of me was relieved that he was letting me in instead of keeping me out, yet my heart ached knowing how much pain he was in.

As I lay there soothing him back to sleep, my mind kept wandering back to that book kept hidden, wondering what world lay beyond the cover.

Chapter 9

Eoin

A reader! He hardly believed it. That momentary feeling of weightlessness—the briefest feeling of peace—left him dizzy with the sheer number of emotions that riddled him as he rode back without delay. His world remained dark. Whoever picked them up hadn't cracked the book open for long.

The quick flash of piercing light that had blinded him wasn't the kind that would normally illuminate his world, adding color—giving life. So, perhaps it was a fluke. Perhaps they didn't really have a reader, just moved from one spot to another—but if they did have a reader, he needed to get back to the palace, back in position, back where his story began.

His mind kept replaying that feeling, the feeling of just being held. He couldn't remember ever being held like that—how gentle was the touch, how reverent it felt across his entire being. As Arian rode on without his assistance, he closed his eyes to revel in it once again.

A moment in time can feel so strong—a touch, a laugh,

a feeling, but the second it's gone, the memory—the sensation of it—can slowly begin to fade. Each imagining, just to relive it, makes it fade even more quickly, but until the next interaction, that's all there is, and I'd give anything to get just another taste of that feeling.

But the thought of not knowing when that reader, who made him yearn for more, would open his book left him reeling. He was at war within himself. For so long, he had fought against the idea of ever having a reader. So adamant that he never wanted to feel the eyes of another, directing his every move—only to live in his life of solitude—now he was yearning for this unknown reader?

Another thought climbed into his head without permission—the memory of that dark void, causing his ending to fade.

What does it mean? What happens if it's still there once this reader gets there, or has it faded even more? Perhaps the reader's sheer presence will be able to avail it.

Eoin shook his head—pure speculation wouldn't do him any good. He had to get back. He needed Valez's help to make sense of it all, to get everything and everyone organized.

Yet, something didn't feel quite right about all of this. How had Valez been so precise in his predictions? Did he know something Eoin didn't, or was it a calculated guess that just happened to be right?

He couldn't think of that now as the one place he always dreaded, the one place he always kept at a distance but never entered was in view, and now he had to return.

As he entered the castle, the great hall looked just as Gorgon's Mount had the night before. The *ceilidh* was alive and well, yet it looked so out of place that Eoin laughed despite himself.

He roared in laughter as he saw Adalind's horrified face. Her mouth turned up in disgust, trying not to be touched by the others jostling around her. He bellowed at Valez's failing attempts to stop the party, eventually giving up and preventing priceless heirlooms from being destroyed.

Eoin briefly wondered if any of them felt the momentary feeling of weightlessness indicative of a reader. He felt a small ball of panic forming at the pit of his stomach—that he imagined a reader—his mind creating such a powerful presence so he wouldn't be left alone with his own ending, his own fate.

The humor left his face, and he was suddenly quite irritated with the frivolity all around him. Valez must have felt his shift in feeling, knowing he was finally not the only one annoyed at this impromptu celebration. With his arms full of crystal vases and porcelain statues, he crossed over to Eoin.

"Eoin, there you are! What the bloody hell do you think you're playing at? Sending everyone here to cavort in this manner?" Eoin had never seen Valez look so harried—so unsure of himself. His heart sank even further.

Surely, the very first thing Valez would have mentioned was that unmistakable feeling of a reader—that he was right all along—not the chaotic state of the castle.

"What are you gawking at me for, Eoin? We need to get everyone under control. Did you not feel the weightlessness while you were away? We have a reader! Finally!"

Eoin carefully hid the feeling of relief that washed

over him and adopted an air of nonchalance, as if Valez had interrupted his daily run, as he did on numerous occasions. "I did, right as I was at the ending inspecting the border. I didn't see any signs of an opening, so we were probably just being relocated to collect dust once again."

Eoin silently prayed to himself this wasn't true. Just hours before, he would have said this with such conviction and sheer force—but to now hope for the thing he ultimately dreaded unnerved him greatly.

"We need to be prepared either way. We don't want the reader to stumble upon *this* when they first open our book." Valez gestured at the party that had gone from carefree chaos to absolute anarchy. "What of the borders? What did you see?"

"Later, I don't want to cause alarm in front of everybody; that certainly won't make getting into positions for this so-called reader any easier." Hiding his anxiety to get everyone ready for this new reader, Eoin casually patted Valez on the back and searched for Sam.

He wasn't quite sure why he wanted to hide his true feelings from Valez—he never felt the need to do so before. They had left things with an argument that was true. Perhaps his pride wouldn't allow him to admit to Valez, with all his wishful thinking and years of badgering, that he was right. Maybe he wanted to hold on to his dignity a little bit longer.

Once again, he needed Sam to gather everyone around for his announcement, which would help maintain his status quo of utter indifference. "Sam, Sam!" His written right hand was a few more drinks worse for wear than when he had last left him. He clapped him on the back for good measure, which only incited good whiskey to be spilled on the stone floor.

"Ah, my liegshe," he slurred, and Eoin took a step back, escaping his overwhelming breath once again. "What a grand idea to have everyone move here! To the King!"

"To the King!" came the rapturous concurrence of all his fellow characters. Though he knew everyone was too far gone to genuinely mean it, an unexpected warmth passed through him, one he never knew he needed to feel.

Before Sam turned back to nurse his glass, Eoin

took him by the shoulders. "Pay attention, my friend. I need you to get everyone's attention. It's very important to me." He mockingly placed his hand on his chest, inciting a humble plea.

Though Eoin was sure it didn't need to take that much convincing at this stage, he didn't want to leave anything up to chance for this reader.

Sam took Eoin's shoulder in turn. "Anything, Milord." He bowed and then turned to the crowd so off balance that Eoin kept his arms out to catch him if need be. "Oi, Oi! The King has something to say, you vagabonds—bunch of riffraff…" He didn't finish as his mouth absentmindedly went back to his whiskey, but it didn't matter as a hush settled over the hall at the mention of "the King," causing that warmth to spread over Eoin again.

He quickly felt like a hypocrite, a pretender, though what he was about to say would definitely solidify him as one.

"As many of you know, we had a brief feeling of weightlessness, which, I can imagine, interrupted a perfectly grand party!" He paused as tankards were raised and "huzzahs" filled the hall. "Nevertheless, this indicates that we have a reader." To his surprise, everyone seemed to sober at this, even if just for a moment—all eyes were bright and clear.

He continued, "Although it is quite possible that we were just relocated, we need to get into position. You lot know where the story begins. Let us be ready, and if we don't see the light, we carry on!"

There were rapturous cheers, but no one moved, looking so unsure that Eoin was suddenly afraid of his position as their leader. It wasn't until a loud belch came from Sam that everyone busied themselves, moving to clear the hall. The minstrels played their somber melody that filled the throne room when the book was opened.

"That was absolutely perfect, Eoin." Valez put his arm around Eoin, pulling him close to his side. "Good show. It shouldn't be long now before our reader returns, and we'll be ready for them."

"How did you know we'd have a reader?" Eoin wrenched himself free and weaved in between characters, making his way to a quiet corner to confront Valez.

"What?" he looked genuinely confused by Eoin's abrupt change in disposition.

"It just seems too coincidental, don't you think? You happen to come by my home telling me our world is fading and to gather everyone in case of a reader, and at that very moment—with everyone back in the castle, just as I reach the end—we feel the weightlessness of a reader. I'm just having trouble wrapping my head around the timing of it all."

"Eoin, you know as well as I do that I have no powers beyond what I act out for the reader when the book is open. I certainly do not have any powers, and that includes seeing the future. It is purely coincidental, I promise. You can trust me, always." Behind Valez's pleading eyes, there was also fear—fear of losing Eoin's trust and friendship.

"Of course, I'm sorry. I guess the thought of having a reader after all this time and seeing that void fading the path at the end has gotten the better of me. Forgive me?" Eoin rested his hand on Valez's shoulder, evoking the same level of pleading.

"There is nothing to forgive." Valez mirrored Eoin's gesture but let his hand drop. "I am a bit worried what that void at the end means, if it will still be there when the reader gets there or if now that we do have a reader, will it just fix itself?"

Eoin shuddered as Valez's words echoed the unwelcome thoughts he had before his arrival. He couldn't think of the end just yet, and he didn't want to think about saying goodbye to this reader before they had even met. "Let's just focus on the here and now and get everything presentable."

"You're absolutely correct, and I'll oversee the cleaning and make sure everyone is at their proper marks." Valez bounded over to the barrel of ale, which hadn't stopped flowing since Eoin arrived, and made everyone disperse—this was the first point of clearing, and Valez saw to it with precision, yet it came with the derision of everyone else.

As Eoin smiled at his well-meaning friend, he felt another presence by his side and he recoiled automatically. Adalind lightly settled her petite hand on his arm. "Well done, Eoin. Seems as if you truly are the leader you were written to be no matter what status the book is in."

She began to stroke his sleeve with her perfectly manicured nails lightly. "Perhaps you'll come to realize you and I could be exactly how we're written as well. This reader couldn't have come at a better time." She chuckled in delight.

Before he could protest and calmly explain to her that, reader or no, there was nothing to rekindle, she was already leading them over to their thrones. This pageantry seemed to change the very atmosphere—everyone else naturally fell into their written roles.

Valez's frustrated efforts went unnoticed, but he smiled as Eoin and Adalind dramatically turned on their platform and raised their hands in the air. Prompted by Adalind, Eoin was left with no choice but to follow her lead. Everyone clapped, not only for their king and queen, but for what they represented. It was a court once more, a court to welcome a long-awaited reader.

Eoin looked over as Adalind played to her adoring crowd. He still couldn't work out whether she truly believed herself the Queen of Caledonia or whether she was the most calculating, talented actress he had ever known.

Either way, it always unnerved him in a way he couldn't quite explain, but if it got them closer to that reader, he wouldn't let it get to him, at least not this time.

Eoin took a deep breath and moved to take a seat on his throne—his starting place. Suddenly, he had no idea how to sit, revealing just how long it had actually been.

***

Days, it seemed as if days passed, and still no sign of that enchanted reader. Eoin felt his heart hardening once more, embracing the thought of his life just a week before, carelessly lounging by his favorite waterfall, going through his routine—a life he had become so accustomed to—rarely feeling anything at all.

Being touched by a reader, or what he foolishly thought was a reader, burrowed itself so deeply in Eoin's heart that the feeling of hope and joy was all at once renewed.

Now, to be so internally wrong, bitterness seeped

its way back and reverberated out. He cursed Valez for getting his hopes up. Of course, no one except Eoin knew the way he truly felt. Valez was physically withered, as everyone knew his feelings on the matter.

Eoin was curled up on his throne. On the outside, he looked bored and uninterested in the whole affair. As he shifted to get more comfortable, he discreetly caught a glimpse of Adalind on her throne. She was reading, perfectly poised as any real queen would beside her king, which always thoroughly annoyed him—that she thought herself a queen even when no one was reading their book.

The corners of her mouth ticked up ever so slightly—she had seen him. He cursed under his breath and lolled his head back over the velvet armrest. Everyone else was asleep, still at their marks, painfully hungover but still waiting.

That was enough; they had waited long enough. He'd let everyone go back to where they chose to spend their unread lives, and he would go back to not caring, finding feeling in what he could in his solace.

He swung his legs, hearing the faint cracking of

joints that went unused. He wouldn't bother waking everyone. He would leave it to his "queen" and "antagonist," who always stayed in the castle to deliver the news—they didn't have a reader, and, his heart turned to stone, knowing they would never have one again.

Eoin got up and grabbed his sack—the same one he had so carefully packed on his journey to the end before his world forever changed for no reason whatsoever. Ignoring Adalind's once smug smile turned disapproving scowl. He made his way to the two oak doors that reached the arch ceiling, which he always found foreboding.

This time, he didn't feel that same consolation of peace spread inside him as he was about to return to his created safe haven.

As his hand hovered over the ornate circular door handles, a familiar pale one was on his sleeve. "Eoin, where are you going? They could be here at any moment!" Valez looked frantic and disoriented—uncharacteristically mad.

"Valez, no one is coming! Now let me go, let the others go when they wake, and we can all go back to the way it was before, the way we all but you want it to be." Eoin made himself believe every word, so Valez wouldn't see his torment.

"It was a reader. I felt it! There must be one, or we won't survive if we aren't read, and you know it. Eoin, please, please don't leave. If you leave, well, there won't be any hope for the rest of us. This is it!"

Eoin lowered his arm, feeling Valez's fall like lead. He desperately wanted to ignore how defeated Valez looked—knowing he saw his own reflection in Valez. Neither could help the other.

He finally placed his hand on Valez's shoulder, urging him to look him in the eye. "I'm so sorry, my dearest friend. I know your heart for this, but it doesn't change the reality of our situation. Maybe fading away has always been our fate. All things come to an end eventually." He moved his hand in comfort. "Come visit me as often as you can before that time comes."

When Eoin opened the door, his world was as dark as the castle walls, the wind blowing everything in sight—it looked just as it had when he was at the end of his book, which he surmised was just the beginning of their book fading entirely.

He solemnly made his way, barely making out the Mealt Falls as mist and fog masked its majesty. He could still see his camp, which was in some disarray since he had left—at least he'd have something to keep him busy for a while, to distract him from the dread that encompassed him.

He made it to the kilted rock, a cliffside aptly named for its ridges that resembled the pleats of a kilt. He looked over across the dark span of the ocean. Oh, how he wanted to be captured by a wave or swallowed by a whale—anything to escape this agony. He turned his head, resigning himself to a solitary life until nothingness took them all.

It was the sudden blast of light that came up over the horizon, illuminating everything it touched, creating colors that didn't exist without the light of the reader's world.

Tears suddenly streamed down his face in pure joy—joy he thought he could never feel again in the hopelessness that had slowly infiltrated his entire being.

Eoin smiled against the warmth of the sun. The enchanted reader had returned.

Part II

Chapter 10

Catriona

For the first time in my life, I was eager for Monday morning to arrive—to get my hands on *that book.* Jeremy was quiet the rest of the weekend, neither one of us acknowledging the time of shared mourning.

It was what went unsaid that revealed exactly how much it was truly needed. He came home before dark Saturday, completely sober. We all sat together to watch the latest episode of *Strictly Come Dancing* that I had recorded during the week.

The next morning, he served Dad and me breakfast—just some sausage rolls and tea from Greggs, but it was the gesture that counted. Dad smiled warmly as his two children ate peacefully with him. It was the first time since Mum had been gone that we had a nice moment as a family—a new family.

In those quiet moments, my mind kept returning to *The Adventures of Accolon,* reliving the touch—how it almost seemed to teem with a life of its own. I had never felt a book like that before. I was an avid reader. I worked with manuscripts every day, but I had never encountered one that appeared to be several centuries old.

That had to be the explanation for what I was feeling. Still, reliving that first encounter had become a distraction, one that I would keep obsessing over until I had the book safely out of the library and in my room—where I could have it all to myself.

I wasted no time getting to work when Monday morning finally came. I hastily made Dad a lackluster breakfast, took the normal amount of time to make sure he took his medicine, but then quickly dashed to the car. I was thankful it was a reading weekend, so I didn't have to fuss over a normal school day and let Jeremy sleep in.

I pushed the speed limit as much as I could. I didn't stand on ceremony as I got out of the car or as I ran to the door of the library. Once inside, I was able to finagle Jonathan's normal ten-minute chat down to five, quickly put my personal items away—keeping a small satchel to stash the book in—and then finally bounded up the stairs.

I came up short when I saw Shona walk out of my workspace. My breath caught, and I searched her hands for any sign of my book. I exhaled as I saw that her hands were completely empty. "Ah, Catriona, there you are. Very nice work so far; it looks like you are ready to begin shelving and cataloging." She glanced back into the room, looking at something I could not see.

She was formulating a question in her mind, wordlessly opening her mouth and shutting it as if she was not quite sure how to ask it. "Catriona," she paused and adjusted her glasses. "Did you happen to find anything of interest? Any books that would belong in my collection?"

I noted her use of "my collection" but bit my tongue. "No, I'm sorry. All new titles, I'm afraid. Good ones, though, good enough to be a lending library, at least." She deflated but eyed my satchel with curiosity.

My eyes darted down to it as well, almost forgetting why I had it in the first place. "I want to start taking books home so I can more accurately recommend them once we have lenders." An objection was rising in her throat, so I quickly added, "I'll run it by Jonathan, of course."

She paused for a moment to mull over the idea,

obviously wanting to equally give her approval alongside Jonathan's, as if it was in her authority to give it. "Well, if he says it's fine, then I don't see a problem with it. Actually, that's not a bad idea. Glad to see your determination, Catriona."

I stood up straighter as if I were truly pleased by her positive assessment of my work ethic. I slumped forward as I heard her descending the stairs behind me. My explanation to throw her off the scent was too good.

Now, I would have to take on additional work—dull at that—all for a future I was determined not to be a part of. When Shona had explained their desired timeline for the lending library, my desired timeline already had me back in Paris.

I realized I had been absentmindedly stroking the strap of my satchel that ran across my body and was reminded once more of its purpose. I spun on my heel to the desk, slid the lid up, and opened the little drawer inside. There, just as I had left it, waiting for me.

I grabbed the book and, without any hesitation, cracked it open to a non-specific page. It smelled wonderfully old—it had a smell that only books have—but before I even let myself get lost in the sensation, I heard footsteps. I closed the book, shoving it hard into my satchel, and threw it into the second room. I was breathing heavily as I saw Jonathan's kind face come into view.

"Catriona, are you all right? You seem out of breath, lass."

"I'm fine. I had…uh… just picked up a stack of books and placed them on the shelf in there and ran back to see who was coming."

"Right, well no need to stand on ceremony if either Shona or I come in. She was just telling me about your idea for our future readers, and I think it's a brilliant idea! You have my full support. Take as many books as you can carry with you until you've got a grasp of what we have here."

"Thank you, Jonathan, your support means a lot to me." I shuffled my feet and looked down at them. My duplicitousness didn't bother me when I used it against Shona, but I was having trouble meeting Jonathan's eyes as he complimented me on what was just an excuse to sneak an old and probably very valuable book out of his library.

"I'm so glad you came on board, Catriona. I know your mother would be proud, as is your father, I'm sure." That smile, the one that always reached his eyes, glistened, reflecting my own as he left me to bask in this brilliant idea of mine.

As I started shelving and cataloging the first room, I chose two books that seemed relatively interesting—*The History of the Scots* and *Scotland's Eight Reigning Queens*—but my mind was still on the book in the other room. I couldn't wait to get home and, after taking care of my guys, settle in bed with a nice cup of tea and read *The Adventures of Accolon.*

When it was finally time to leave, I was happy to see Shona bent over a collection of antique maps. When my foot hit the first step, I heard her clear her throat as she addressed me. My heart jumped as I took a step back up and turned around.

"Catriona?" I put a protective hand over my satchel and swallowed hard. "Did you pick out a couple of books to start with?"

I plastered on a smile and patted my satchel with the "two" books. "Yes, two on Scotland's people and their queens."

"Acceptable choices. I can't wait to hear a full report." She gave me a tight smile and resumed her study. I inwardly rolled my eyes and flew down the stairs.

I waved goodbye to Jonathan and hastened my steps, not giving him the opportunity for a long goodbye.

***

Eoin

The light was gone as quickly as it came. The absence of its warmth left Eoin chilled but nevertheless hopeful. He smiled, and he felt his heart leap in his chest. He had seen her; he had seen their reader. He knew by her touch that she intended to read them, which meant he needed to return to the castle immediately.

Just as he was about to make his way back, an invisible force threw him to the ground—knocking the wind out of him. As he was catching his breath, the ground began to shake and shift, causing him to tumble repeatedly until he fell over the cliff's edge, barely managing to hang on.

What was she doing with them? A laugh escaped his lips as the world straightened itself out, and he was able to hoist himself up and roll onto his back.

He looked up at the sky—still gray and foreboding—unchanged, yet everything had changed. That empty, dark void had left his heart, and something new was taking its place. He didn't know exactly what it was, but he was just happy to have it there.

His world stayed straight and unmoving for the journey back. He was bemused as he imagined what she had done to cause his world to overturn and if she only knew what it did to him.

As he approached the same tall doors that he vowed he'd never lay eyes on again, he was just fine with being wrong. The doors burst open as his hand came into contact with the wood and iron, and he was thrown to the ground for the second time today, but this time, he was not entirely alone.

"Eoin!" Valez lingered on top of him longer than

necessary but made a quick recovery. He cleared his throat in embarrassment. "I'm so sorry, but I was in a hurry to find you. Did you see the light? It just came through the stained-glass windows, piercing the hall with such color, my eyes filled with tears at the sight!"

Eoin closed his eyes to visualize it, but he wouldn't change the encounter of experiencing the reader alone.

"Aye, that's why I'm here; we don't know when she'll begin to read in earnest."

"She?" Valez brushed off the dust that clung to his cloak from their fall and brushed some off Eoin's tunic as well.

"Aye, I caught a glimpse of her. It wasn't for long, but just the look in her eyes, I could tell that she intends to read us." Eoin looked wistfully past Valez, visualizing that angelic face that came with the sun.

Valez stopped his lavished attention on his friend and took a step back. "I didn't see anything. After admiring the light, the whole court was thrown to the floor. We were sliding back and forth until we hit the far wall, and the world finally straightened itself out. Don't know what she was doing, intended reader, indeed."

"Well, believe it. Now, we must get into position." Eoin saw the skepticism in Valez's eyes about his new-found attitude at having a reader, but he didn't want to hear it, and he couldn't wait any longer to enter his castle, sit on his throne, and wait for her to return.

The room fell silent as everyone paused—surprised faces followed his path until he turned around to sit on his throne, and the sound of busied conduct filled the air as if he had been there all along.

Adalind was sitting in hers with a mirror in one manicured hand, putting the last of her auburn hair in place with the other. Eoin chuckled at the picture of Adalind tussled from the reader's unconventional handling.

"Good God, Eoin, the way that reader is treating us, I never! Well, at least we have one—at least I hope we do." She looked sidelong at him. He wasn't paying attention to her thesis on what had just occurred. His thoughts were on someone else.

Before she could demand his attention, he stood to

address his fellow characters. "Everyone! We have our reader!" Murmurs quickly filled the room. He felt their hesitation and doubt as many held their heads, hands, and elbows in pain. "Truly, I saw her face, and she very much intends to read us. It's not a matter of if but when. So, we must be ready. To your marks!" Still, they hesitated.

"You heard the King, to your marks!" Sam echoed Eoin's command, and everyone scurried to their places. Eoin smiled, wondering why he thought him so insufferable all these years. He sat back down and sighed contentedly.

"Her?" Adalind hissed.

"Aye, her." He turned his head away and began to wait once more, but this time with absolute certainty.

***

Catriona

I rushed home, knowing I pissed off several fellow drivers as I cut in and out of intersections, hearing the fading sound of blaring horns, but I couldn't be bothered. My mind was on the book hidden in my satchel. Not the two obligatory ones both Jonathan and Shona were eager to hear about, but the one I felt I was meant to find.

I had about an hour before I would have to start dinner for all of us. I knew I wouldn't be able to properly read in that time frame—that would have to wait until tonight when all was quiet— when everything was still.

The house was in stark contrast to that as I entered. The Telly was blaring, but its main consumer was not in his chair—it was the overwhelming smell of smoke and the blaring alarm that indicated where he was.

"Dad!" I ran over to the stove and turned both the oven and gas range off. Then that's when I saw him—helplessly sprawled on the floor clutching his arm. The pot and surrounding water told me exactly what had happened. He was silently weeping, eyes tightly closed. I ran a cloth under cold water and gently placed it around the burn.

Not letting myself panic, I held it softly while I called an ambulance. He kept his eyes closed, not allowing himself to look at me, knowing the look of worry, pity, and guilt would injure his pride far more than his accident.

When the paramedics finally arrived, they loaded him onto a stretcher, and only then did he open his eyes to look at me. I did my best to eliminate any feelings of fear and I gave him a reassuring smile, but he adverted his gaze, resigned.

"You comin' with us, love?" The older paramedic looked at me expectantly as I clutched my phone to my chest. I looked at the mess around me. Jeremy wasn't home; he'd had the day off, so God knew where he was, but tomorrow was a school day, and after the precedence he set this weekend, I was worried.

"Aye, I'm coming." I jumped in after her and dialed Jeremy as I sat in the seat closest to the door. Dad seemed to be asleep as they put an oxygen mask over his mouth. I suffered through Jeremy's annoying voicemail that referenced a 1999 beer commercial—*"Wassup?"*—until it finally beeped.

"Hi, Jeremy, umm, I don't know where you are or when you'll be back, but Dad's had a bit of an accident and we're headed to hospital now. He's just burnt his arm a little. Don't bother coming, we should be home soon…but if you get home before we do, can you clean up the mess in the kitchen? That'd be a huge help. Thanks, Jer. Love you. Bye."

I let out a shaky breath and stared at my dad, so helpless and weak without Mum. Tears stung my eyes.

The middle-aged woman leaned over and touched my wrist. "He'll be all right, love. The burn looks worse than it really is. They'll patch him right up when we get to hospital." She smiled reassuringly and took her hand away. Its warmth vanished, causing me to shiver. I mustered up some sort of smile, and she went back to her place as we approached the entrance.

They rushed him to the first available bay and closed the curtain. After several protests, they sent me to the waiting room, reassuring me that the doctor would speak to me soon. I sat down on the multicolored seat with a pattern from the '70s—dulled and stained with time, ignoring the other possibilities. I checked my phone. Nothing from Jeremy.

A message from Gemma came through before I clicked it off. "Hey girl, I haven't heard from you since you first got that job! How's it going?"

"Hey, I'm fine. I miss coming into the office. How is everyone there?" I wiped my nose on my sleeve, breathing deeply, trying not to burst out into tears in front of a mother and her teenage son who had a broken arm or the elderly gentleman in the far corner with his portable oxygen tank. If I told Gemma where I was and received her heartwarming concern, then that would definitely be the case.

"Good, everyone misses you. Ludo talks about you and brags about his star editor all the time."

I swallowed a sob. "He does not!"

"Swear to God he does. I miss you too, lady." Three ellipses faded in and out as she continued. "So, Gabriel and I are going to have our engagement party at my parents', partly because they offered, but also so it'd be easier for you to come! I know it might be a lot for you to get away, but just think about it. It's in December, so you'll have about a month to make any arrangements if you decide to come. We also decided to move in together!"

I covered my mouth and squeezed my eyes tight,

causing tears to escape even faster. I sent her a heart emoji and set the phone down on the seat beside me. I leaned forward, putting my face in my hands, wiping away the stream of tears, not wanting to acknowledge my waiting room audience.

I slowly opened my eyes, clearing the tears that caused a blurred lens across my vision. It was the form of my satchel nestled beside me in the chair that dried my eyes completely. I sniffed loudly as I realized that it was here and, more importantly, what it contained.

My fingers skimmed over the two books I cared nothing about and came to rest on the red and gold-ridged spine of the book—*the book.* I exhaled as I pulled it out of my bag. This was the moment I had been waiting for, but I never imagined this was how it would begin.

I ran my thumb up and down the rounded edge of the cover that bordered the pages as my other hand cradled the spine. I took my thumb and ran it over the rough edges of the pages, viewing the blocks of text in rapid succession as they continually fanned until I reached the last page.

I closed it fast so as not to see the last word and ruin the ending. I found solace for a few moments in just rubbing the surface of the back cover.

As I flipped it over, ready to start with the first chapter, the first page, the first word, I heard my name called many times in the small room as the faces of new patients looked over to me and the doctor followed their gazes.

"I'm sorry." I put the book back in my bag and stood to shake the doctor's waiting hand.

"Ms. Lamont?" The doctor clarified, and I nodded. "Your father is in stable condition and asleep from the pain medication we gave him for his arm. The damage isn't as bad as we feared. The paramedics told me of the cool compress you put on before they arrived—that helped a lot. We have it bandaged, and here are the instructions for cleaning it over the next few days." He handed me a packet of papers that resembled a university syllabus.

"So, he's going to be…ok? Can I take him home tonight?"

"I'd like to keep him overnight just for

observation." He must have seen the worry and confusion written on my face. "He's had quite the ordeal, and his blood sugar is still a bit high. Should go down by tomorrow as he sleeps, but just in case, I'd feel better if we kept him overnight. You're welcome to stay and wait, or if you'd like to go home, we'll phone you when he's ready to be discharged."

"Okay, thank you." He gripped his chart and left me with my choice to stay or leave. It was the only choice that I seemed to have these days.

***

Eoin

Eoin and the rest of the court tumbled in chaos. He noted that only one of his elbows took the blow as they hit the ceiling, both walls and the floor, with each unending cycle. His body came into contact with countless others, not knowing who hit what where.

When they finally came to an abrupt stop, all he heard was the moans and groans of incited pain, including himself, until he heard Valez's piercing voice say, "Ugh, I hate it when readers flip through the pages like that!"

Eoin chuckled as he knew that was a telltale sign a reader was about to start their story. He blushed at the memory of her touch right before she caused their world to spin.

He recovered quickly, taking inventory of everyone's condition. "Well, Valez, we can't very well tell them what it does to us, now can we? But what we do know is that it is a clear indication she is about to read us, so…."

"…we must, uhh," Eoin paused and looked around. He was suddenly standing on Gorgon's Mount. He noticed his finger still aloft as if he was about to give instruction to a room full of courtiers and subjects.

Upon hearing Eoin's voice, Gorgon came out goodhumoredly with his tongue freely hanging from his mouth. "No, boy, go back in. It's not time for your cue yet." Gorgon tilted his head in confusion. Eoin didn't have the heart to send him back to his cave alone.

As he went over to pet Gorgon, a sudden burst of light that revealed the tiniest detail of every nook and cranny of the craggy mountain alerted them both to her presence.

She was reading. *She's reading right now? Why start in the middle of the book*?

Before Eoin let himself panic, he felt her eyes on him, directing his movements. He heard the lines in his head and knew exactly what to do. He knew Gorgon's terrifying written entrance was coming, so he prepared to "fight," but then his world went dark, and in the blink of an eye, he was back at the beginning.

He barely had time to react to what had just happened or to everyone else's bemused looks before the light was back once more.

***

Catriona

I decided to stay the night in the dimly lit waiting room. Jeremy still hadn't phoned, so I messaged him an update. Several patients with a variety of ailments filled in and out of the room until around midnight; only then was I entirely alone.

I looked back and forth between my phone and the far wall in front of me, half tempted to call Henri and tell him about Dad. Surely, that was a good enough cause to call my boyfriend—just to hear his voice. *He is still my boyfriend, isn't he*?

I clicked on his name and waited as each ring matched my heartbeat. It stilled when I heard his voice—it was hoarse—he must have been working late into the night. He only smoked his rolled cigarettes when he was deep in a painting. *"Oui?"* He cleared his throat. "Hello?"

I hesitated, unable to find the right words. It was the sound of female laughter and a fake French accent that finally crushed what was left of my voice.

"Baby, who is it? Come back to bed, *mon cherie*." He dismissed her with a sharp hush.

"Hello? Catriona?" At the mention of my name, I hung up and muffled a moan. It rang again, and I flung it in my bag to let it ring unending as I stood to pace the room. The thought of Henri in the arms of another woman—not just any woman, but who I presumed to be Lou-Lou—made me retch.

I didn't let my mind wander to the nagging thought that this wasn't the first time. Instead, I forced myself to focus on the present implication. I thought we were just on a break, not a breakup that allowed us to see other people.

Quiet sobs seamlessly turned into an anxiety attack. *Lucky I am in a hospital*. I let out a sarcastic snort, but I didn't want it to escalate to the point of admission.

It was the sight of the book that finally calmed me. I sat back down and thumbed the pages and opened it to a random page—just to feel it, to smell it, to connect with it. My gaze inadvertently caught one sentence in the middle of the book as I followed the path of my fingers.

A man named Eoin was about to encounter a ferocious dragon on a dark and rocky mountain. As the action began to rise, I forced myself to close the book so as not to spoil the story, no matter how taken I was with it, even at first sight.

There was no chance of sleep now that the story had taken its hold on me. I had hours to kill and a quiet atmosphere to properly begin. I reverently opened the ornate cover and lightly turned the inconsequential pages to get to the first chapter.

The edges of my reality began to blur as I was transported into a dense forest—full of darkness—with dulled colors of evergreen, midnight blues, and rich browns. I could smell the distinct scent of minerals from the translucent waterfall ahead.

How I longed to be lost in this forest—in this ancient world—rather than in the overly bright sterile room of a hospital. I was weaving between two worlds, and I could only be immersed in one.

At that, I was whisked away to an ancient castle. It was described as any medieval castle in Scotland, but instead of the makeshift modern-day replications that filled them, this castle held an essence of jovial usefulness.

There was something about the dark, stone fortress in contrast to its pastel-colored gardens, where nobles would take turns with each other to escape the dreariness of a long winter spent within the damp, cold walls.

Inside those walls, in the throne room that held two red velvet thrones and matching draperies of embroidered gold, silver, and violet, I was first introduced to the king of this brooding castle and his mysterious kingdom of Caledonia—Eoin of Accolon.

"Catriona Lamont?" I was forcefully pulled out of Eoin's world and back into mine by a well-meaning nurse. "Your father has just woken up and wants to see you." I placed a scrap of paper in place of a bookmark with the mental reminder of acquiring a real one and reluctantly put the story on hold… *for now.*

***

Eoin

Eoin's introduction to the reader at the beginning of the book included a brief physical description, along with his title and status. He was described as broad, with thick golden-brown hair and piercing green eyes, abnormally tall, with muscle definition that would not only take years to perfect but daily anguish to maintain, yet this is how his author had described him, and this was how he would effortlessly appear.

It hadn't slipped Eoin's notice the way female

readers would respond to this paragraphed description, along with the flattering descriptions of his "broad and graceful" movements throughout the rest of the book, which caused him to think that men in the real world didn't naturally possess his appearance or abilities. He begrudgingly knew this was one if not the main reason people read his story.

When Catriona had all but rolled her eyes at his description, he was elated that he might finally have a reader who appreciated him—for his story told. *Catriona.* He had heard her name spoken aloud. He relished in knowing, even if it was just one small detail, who this reader was.

His elation was quickly abandoned as darkness filled his world, and she was gone before he could deliver his first line. He kept his eyes trained on the ceiling, desperately willing her presence back to him. It wasn't until he detected movement that he knew she would be gone for longer than just a moment.

"Did you see her, Valez?" There never seemed to be a good time for Eoin to really look at her as he waited for his cue to speak and introduce his world to her. He hoped that Valez at least saw what he had briefly seen when she had first opened his book—when he had stood on that cliff contemplating the abyss, then felt the sudden rush of warm sunlight that cascaded around her face.

"No, I was too busy waiting in the side wing to hear my cue to notice. This reader, she's so elusive. She's not taking the proper time to really read and know our story. She's in and out, in and out, I can't keep up! She's even causing your head to spin."

Eoin adverted his gaze. Valez had noticed Catriona's brief yet powerful effect over him that Eoin thought he kept well-hidden.

Adalind sidled up next to him just as he was about to contradict his friend. "You're absolutely right, Valez; such an annoying habit this reader has developed. What could she possibly be doing with her time? The real world can't be as fascinating as ours, can it?"

Eoin rolled his eyes. Of course, the real world was far more fascinating than theirs, and he longed to be there. He felt a surprising tug that perhaps now there was another reason to be there—to truly brave the jump into the void.

"Quite right," Valez said through a mouthful of bread, pausing briefly to wash the rest down with wine. "She's already captivated our poor Eoin here." Valez chuckled as Adalind's head snapped towards Eoin with the fiercest look he had ever seen.

"Don't give yourself whiplash, my dear. You won't be able to perform for our reader with a snapped neck."

"Is that a threat?"

"Take it as you like. Think of it as me caring for your well-being for all I care."

"Damn, this reader really does have your head spinning. It should be you who is worried about a snapped neck, Eoin." Valez jeered him with the slightest edge Eoin didn't fail to notice.

"Can you truly blame me for getting caught up in all of this? We haven't had a reader in decades. I'm just getting adjusted to playing the part, that's all—your charismatic, head-over-heels romantic king, remember? Now, if you'll excuse me, I need to boost morale for the rest waiting for their cues."

Just as he suspected, everyone was losing their interest as most slumbered against the wall and even against each other. He heard quiet mumblings of returning to Gorgon's Mount to resume the revelries that had once kept them captivated for so long without a reader. He understood that was all they had known for some time.

Sam snapped to attention when he saw Eoin approach and kicked at those who slept. Eoin nervously cleared his throat, "I know waiting for our cues can be challenging; we don't know the life of the reader beyond the pages, what keeps them from delving into our story for a long period of time, especially at the beginning, but we do this for the reader. She gives us purpose."

Unenthusiastic moans filled the corridor in response. He needed a more resounding agreement—for Catriona's sake. "Remember, a reader has the power to make our world come to life. It's not our doing; it's the reader. As long as she's here and reading, we press on when our world is dull and lifeless for a time."

He rubbed his hands together, anticipating that

feeling of being accepted as their beloved leader that would come with his next announcement—though he wished it came alongside his own enthusiasm about Catriona's presence and the reader's influence. "Now, feel free to help yourself to the castle's food and ale until you see that familiar light; then it's time to have purpose once more!"

To that, he got the resounding huzzahs he anticipated, mainly from Sam, but everyone followed and started for the kitchens to refuel for the next time Catriona cracked up their book.

Eoin knew that when Catriona returned, she'd fully settle into his story and begin to know him and his world, just as he would begin to know her and her world.

Chapter 11

Catriona

I brought Dad home from the hospital after a tortuous night by his bedside, not able to do anything but hold his hand for him to sleep after a fitful attempt before the nurse came and got me. I was just about to dive into a dialogue between Eoin and his knight commander, Samuel Ward, when I was interrupted.

The interruption was disconcerting at first—it was that feeling when you first wake up, and you don't know where you are or how you got there. After the slight irritation of abruptly entering reality once more, realizing that my dad needed me by his side was more important than the book.

It was already ten in the morning when we pulled into our driveway, and I was officially late for work. I had missed a couple of calls from Jonathan and immediately phoned back, explaining what had happened the night before.

I'm sorry to hear that, Catriona. Please take the rest of the day off.

And do not ever hesitate to ask for time off when needed, especially when it comes to your family.

When Dad and I entered the house, it was as if we had never left. His accident in the kitchen was frozen in time—the floor still sopping wet, the gray pot turned over, and the last strands of smoke wafting in the morning's first light. Jeremy hadn't come home, or if he had, he ignored my only request to help clean up.

I quickly steered Dad away from the entrance and into the living room before he could be reminded of his accident. I settled him in his chair, changed his bandages, gave him his medicine—both old and new—haphazardly cleaned the kitchen, and then, without hesitation, charged towards Jeremy's bedroom—not even bothering to knock. It was empty, and his bed was still made—he hadn't spent the night here.

I wanted to vent my frustration to Dad about his selfish, inconsiderate son, but he was sound asleep with the game on. Even if he weren't passed out, in his current state, he wouldn't be the soundboard I needed. I backed out of the living room and headed straight for my room.

There was no conscious effort to try and do anything else but sleep as soon as I laid down.

I was awakened by my buzzing mobile, lightly shifting back and forth on my bedside table, the Telly on full volume in the next room, and the sound of Jeremy's voice yelling at the game.

I absentmindedly checked my phone; it was Henri calling—*again.* I ignored the incoming call and noted the time. I had only slept for about an hour—still feeling the last tendrils of remaining dreams that I couldn't quite grasp and the pangs of awakening without the proper hours of restful sleep.

I heard Jeremy's voice again, which reminded me of all the unanswered questions and anger I had when it came to his actions from the night before.

Jeremy was noticeably unwell — sweat beading on his forehead and upper lip, his eyes bloodshot, and floppy hair in complete disarray — all unbeknownst to our father, who was just happy to have a familiar companion watching the game with him. There was something wrong with this picture. Jeremy was home in the middle of a school day.

I went back to my room and phoned his school, asking if they could excuse his absence due to a family emergency the night before. I conveniently left out that Jeremy wasn't even present for the accident. They graciously excused him, offering him the next day off as well, if needed, but just to call and let them know. After a polite "thank you," I hung up and stormed into the living room.

"Where the hell were you last night!" Startled by my sudden presence and the apparent harshness in my voice, Dad whipped his head towards me and then to Jeremy in utter confusion.

"Hey, sis. Come on, s-sit down and join us." He belched unapologetically and sipped a beer that had slipped my notice before.

"Give me that!" I grabbed the can as he tilted it to his lips.

"Fuck, Cat, I could have cut my lip!" He got up and headed for the kitchen. I noticed movement behind me. Dad was shaking his head as he headed toward the bathroom, unable to cope with our fighting. Jeremy stood by the sink holding a tea towel to his lips, periodically checking for blood.

"You didn't cut yourself." I snatched the towel out of his hand and gestured to the kitchen floor. "So, this was a completely different scene last night. Dad tried to cook for himself—boiling water with the oven on. I came home to find him in the fetal position, clutching his burnt arm while our house was filled with smoke!"

He couldn't meet my eyes. "I didn't cut myself; you did," he said under his breath.

"I don't care! Where were you last night? Why couldn't you have waited for me to get home before you went out? Why didn't you answer any of my messages? Why didn't you come home and help me clean up, then go to bed so you could get up for school?" I stopped to catch my breath, hoping for a reasonable explanation so we could move on and be as we had been just the other day.

"I went out with my friends to score."

"Score? Score what?" I began to feel ill as I already knew the answer.

"It doesn't matter. I'm never going to do it again, Catriona. I just needed to escape for a bit. Sitting with Dad hour after hour, him not speaking, not having Mum…" His voice cracked, and he couldn't finish. He broke down and cried. He slid down the cabinet until he was sitting on the floor with his long legs crossed over each other. I stood there and looked at him. He looked so small—like a child who feared a monster under his bed.

I swallowed a sob before I stooped down to hold him and then pulled him up. I let him cry on my shoulder, and just like a child, I guided him to his room—onto his bed—and tucked him in. I brushed his soft, wavy hair away from his eyes for just a moment as his sobs quieted, and he fell asleep.

I went back out to find Dad's face wet from crying. I bent over him to wipe his tears away. He grabbed my arm and gently kissed my palm. I placed it on his face for just a minute and went back to sort our lunch and eventual dinner.

***

Eoin

Eoin still waited for her in the middle of the throne room, right where he would deliver his first line addressing Sam about the darkness slowly poisoning his realm. Sam had left mere seconds after Catriona's departure, and everyone followed his lead—all but Eoin. Adalind stayed perfectly poised on her throne, and he felt Valez's eyes trained on him from the shadows.

Lingering doubts trickled into his mind. The shadows of a reader-less life that he once embraced, along with terrible memories of other promised readers that came before Catriona rushed in like a flood, overwhelming every one of his senses.

Eoin let out a pained sigh and burst from his position. Before he knew where his feet had taken him, he was out of the castle and back at his camp. He felt immediate solace and blocked out all sensations of fear that began to threaten his state of mind.

Everything had changed so quickly. Living alone for so long with no hope of a reader, then discovering the end of his story was fading, which was still unresolved and seemingly forgotten—*until now.* All of that went away when Catriona found them and began to read, but she was taking so long to delve into his story.

He shuddered at the thought of her never returning and discarding them back from whence they came. Something like a vice suddenly gripped his heart. He didn't want to think about that, didn't want to even fathom the feeling of never seeing her again—feeling the warmth of her light splayed across his face.

He stripped down, discarding his clothes that now felt constrictive. He ran his familiar course as long as possible, eventually free-falling into the loch below. Burnt out and feeling nothing, he allowed himself to freely float on the surface of the water that he could never truly feel—he knew it ought to feel cool and refreshing, look clear and inviting, yet, in his world, it lacked everything it needed to be real. Somehow, when they had a reader, their world seemed to come to life, not fully, but enough to forget the dull, lifelessness of it all.

He kept his gaze firmly fixated on the sky even when he heard rustling on the bank, knowing exactly who had followed him. He eventually went underwater and came back up, smoothing back the hair away from his face. He squeezed the excess water from the tips that fell right above his shoulders.

"That was quite the show, Eoin." Valez wrapped his elaborate black and crimson robe around him as he sat on a log that Eoin had strategically placed for times of deep contemplation.

Eoin made his way out of the water, carefully concealing himself. He dressed without meeting Valez's gaze. "I was feeling overwhelmed, that's all—needed some air."

"Overwhelmed? By what?" Valez played with a pulled piece of grass, seeming to already know the answer.

Eoin came to sit by him with his arms resting on his knees. "Events over the past few days have happened so quickly that I hadn't had the proper time to process them, and then, in her absence, it all came flooding back. At that moment, I realized there was nothing within my control as it had been before Catriona. There were some things within my control at the first sign of her. I have none now."

He looked down at his feet. He gave everything he had to Valez, gave him everything he thought and felt and waited with bated breath for his response.

Valez shifted his legs towards Eoin. "Well, I know I have been giving you a hard time about this reader, but truth be told, it's nice to see you so invested. I'd been trying for years to get you to care about our purpose and our world, and it pained me to see you so withdrawn and listless." He paused to suck in a large breath and let it out with a defeated sigh. "I suppose I was also a little jealous of what this reader was able to do with such little exposure that I could not in all that time."

Eoin met his eyes as Valez gave him a weak smile. Valez had returned his vulnerability, and he was relieved that they could be so open with each other just as they had from the moment that they were both written into existence.

Valez stood and offered Eoin his hand to pull him up. "I know you still feel worried about what you saw at the end, but I have a feeling that it will all work out now that this reader has arrived."

"How can you be so sure?" Eoin searched Valez's eyes, knowing Valez carried more wisdom than half their cast of characters, himself included.

"My theory is that the fading pages are due to the lack of a reader to care for us and to give our world its sole purpose. We shall see how this Catriona takes care of us when she takes the time to read our story in its entirety."

"I hope you're right, my friend, but the memory of those dark voids at the end are still plaguing me."

"I know, but you won't have to worry for long." Valez placed a soft hand on his shoulder.

"I don't? Why?'

"Look." Valez pointed to the horizon, a soft blue hue was slowly coming over the mountains.

Eoin felt his eyes start to well with unshed tears. He turned back to Valez. "Well then, we haven't much time." They smiled at each other. "Race you!" Eoin didn't wait for a response as he sprinted the other way. He heard Valez's joyous laughter come up behind him—quickly catching up so they were side-by-side.

With the light at their heels, they ran at full speed toward the castle.

***

Catriona

I sank into my bed after a long night spent in hospital and a long day catching up on everything else. This was the moment I had been waiting for ever since I found Eoin's story.

I didn't hesitate as I opened the book and found exactly where I had left off—with Eoin's first line of dialogue. I held my finger to the spot and paused to reflect on what I had read the night before.

Although I had initially dismissed Eoin's description as terribly cliché, I had to admit that I couldn't stop thinking about him or the way his piercing green eyes seemed to bore into my soul through the pages of the book. I blushed at his description but also at the way I was reacting to it.

Embarrassed by my own thought process, even though I didn't voice it to anyone, I still felt the need to internally justify myself—*everyone falls for the main character of a book. It happens, but everyone knows the hero always ends up with the heroine—who is effortlessly gorgeous, fearless, and nonsensically irresistible to him the first time he sees her.*

I hadn't met Eoin's love interest, but there was a part of me that already knew I'd like her and would eventually root for their undying love.

The thing about these types of stories is how the heroine will start off so ordinary and normal, a self-described nobody, and then, with the one thing that matters—the key that unlocks the entire plot—she suddenly becomes irreplaceable—the only one the hero sees and falls for first.

That doesn't happen in real life. I sighed and cursed myself for allowing Henri to enter my heart and mind without permission. The world is full of men like Henri, not romantic heroes like Eoin—that's why authors and readers alike seek them out in fiction—in that way, at least, we can feel set apart.

I managed to read a couple of more chapters—it was just enough to be properly initiated in Eoin's world and his initial dilemma. I met Eoin's love interest, Adalind, and she was just as I suspected—she was utterly divine and irresistible. She had flowing red hair, eyes the color of the morning sky, and was incredibly fierce and independent—not yet falling for Eoin's brash and arrogant bravado.

I wasn't able to get a good read on Valez, although knowing the era in which this book was written and the fantastical, medieval world in which it was set, I suspected him to be the villain—masquerading as Eoin's advisor.

Exhausted from the previous night's events—Dad's accident, Henri's affair, and Jeremy's overwhelming grief and how it was manifesting—I wasn't able to finish Valez's initial description.

I found I could no longer keep my eyes open as tears blurred my vision, and the only release was to ignore the heavy onslaught of emotions and just give into my body's demand—to finally sleep

***

Eoin

Eoin's action came to its natural conclusion at the end of chapter three. To his delight, he was able to steal a glance at Catriona's lovely oval face as she briefly paused before closing the book.

As her face began to crumble and sparkle with fresh tears, he found himself longing to reach out and wipe each and every one away with the pad of his thumb, to softly ask what was causing her so much pain—to know everything about her. He could almost feel a soft mist on his face—the taste of salt on his lips—as her tears splashed onto the page, filtering into his world.

As he lingered on that overwhelming need to comfort her, her face slowly faded away, and his world darkened. He tried to steal one more glance until all he saw was her Peter Pan bookmark with the inscription, "Second star to the right and straight on 'til morning," which assured him that he would see her again—*in the morning.*

When he finally removed his gaze from above, he saw that all his fellow characters stood in place in case she opened the book to return to their story. He reluctantly shook his head, knowing she was done for the night. He quickly left the scene, wishing she had spoken her inner turmoil aloud.

***

Catriona

A few weeks went by without incident. Nothing as dramatic as Dad's accident or Jeremy's experimental drug use. Work kept me busy, as I had to keep up the charade of taking various books home at a time and reporting back, mainly to Shona, their content and predicted performance in the lending library, all the while hiding the book that started it all.

I took every opportunity to read, but that was few and far between. Taking care of my dad, keeping up with Jeremy's schedule, and paying close attention to his level of grief, along with my part-time schedule at the library, took up most of my time.

The only real time I had with Eoin was at night when everyone was asleep and I could snuggle comfortably in bed and truly escape, but, as was always the case, no matter how hard I tried to fight it, sleep would inevitably consume me, and I would awake with the book open on the other side of the bed—*it is the closest thing I had to a lover at the moment*.

Henri's calls had slowed, but he would still phone periodically, and I always ignored them. In his voice messages, he never once apologized for his unfaithfulness. Instead, he insinuated that I was in the wrong for calling at that time of night.

I began to realize how he truly made me feel. He made me feel like, in every feeling I had about us—no matter how justified I would feel on my own, once we were together, it was only me who was in the wrong—that I was crazy. It felt so hypnotic that just being in his presence—the way he made me feel—I would eventually take everything back and apologize to him for *my* behavior.

Time and distance made me see that I was the one who clearly deserved the apology, but deep down I knew I would never get one—I would never receive closure. He knew the power he had over me. He knew I was tangled in his web, and no matter how far I thought I had gotten away from him, he would pull on our connecting string, and I would come crawling back.

Our web seemed to dissolve as I read about Eoin and Adalind's intimacy—a love so pure, uninhibited, and undeniable. A love not manufactured, controlled, or sought. I found that settling for less out of fear—that no one would love me as Eoin loved Adalind—was no longer what I wanted.

The fear remained, but it would not dictate my actions any longer. Even so, my heart still seemed to bleed as I read of the small intimacies shared between Eoin and Adalind, making me lose all my resolve.

I sat comfortably in my newly bought chair with a matching ottoman so I wouldn't have to think of the unoccupied one in the living room. I even ignored the fact that the living room lay uncharacteristically bare for the first time in our lives as Christmas was just around the corner.

I ignored the snapshots of memories of Mum putting on Bing Crosby and dancing around the tree as she strung up its lights, and, instead, I read. I became rather immersed in how Eoin and Adalind found ways to escape the demands of monarchy and Valez's growing threats as they reclined in the forest grove, perfectly hidden from the castle's overbearing view.

What Henri and I shared never reached the depth that Eoin and Adalind clearly had. My soul ached knowing I had never experienced this, only my imagination could carry the weight of their stolen moment, and I found myself crying as I longed to one day experience this type of love, not having to rely solely on my imagination that I knew wasn't enough—that perhaps I wasn't enough to deserve it.

I dashed away any remaining tears that had to do with unrequited love, Henri, or the fact that I would be faced with this same dilemma at Gemma and Gabriel's engagement party. I gently closed the book, realizing I had voiced each thought out loud even though no one was in the room—it was out of place for me.

Clearing away that oddity, I placed the book in my purse and went to pack the remainder of my clothes and supplies that I would need for a weekend away in York.

***

Eoin

As Eoin gently stroked Adalind's back, he felt the familiar mist of Catriona's tears. How he longed to tell her that this was all an act. More than that, he wished he was caressing her with genuine intimacy rather than with his costar, for all intents and purposes.

Adalind sat up quickly, wiping away Catriona's tears from her face and arms when the book was closed. "Ugh, I mean honestly, does she need to cry every time she reads a passage of our lovemaking? I'm always sodding wet after!" He stifled a laugh at her unintended and, most likely, unaware double entendre. "I don't ever remember feeling anything from the reader's world like this, have you?"

She continued to wipe herself down as Eoin stayed in his languid position, content with the lingering feeling of Catriona on him, "No, but perhaps no one connected with my story in the same way Catriona does; she truly seems one of a kind." He sighed and twirled a piece of grass around his finger, picturing her lying next to him.

Adalind craned her neck at such a painful angle that Eoin thought it would indeed snap off this time. She smiled wickedly and turned her entire body to face him. "This Henri she speaks of seems to grasp her attention more than you. She cries for what she will never have with him—for the true love that *we* share." She continued to smile menacingly at him, waiting to see what affect her words would have.

"She doesn't know that what you and I have is fake, Adda. Thank God our author didn't go into specific details of our lovemaking." He convulsed at the thought of actually making love to Adalind just for the sake of the story. "Besides, you did not hear her correctly. She is done with that cad known as *Henri*. His poor treatment of her makes me want to spring out of this book and run my sword through him."

"It is quite humorous the way this reader has you wrapped around her little finger. Sad really that this relationship you seem to think you have is only one-sided—that you will know everything about her, but she will never know you, well, not in the same way I do." She made a move to caress his face with her fingers, but Eoin stood abruptly, no longer able to ignore the person ironically written as his true love or endure her cold touch.

Not seemingly dissuaded by his outright rejection, she continued, "I do love how she re-reads the romantic gestures that pass between us—that we get to act them out over and over again. You get to stroke and kiss me more than what's written, where some readers only read it once and it's fleeting. Catriona seems to relish in the intimacies we share," she laughed sardonically as Eoin pushed past the leaves and branches, not bothering to wait to hold them aloft for her.

He headed straight for his camp to cool down and ultimately rest until he felt Catriona's familiar touch as she picked him up again. He would wait for her in his hammock, imagining what her touch would feel like on him—he moved his hand slowly up and down, increasing his speed and bucking his hips to fully erase Adalind's words and even her touch from his mind and, instead, pictured Catriona spread out in the glen before him as his rightful queen.

***

Catriona

Jeremy gave me a lift to the train station. He had become very pensive, far too focused on the road than was necessary. I had given up on all attempts of casual conversation as we exited our neighborhood, but I noticed that we both turned our heads away at the exact same time as the giant Christmas tree in the middle of the town's centre came into view.

I thought about Dad and how he seemed to be doing better. He started grunting at us to signal his wants and needs. The doctor said that was definitely a sign of progress in his diagnosis of complicated grief, which gave me peace in going away for the first time since Mum's death—*three months ago.*

As we pulled up to the station and came to a rather forced stop, the sound of Jeremy's voice cut through my cordial and scripted goodbye.

"Cat, I…I hope you have a good time. It'll be good

for you to think about yourself for a change."

"What is that supposed to mean?" He sounded alarmingly concerned rather than congenial.

"I just… what, what I'm trying to get at is… you haven't seemed to take time for yourself to mourn Mum or even acknowledge how you feel about what happened." I turned my head away from him as his carefully contained frustration suddenly boiled over. He paused and then I heard him sigh and whisper, "Cat, you never bring her up, unless it's about how I feel or it's a clinical response to Dad's condition. I'm just worried about you is all."

"What are you talking about? That's all I do!" I burst, flailing my arms. "I'm constantly confronted with it; what with you and Dad falling apart all the time since she passed."

"That's what I'm saying. You've been so focused on me and Dad, our grief, and taking care of our day-to-day concerns that you've forgotten about your own. If you keep ignoring it, it'll come up one way or another, and I'm just afraid of when and how it does." He looked straight ahead, refusing to meet my eyes. "Tell Gemma congrats for me, will ya?"

"I will." I collected my bags from the boot of the car and slammed it shut, refusing to acknowledge that I knew exactly what he meant. Perhaps I was angry that he could see what I was trying so hard to hide and run from all this time, what I still wanted to keep hidden, even from myself.

Jeremy was right about one thing: one way or another, it would come out. I was terrified of the day when he and Dad no longer needed me, and I'd be faced with my own gnawing grief.

This trip to see Gemma and Gabriel was not the time to dwell on any of this. I was also glad that I had Eoin's story to keep my mind focused until I got there—to enter a world where my Mum hadn't died.

I arrived at the York station as the colors of the sky began to dull from late afternoon to evening. I saw Gemma wave and run over as I exited the platform along with the other passengers who scattered to their own lifts—either taxis or considerate friends picking them up like me. I breathed a sigh of relief that she was alone, that Gabriel stayed behind at her parents' house.

"Catarina!" She squealed unabashedly and jumped into my arms. I didn't fail to notice another endearing nickname she decided to bestow upon me. "It's so good to see you and to hold you after so long. Let me look at you!" She looked me up and down dramatically. "You look good after dropping so much dead weight."

I rolled my eyes. "Yeah, yeah. I bet it feels good not to have to hold back about how you really feel about Henri. Go on, take your best shot; I'm ready."

"Honey, I told you how I felt about him on day one, but I'm just chuffed you have about 130 pounds of useless Frenchman off of you."

"Gemma!"

"What?"

"He was more like 120 pounds." I laughed despite my unresolved feelings for Henri that I wasn't ready to let Gemma be privy to.

"Ha! There's my girl, that's right!" She took my rolling luggage and hooked her arm in mine. "We got a takeaway from my favorite pizza place, and my parents have already thoroughly embarrassed me. As I was leaving, they were showing Gabriel volume three of my baby photos. God knows what number they are on now—only child problems, huh?"

"Sounds like champagne problems to me. I only wish I had both a fiancé and two parents without a troubled sibling to embarrass me." I blanched as I fully digested what came tumbling out of my mouth. Gemma had stopped her buoyant strides and stood completely still, waiting. "Oh, Gemma, I'm so sorry, I didn't mean…" She let go of my bag and swept me into her arms, holding me as my eyes began to sting from forcing back my tears.

"Lady, are you sure you're okay to be here this weekend? There's going to be a lot of people, family, unnecessary hugging, and lovey-dovey talk… and Christmas…I would completely understand if it's too much and you'd rather go home." We stayed in our embrace until I could talk without compensating for unshed tears stinging my throat.

"I'm sure I'll be fine. I think Jeremy got to me when he dropped me off, and not seeing you every day, and the last time that I did see you, well, you know, it wasn't the best day."

"I know, sweetie. Only if you're absolutely sure." I nodded, and she let me go to grab my luggage as we headed towards her mum's beige crossover. "Oh, what did Jeremy say? I'll kick his puny ass for that and all the shit he's been pulling lately."

"I appreciate that, Gem. He just said some crock about being worried about me." Gemma cocked her head, allowing me to elaborate. "He just said something like I'm more focused on him and Dad instead of myself and my grief. I mean, that's the whole reason I'm here and not back in Paris with you." I scoffed, expecting her to join me, but she just looked at me over the car before disappearing from view and settling into the driver's seat.

"Well, he doesn't sound entirely wrong, does he?" I slid into my seat, placing my purse, with the book inside, between my feet. I refused to respond and turned my head toward the window. "Well, this is your first weekend away, so let's make the most of it, huh?"

It wasn't long before we pulled into a stately

neighborhood that consisted of all brown-stone mansions but varied in structure so their occupants could tell each house apart. "Gemma? You're rich?!" She was pulling out my luggage and didn't meet my eyes.

"I'm not rich; my parents are rich." She said it like even she didn't entirely believe it either.

"In Paris, you live so modestly, and the way you hardly talk about home, well, I just figured."

"Yeah, well I don't want to rely on their money, they only helped me when I was first getting started, but I intentionally picked a flat there that I could support alone on a publicity assistant's salary, all right?"

"All right, not another word. So, does my room have a jacuzzi?" I yelped in surprise as she slapped my ass.

"No, now get in there before I convince my parents to stick you in the dog's room."

"Your dog has its own room? Oh, Gemma."

"Get in there!" She moved her hand to slap me again, but I dodged, skipping to the walkway.

Gabriel must have heard the commotion as he came out and took my luggage from Gemma's hands and kissed her for an endearing moment. He had to stoop rather low to reach Gemma's five-foot-two stature in accommodation to his height of six-foot-four. His dark blonde hair looked brighter against her dark brown braids—*they are a gorgeous couple.*

"Catriona, it's good to see you." He gave me the French welcome—kisses on both cheeks, which I was well-acquainted with but didn't entirely miss. "I was so sorry to hear about your mother; I'm sorry I couldn't come with Gemma to the funeral."

"Thank you, I appreciate that, but Gemma's presence and support ended up being all we needed. I don't know how I got so lucky to have a friend like her." Her eyes glistened brightly in the light from the front porch lamps and the dozens of Christmas lights that lined the roof that I knew mirrored my own.

"Dinner's here. Let me help you get Catriona settled, hmm?" He took Gemma's hand in his, leaving me to follow behind. I instinctively reached for the book in my purse for comfort as I looked on at their adjoining hands, and I suddenly felt less alone.

After too many slices of pizza and countless glasses of pinot grigio—to counter the overwhelming amount of red and green that glittered every surface of their house—Mrs. Bell offered to lead me to one of their many guest rooms.

Gabriel had to carry an unbalanced Gemma to their room as she had twice as much as me and was in no shape to walk, let alone show me to my room herself.

"Come on, love, let me show you where you'll be staying this weekend." Gemma's mum stood up and helped me, as even I stumbled a bit from this evening's pre-celebrations. I quickly apologized for being so inebriated in front of my best friend's mother—whom I had just met.

She waved off my apology good-humoredly as she led me up the dark oak staircase lined with garland that came to a brief landing and continued with another set of stairs. When she thought I was secure, she kept going to prepare the room and was already up to the corridor when she looked back to see that I was only halfway there.

She glided back down the stairs and gave me her

arm once more. "You poor dear, we're almost there." We walked arm-in-arm until we reached the room designated for me. She slowly detached herself from my hold and went over to a creamed-colored wardrobe. I hovered close to the doorway and took in the beauty of the room.

The walls were painted teal with blue and white stenciled vines, leaves, and lilies. In the middle of the room, there was a large canopy bed with spiral beams and an elaborately detailed headboard. It was draped in teal-colored silk with a white-patterned duvet that perfectly matched the walls. The carpet was a heather gray and looked just as soft as the bed—it was an exquisite room.

In the corner, there was a small white Christmas tree with blue and silver ornaments that didn't seem to bother me as much as the many traditional ones I couldn't quite ignore, no matter how hard I tried.

"The towels are in this wardrobe here and the bathroom is just through there. Let us know if there is anything you need, dear." Mrs. Bell was the most elegant woman I had ever seen. She was taller than Gemma, but they had the same oval eyes with the longest eyelashes that made them look like models with or without makeup. She wore a tan cashmere cardigan on top of a white lace dress, which swooshed around her ankles as she made her way towards me.

"We're so glad to have you here to celebrate with us. Gemma has told us so much about you, and you're just as lovely as she said." She hugged me tight, and, to my surprise, tears pricked the corners of my eyes. My lungs burned as I contained the onslaught of impending sobs. I didn't realize how much I missed the feeling of a hug that only mothers know how to give. I wrenched myself free and quickly dabbed at my eyes.

"Thanks, Mrs. Bell. I appreciate the invitation and you and your husband's generosity."

"Call me Patricia, please. Oh, sweetheart, it's no trouble. Gemma told me about your mother; I'm so sorry. If you ever need anything, you're always welcome here, even when Gemma is back in Paris. And here's my number if you ever want to call and just chat." She wrote down her mobile number on a notepad that sat on a glass desk and hugged me one more time before she quietly closed the door behind her.

I wouldn't allow myself to break down and cry again. I unpacked a few things and took extra time to get ready for bed in such a luxurious place. There was something about sleeping in such style and class, relishing in every fiber of the blanket, sheets, and pillows. My room did, in fact, have a jacuzzi tub, and after a long, relaxing soak, I settled right in the middle of the king-size bed and opened *The Adventures of Accolon*.

Eoin and the other characters were becoming so familiar to me; it was as if I had friends that were just mine—Adalind, Isla, the village healer, and Samuel—all waiting for me every time I cracked open the ornate cover.

I fell into my regular rhythm, not daring to put it down as I read of Eoin's harrowing journey to Gorgon's Mount to face Valez for the first time since his betrayal, but encountering Gorgon instead, who fearsomely stood between Eoin and Valez.

I awoke to a blinding light coming in through the floor-to-ceiling window opposite the bed. I found I could only open my eyes in mere fractions to absorb my surroundings, which only meant one thing—snow! I had no idea what time it was. Judging by the lack of noise outside my door, I figured it was still very early.

I wanted to stay in bed as long as I could—anxiety filled me at the thought of leaving this room. Here, I could ignore what would transpire later in the day, coping with Gemma's relatives whom I had never met, practicing cordiality, and viewing a life I wished to have. I was lying on my back, staring up at the canopy, when I felt the weight of a book on my stomach, still open with my bookmark nestled within the crease.

I sat up without compensating for a hangover I suddenly realized I had. I ignored the onslaught of nausea and pressed on to read a little more before I was forced to leave the warmth of my newly found sanctuary.

***

Eoin

Eoin watched as she slept peacefully. It was as if the weight of the world was finally off of her, and she could finally breathe—the planes of her face were smooth and relaxed.

At some point in the middle of the night, as the light of the moon illuminated her surroundings, he noticed she was not in her own bed, and panic seeped into his chest. He peered as far as he could to see if she was with somebody, or God-forbid, with Henri. Alas, he could not see that far, so he, too, let sleep claim him.

He didn't know how long he had slept when he first felt the comforting strokes of her hand. He stayed frozen in place as his world lost its gravity, and he and Gorgon floated in mid-air.

They eventually settled softly back on the ground, indicating she was in her familiar reading position. He could now tell her true intent based on how she handled them, how his world responded, and how she made him feel.

Eoin nudged Gorgon, who was still somehow slumbering as he tried to nuzzle further into Eoin's side to fall into an even deeper sleep. Gorgon blew a puff of smoke and fire in alarm at Eoin's third attempt to wake him.

"Shh. Calm down. She's about to read. Be alert. She

could begin anywhere, and we must not diverge from what's written." Eoin shifted his gaze outward before he heard her voice directing the story in his head.

The book was slightly tilted. He let out a breath he hadn't noticed he was holding to find that she was alone in this new bed. He was surprised as she began to read in earnest, but halfway down the adjoining page, the narration in his head abruptly stopped.

"What is she looking at now?" He muttered to himself. He stayed in position but freely looked up at her. Her gaze had left the page, and she was distracted by something unseen by him.

His poised demeanor was about to shift into frustration until she tilted the book even more so that he could see why she had paused her reading. It was snowing. Eoin's breath caught in his throat. He had never seen snow in the real world before.

As he looked back at Catriona, he wished she would keep her gaze fixed on the snow just a bit longer. For far more beautiful than the falling snow was her face appraising it. It was obvious that she loved the snow in her world, and he hoped, one day, that she would look at him in the same way.

She looked back at the book, and he took a moment to look into her eyes, imagining she could see the way he was looking at her, but the spell was broken as he heard loud thumping coming from her side of the book, "Catriona, love, are you awake?"

"Yes, I'll be right down!" Catriona shouted back to an unseen woman. "Until next time, Eoin." She smiled sweetly at him, with just a touch of melancholy, until her face finally faded and was replaced by darkness.

Eoin sunk to his knees and onto his back. She spoke to him. She said his name, addressing him as if they were dear friends. Perhaps she was sad to have to leave him behind—to deal with whoever was calling her away.

He almost couldn't believe or dare trust the way she was making him feel. A subtle movement out of the corner of his eye interrupted his delightful ruminations. A tiny sapling had poked itself out from beneath the surface and was continuing to grow. It was so small, but its bright green pigment, in contrast to the dark dust of the mountain, made him realize it was alive.

Nothing looked like this when the book was closed. Descriptions of plants that inhabited his world didn't even look like this when a reader's light illuminated them. A shadow slowly cast itself over the plant.

"Valez, do you see what I see?" Eoin didn't dare look up at him but kept his gaze firmly fixated on the plant in fear that if he looked away, even just for a moment, it would disappear.

"I do," Valez breathed out. Eoin eventually tore his eyes away to look up and saw a single tear resting on Valez's high cheekbone.

"What does this mean?" Eoin felt tears pricking the edges of his eyes as well.

"I have no idea." Valez bent down to touch it.

"No! We don't know what this is or what it means. Until we do, we tell no one what we have seen and leave it be."

"What about the giant 'puppy' in there? He'll squash this precious sapling the moment he sees it." Valez rolled his eyes at the overwhelming contrast between their

Gorgon and the reader's Gorgon.

"Well, luckily, Gorgon doesn't come out unless he's cued by the reader. He'll be no trouble to distract once we are acting our parts, *ye ken*?" Valez nodded in agreement and grew silent.

Both men just stood and stared at the plant, wondering if this had anything to do with their newest reader, or if it was one of the many changes that was happening within their book that could not be explained.

As for Eoin, this signaled hope for a brand-new future, one where maybe, just maybe he could decide his own fate—a fate unwritten.

Chapter 12

Catriona

After a lovely English breakfast with just Gemma, Gabriel, and her parents, I went back to my room to get ready for the party. I savored the time with just the five of us as I knew in a few short hours, there would be a house full of guests all vying for Gemma's attention, leaving me to make idle chit-chat with complete strangers. I seemed to cope just fine in the moment, but I always had anxiety beforehand at the mere thought of unknown circumstances.

I decided to focus all my thoughts on getting ready, along with what was happening in Eoin's story thus far. I first took a long, steamy shower. As the warm beads of the rain-shower head cascaded around me, I began to imagine that I was under the Mealt Falls—Eoin's favorite place to find solace when he became overwhelmed or scared.

I briefly pondered what it would be like, what it would feel like if neither of us was entirely alone under those falls if he were to hold me just so. If I were to run my hands through his soft curly hair as he ran his lips down my neck, feeling his large hands caressing my back and settling on my ass. If I were to splay my hands on his hard chest that had proportionately placed hair. If his piercing green eyes were to bore into mine, feeling his erection against my hip just before taking me against the rocks…

I shook the ridiculous fantasy away as shampoo ran down from my head, threatening to enter my eyes. I dried myself off, taking more time than was essential, and relished the feel of the thread count of the towels on every part of my body. I sucked in a sharp breath as the fantasy returned.

If Eoin would take his time, linking our hands above my head before sliding inside of me with that first thrust, my breasts sliding against his chest—pleasure igniting my nipples with the friction...

The threads of the fantasy slowly dissolved as my mind wandered to the evening ahead—surrounded by mostly strangers making small talk for hours on end with only alcohol and occasional glimpses of Gemma as consolation.

With my mind mainly on autopilot, I dried and

straightened my hair, which I only did for special occasions as it took forever to achieve that level of sheen, considering the length and volume of my natural hair. I would normally just let it air dry, resulting in passable waves and curls, but I wanted to look my best for Gemma.

I was very pleased with the result that I saw in the mirror. I had bought a navy-blue lace dress that had a more daring neckline than I was used to for the occasion, with matching satin high heels. I also went with a smokey eye with just a hint of dark blue to go with my dress. My hair fell past my shoulders and exposed chest.

The tendrils of the fantasy began to return as I stroked my hair—lost in the sensation as it went from skin to dress and ended right below my breast. I imagined someone coming up behind me, weaving his hands around my waist, nuzzling my neck, and whispering seductively in my ear about how gorgeous I looked tonight.

The image my mind's eye had conjured was a modern-looking Eoin, wearing a perfectly form-fitting navy suit and pinstripe tie. Still dreaming, I reached my hand back to caress his face to urge him closer to my lips but found nothing but air—I shivered in contrast. I looked back at myself in confusion with the picture of the perfect couple now gone.

Why didn't I picture Henri in that position? He'd done it a thousand times—it wouldn't be hard to recreate the sensation, but instead, I was picturing a fictional character—that admittedly felt more palpable than my actual memories.

A loud knock rescued me from further pulling on that thread.

"Come in." I busied myself in the mirror, hoping to come across as normal as possible for whoever came through the threshold.

"It's just me, Cat in the Hat." Silence filled the room, and as I saw her reflection behind me, I suddenly felt ill at ease.

"What, what is it?" I turned around, but she still didn't say anything. "Are you nervous about tonight; not getting cold feet, are we?" I laughed, trying to dispel the uneasiness that kept knocking at my heart, but she smiled sweetly back at me.

"No, what? No! Of course not. I've just never seen

you like this, Catriona Lamont. You are seriously hot!"

"Come off it, Gem. But you should hurry and shut the door so Gabriel doesn't find us out, hmm?" I laughed and turned back to reapply more red lipstick.

"Yeah, you wish. Or maybe I wish, who knows?" She came over and applied blush to both my cheeks. "Oi, I do have a cousin I can set you up with tonight. He's cute… in an awkward, charming sort of way." She applied the same blush to her cheeks and stepped back to examine herself. "So, what do you say? You and Edmund… if *yous* get married, then we'd be related. Hello? The dream, am I right?"

"While that is absolutely *the dream*, I'm not ready to be set up quite yet." *Apparently, at least not with real-life men,* I internally rolled my eyes at myself. Gemma gave a dramatic pout. "I'm still working through unresolved things with Henri, you know." I brushed at my cheeks to blend the blush she had overly applied.

"Not about getting back together or anything, I hope." She moved away from the mirror and sat on the little white settee at the foot of the bed, almost blending in with her white-silk dress.

"No, nothing like that, but he really hurt me, Gem, and until I feel like I can fully trust someone of the male species, then I think I need to be by myself." I came over and sat beside her. She motioned for me to rest my head on her shoulder.

"I know, sweetie. And just calling them the 'male species' really screams *not ready*." She paused, and we sat in that quiet moment together. "Right." She kissed my forehead sharply, breaking the moment. "We need to get downstairs and help Mum set out the hors d'oeuvres and welcome our guests." She couldn't help but let out a little squeal of excitement.

"Gemma? Hold on for just a sec." I grabbed her hand, and she turned to face me. "You look stunning tonight, and I'm so happy for you and Gabriel." Her eyes began to glisten, which surely reflected my own. "Just wanted to say it first before you heard it a million times tonight." I wrapped her in a tight hug and savored the calm before the storm.

"Thank you, Cat." She let out a loud sniffle and

broke our embrace in an instant. "Okay, we seriously need to stop, or I'll have to reapply my entire face and be late to my own party; really pissing off my parents."

"That would actually quite fit the Gemma I've come to know and love, but yes, no need to upset Mick and Patricia." I began to follow her, but then I felt an inkling of total exposure.

I turned my head and spotted my book. "I just have to grab one thing. Go on down. I'm right behind you." I grabbed my clutch and gently nestled the book inside. I felt a soothing calm wash over me—with the book just in reach, I didn't feel quite so alone for whatever this evening might hold.

The house was filled with guests in less than an hour. When an elegant, slender woman and her daughter, who was almost identical in appearance, entered, Gabriel's eyes lit up, and Gemma smiled in warm welcome. They both moved forward and took turns kissing each woman's cheeks.

When the women turned their attention to me, Gabriel sidled up next to them to introduce me, "*Maman,*

Emily, this is Catriona, Gemma's best friend and maid of honor. Catriona, this is my mother, Josephine, and my little sister, Emily.

Josephine looked like French royalty with her graying blonde hair in a tight chignon at the base of her neck that paired well with her form-fitting feather-gray dress. Emily looked to be around Jeremy's age, with bright blonde hair that was straight as a pencil falling down past her lower back.

Josephine stepped forward and kissed my cheeks, "It's lovely to meet you, Catriona. What a lovely name."

"Thank you so much. It's nice to finally meet the woman who raised Gabriel. He's such a gentleman and treats Gemma here like a queen."

"*Merci.*" She turned her face to look at the happy couple and beamed at her pride and joy.

I turned to Emily as the three of them spoke, "It's nice to meet you too. I have a brother who I believe to be about your age."

"Really? Is he here?" Emily looked around, clearly desperate to have someone her age to talk to rather than a house full of adults.

"No, he's back in Scotland, I'm afraid."

She deflated, but relaxed when her mother was done speaking and they moved into the house to greet Gemma's parents.

After meeting Gemma and Gabriel's closest families—I made my way inward undetected. My cover was making sure that the food and drink supply was still plentiful and that I could be readily on hand in the kitchen if Patricia needed anything, as she seemed to float in and out with sheer poise.

Once she forced me off duty, insisting I join the party, I couldn't refuse without seeming rude or inciting worry. I grabbed my clutch off the counter and held it in front of me as I entered the main area.

Gemma flagged me down and steered me toward the group where she and Gabriel were encircled. Surprise recognition struck me as her circle of well-wishers were some of our Parisian coworkers.

"Catriona!" Everyone said in unison and came to kiss me on one cheek as I simultaneously reciprocated.

"Hi, everyone! Oh my gosh, this is quite a surprise! I don't know how it could have slipped my mind that I'd see you all tonight." I feigned embarrassment, but truth be told, I wasn't too keen to see anyone from my past life. It was just another reminder of the life I couldn't have at the moment…and the ultimate reason why.

"We all miss you at the office, Catriona. I'm so sorry to hear about your mother. I can't imagine what your family is going through; that must be so hard." Marguerite, an accounting assistant and absolute bore, said, placing her hand over her heart in sympathy.

Everyone chimed in agreement with sympathetic murmurs, but feeling the encroaching uncomfortableness, they all turned back to Gemma and Gabriel to hear details of their upcoming nuptials—to my relief but also disappointment.

I stayed and listened as Gemma gave details of the wedding. Most I knew about, but some came as a surprise that she must have thought of quite recently and hadn't had the chance to tell me. I shifted my gaze outward as the others disengaged from me and went back to listening to

Gemma and Gabriel's love story—which I had already witnessed firsthand.

There were other small pockets of people talking and laughing boisterously, compensating for the atmospheric Christmas music and chatter all around. Everyone with a glass of champagne or wine in hand seemed to be having the best time, and I found that I was quite envious of each and every one of them.

I accidentally locked eyes with Gemma's cousin, Edmund, whom she had introduced me to when he first arrived, trying once more to set us up. She must have said something to him before she talked to me about it because he lifted his glass of champagne at me and attempted a seductive wink, which was more of an exaggerated blink if anything else through his thick-brimmed bifocals.

As he tilted his glass to take a drink, most dribbled out onto what would clearly be the winner of an ugly Christmas jumper. I nodded but quickly adverted my gaze so he wouldn't see it as an invitation to come over.

Out of the corner of my eye, I saw a familiar figure. He stood alone in the corner of the room by a built-in bookcase, nursing his glass of mulled wine and intermittently perusing the books. When his eyes met mine, his face lit up with a smile so warm that the ball of anxiety that set up residence in my throat left, and I felt safe. I couldn't contain my own smile and let out a relieved laugh as I saw Ludo put down his glass and make his way towards me.

"*Excuse-moi,*" I whispered to the group, who didn't even acknowledge my polite exit as I met Ludo halfway.

"Catriona." He opened up his long arms to me, and in our embrace, I felt like I had finally come home. My home in Paris, rather. I had no memories of hugging my dad until recently. Yet this one and only hug from Ludo, which lasted less than a second, is what I imagined normal people experienced with their fathers.

"Ludo? I can't believe you're here! It's so good to see you. How's the office doing without me?" I laughed goodhumoredly but halted as I saw the humor drain out of his light brown eyes.

"To be honest, it's not the same without you, Catriona. When Mademoiselle Bell first invited me, I wasn't sure I'd be able to make it, but when she told me you'd be here, I booked the first flight available." He looked down at his hands in confusion and looked back at the end table, realizing he didn't have his wine to channel his nerves. "I know I was there, and I have said it countless times since, but I am so sorry about your mother, Catriona."

"Thank you, Ludo. I appreciate it more than you know." I smiled trying to get past this moment but feeling a strong urge to grab a whiskey and go off and read in a quiet corner.

"How is your family doing *now*?"

"My father is still not able to talk, but he seems in better spirits these days. Jeremy, well Jeremy, is just, I'm not sure. One day he seems like he's on the mend, but then he'll regress." I paused, shocked by my own candidness, offering more information than what was customary in this setting. It seemed as if the party around us had faded, and it was just me and him, and my *Series of Unfortunate Events*-like family drama.

I shook my head. "I'm sorry that I just piled that on

you, Ludo. I haven't even had a drop of alcohol to blame it on." I wrapped my arms around myself, feeling incredibly self-conscious. I looked around to find the drink counter.

"Please don't apologize. You may confide in me any time with anything. Please know that." His attempted smile made him wince instead. "So, they still need you by the sounds of it?"

"My family? Yes, I believe so. Is that okay? I mean, I could do some work from home, I can quit my part-time job at the library and take on my responsibilities, you know, remotely?" I became alarmed at where this line of conversation was going, and panic flooded in as I rambled—my voice rising an octave with each word.

"Catriona, I'm so sorry, but umm, we desperately need somebody in your position who can be in the office, in Paris, to meet with writers and have access to our systems. It's just impossible. If there were a way, believe me, I'd keep you on in a heartbeat."

He reached for me, but the room began to swirl around me, and heat crept up my spine to my face. I slowly began to back away. "Catriona, whenever you are able to come back, I'll do everything in my power to make a position for you, I promise. Here, let's go somewhere quieter so we can sit and talk."

Worry filled his eyes as he placed a soft hand on my elbow. I choked on a gulp of air, threatening to escape with a flood of tears. I whispered I was fine and thanked him for his kind offer.

I broke from his hold and made a beeline for the drinks, grabbed a bottle of whiskey, and made my way to the far side of the manor, where I knew there was a small sitting room with one chair and wall-to-wall bookshelves. As the number of people on this side began to thin out, I was confident no one would be in there.

I sat down in the plush beige chair and let it envelop me. I still had a sightline of the party down the long corridor as I watched everyone mingle and celebrate without a care in the world.

I had always felt like an observer of life instead of an active participant like all those around me. I used to think that there was something wrong with me, and maybe there was, but there was some comfort and safety in being just an observer.

I took a swig from the large bottle of whiskey and winced as the burning sensation ran down my throat, then sighed as, in an instant, it was replaced with a toasty warmth that spread throughout my entire body. I don't know how many swigs I took, but after a while, I felt completely numb, feeling next to nothing, and that scared me more than death itself.

After hearing that I had lost my dream job in Paris by a man I saw as a father figure, not knowing if there was an end in sight for my dad or brother and having to relive the day my Mum died with people I didn't know and could care less about, I should feel *something.*

I desperately tried to feel anything, anything at all, but I couldn't. What came close to a feeling couldn't break through the icy ceiling. I muffled a fake cry with a small throw pillow with obnoxious tassels on each corner in an attempt to feel without alerting anyone of my presence, but nothing seemed to work.

As I situated the pillow back in its place, I noticed my clutch on my lap and pulled out the book with shaking hands. Only when I had opened it and started to read, did my hands still. Perhaps I could bring the magic I felt from reading to reality since reality had nothing else to give.

***

Eoin

Eoin and Valez sat in companionable silence, just looking at the plant. It had stopped growing, but it still maintained its bright hue, and the longer Eoin stared at it, he noticed flecks of yellow in perfect harmony with the green. It stopped growing when Catriona closed the book, but Eoin had no doubt that once her light returned, it would keep growing until it reached the sky.

"You know something, Valez?" Eoin broke the silence without breaking his stare. "This tiny plant has changed the way I see our world."

"Aye. Me too, actually."

"Really? That's reassuring. I don't know if it's possible, but it's making me think, if things are changing, then I could potentially change my own fate." He wasn't entirely sure he wanted to confide in Valez everything he was thinking about the sudden appearance of this plant—his ever-growing feelings for Catriona, his lifelong dream of leaving the book and entering the real world.

Somehow, he already knew Valez wouldn't understand or even approve. He stopped himself before receiving an impending reprimand.

"I don't know how our fate can be changed, Eoin. We exist to tell this story so readers can escape in fantasy, and once they've finished, we wait until the next—that is our purpose." Eoin looked over at Valez, and it seemed as if he, too, was holding something back, not quite believing his own mission statement. He let it go, as he was hiding his true intentions from his friend, as well.

They continued to stare at the plant until it and the surrounding ground began to vibrate. Their necks both snapped in the direction of the mountain's entrance. Gorgon was coming to join them as he bounded from one side of his legs to the other in blissful ignorance.

"Oh, no, Valez! We can't let him come near the sapling, or he'll over-excite himself and tear it to shreds!" Eoin stood quickly and got into his well-known fighting stance, blocking the plant.

"Indeed, we have to distract him until the reader returns, so he'll have to go back to his cave until his action is cued."

"Aye, come by my side." Eoin pressed his arm against Valez's but did not break even when Valez tensed from the contact. His main focus remained on blocking Gorgon's view as they coerced him back to his cavern.

"Gorgon!" Eoin yelled as they were almost to him. Gorgon crouched down, about to pounce on them in welcome. "No, no, boy! Stay there." For if he would knock them to the ground, the plant would grab his eye.

He broke from Valez's touch but stayed almost parallel, holding up his hands for Gorgon to stay, even enticing him to touch his nose to Eoin's outstretched hand. Gorgon reacted as Eoin designed, but through Eoin's splayed fingers, the plant was in view. Eoin looked back, realizing his mistake, and sighed in the knowledge of what was to come, unable to stop it.

Gorgon leaped, causing dirt to rain over both Eoin and Valez. Eoin shielded his eyes from the downpour.

When it had finally cleared, Eoin looked in horror as Gorgon hovered above the plant—the gust of wind from his wings barely kept the sapling intact.

"Gorgon! No! Get away from there; that is none of your concern!" Eoin was about to sprint and dive on the plant to keep it safe when he felt Valez's hand on his shoulder. Valez must have anticipated his thoughts—both knowing he could not get there in time.

It was Catriona's face and the soft light that cascaded around her that distracted Gorgon from his intended target. He looked up and flew straight into his cave.

Eoin sighed in utter relief and smiled at Catriona, taking a moment to look at her. She was a vision. Her hair shined like the sun and looked smooth as silk—if only he could run his hands through it, he would capture it between his fingers as he cradled her neck to gently kiss her, weaving them in and out as he would part her lips, deepening the kiss.

He moved his eyes down from her red lips and noticed what she was wearing. She looked so elegant in what he presumed was a dress. He blushed as he couldn't help but notice the top of her breasts curving over the neckline of the lace trimming.

He averted his gaze, embarrassed to have lingered so dishonorably. He cleared his throat and moved away from her image as he met Valez's harsh gaze.

"Get a hold of yourself, man. She's about to read," Valez scoffed. Eoin got into position but huffed at Valez's chastisement—he could never understand this feeling. Eoin believed Valez incapable of this type of love. In retrospect, he was glad he didn't tell Valez of his true intentions as they gazed at the plant, envisioning a future of his own making.

Valez left Eoin's side to get into position. Eoin took his stance, ready to hear the soft lilt of her voice in his head to continue the story. As if on cue, he could hear every word she read that prompted his action.

He was meant to fight Valez to the death as Valez guarded Gorgon on the Black Cuillin Ridge, but there was something different tonight in Catriona's reading. He could feel that something was wrong, but he couldn't quite put his finger on it.

Her reading was lagging so much that instead of bounding up the mountain as the story described, his actions were measured to mere fractions of a movement. His legs moved in slow motion, his knee rising parallel to his abdomen, then descending back to the ground.

Then, as his right foot hit the ground gradually, he suddenly emerged right in front of Valez, having sprinted up the mountain at warp speed. Valez snorted, barely containing his amusement. "Your lover appears to be drunk, Eoin."

They both lifted their gaze without shifting their heads. Eoin saw she was bleary-eyed, with her mouth ajar. She shook her head to no doubt clear the fuzziness and looked away from the page.

As she began to read once more, he materialized back down at the foot of the mountain. She was re-reading what he had just done, but this time, he made it to the top at the speed in which the story required.

He knew she was about to read the beginning of a five-page battle between hero and villain, but both were stopped short at the sound of yelling coming from Catriona's side.

Eoin glanced up as he saw the confusion written all over her face transform into indignation as she set him down. All he could see was white, but her pained voice reverberated throughout her world and into his so clearly that he might as well have been standing right behind her in loving support.

***

Catriona

I was having a hard time concentrating on Eoin's story as the numerous swigs of whiskey infiltrated my mind. I was reading each word painfully slow, but as the alcohol settled into my bloodstream and began to seep back out of my brain, I read rapidly through the details of Eoin's climb up Gorgon's Mount as he, as he… I was distracted as I heard shouts and glasses clinging, and the word "toast" was thrown about, but I couldn't be quite sure that was the word being said in my inebriated state.

I looked down at the page, squinting my eyes at the

blurred words. I couldn't remember what I had just read. I picked up at the beginning of the page.

Eoin ran past the emerald pools of long-ago fairies and came to stand at the foot of the ridge, where he could see the eerie red glow radiating from Valez's staff.

I remembered his jagged run up the ridge, dodging blasts of magic that were aimed to kill—dirt flying over Eoin's head as he nearly avoided the wizard's shots. My heart jumped in my chest as Eoin narrowly escaped death—relieved I had some semblance of feeling, even if it was in response to a work of fiction.

As both Eoin and Valez squared off, my heart settled back in my chest just for it to jump back in my throat again as I heard Gemma screech my name, and its echo reverberated off the walls.

"Catriona! What the hell?" She barreled into my fortified place of solace, not just in this room, but in Eoin's world, as well.

"God, Gem. Not so loud. What did I do?" I held my hands to my head as sharp jabs pricked at every angle.

Gemma looked around the room. She first saw the

book in my lap then spotted the almost empty bottle of whiskey on the oak end table. "Very nice. You leave my engagement party to read and get drunk alone? I mean, I wouldn't care if you got drunk at the party with the rest of us, well some of us, I won't say who, but, for fuck's sake, Cat, you missed my fucking toasts!" Her voice cracked, and tears began to streak her cheeks.

I sighed in resignation, "I'm sorry. I just needed a minute to collect myself after Ludo…" She lowered her eyes to the floor. "Hold on, did you know? Gemma, look at me. Did you know Ludo was giving away my position?"

I realized I had stood up, placing the book face-open on the chair, but I set my sights back on Gemma, who still couldn't look at me. "Well?"

"I did, but I didn't want to be the one to tell you—you're dealing with so much at home, you haven't truly dealt with your Mum's accident—I just thought you'd realize it on your own. I also knew that Ludo would be able to hire you back when you were ready."

I shook my head in disbelief at her betrayal. "Good lord, Gemma! I was completely blindsided!" I put my hands on my knees to steady my breathing. "You know, I woke up every day in Paris feeling like anything could happen to me. I don't feel that here. In fact, I feel absolutely nothing! Not going back to Paris scares me; staying here scares me even more, but not being able to feel anything scares me to death! And you didn't tell me? My supposed best friend lied to me for weeks!"

"Well, *my* best friend missed something that meant the world to me! Hell, as maid of honor, you were supposed to give a goddamned speech yourself. It was so awkward as we called your name several times before everyone just weakly shouted, 'To Gemma and Gabriel.'"

"Well, I'm sorry. I'm sorry I wasn't there to tell you how wonderful your life is and congratulate you on meeting the love of your life as your whole family stood around you in support." I choked out the last words through uncontrollable sobs.

The stronghold—the wall I had carefully erected the night of my mum's death—finally broke through the weight that had been holding it so carefully in place. "But my Mum's dead! She's never coming back!"

My eyes filled with tears, and I shifted my eyes back and forth to clear them away. "I have to get out of here. I'm sorry." I lightly touched Gemma's arm, grabbed my open book, placed it back in the safety of my clutch, and ran straight to my designated room.

I changed my clothes and packed as fast as I could, wanting to avoid everything and everyone. I would call for a taxi outside, even if it were below freezing. I would do just about anything to get out of here. I descended the stairs, phone in hand, when Patricia came into view. I paused and shoved my mobile into my coat pocket.

"I'm so sorry, Patricia, for everything, but I, I can't stay." I hung my head, hoping to pass her by quickly and apologetically.

"I know, dear. I already called you a taxi. It'll be here in five minutes." She didn't warn me in any way as she hugged me fast, and I couldn't help but fall into her embrace like a child.

"Please tell Gemma how sorry I am. There's just so much…" Her shoulder absorbed my sob. She stroked my back in soothing circles. The sound of the taxi's horn stopped what was short of a breakdown. "I've got to go. Thank you so much for everything." I gathered my things and left without a backward glance.

On the way to the train station, fear gripped me like a vice. I wasn't ready to go home. I wasn't ready to admit to Jeremy that he was not only right but that we would all fall right back into old patterns—where my grief was forced to take a back seat.

I flipped open the book to my marked page and saw something. Eoin's battle against Valez took place at the Fairy Pools in Skye.

An idea hit me like a ton of bricks. I could delay *that* reality for a day if I traveled to Skye and visited a place right out of a fairytale. I searched for the most efficient way to get there from York. I could take a train from York to Manchester, book a flight to Inverness, then rent a car and drive the rest of the way.

I had cried myself to sleep on the short train ride to Manchester, and sleep claimed me in minutes on the Red Eye to Inverness, so I had no time to read, but I knew I wanted to save that exact moment in the plot for Skye. I realized I hadn't been there in years. The last time that I was at the Fairy Pools, I was with my mum.

***

Eoin

Eoin heard it—he had heard it all. Catriona's mother had died. Right before she found him, from the sounds of it. He was busily trying to piece together their timeline together in his mind, recalling what he had seen and heard in her world, all culminating in this one truth. She had only found him because of her mother's untimely passing, and her family's grief kept her in Scotland until she was forced to take a job she barely tolerated.

Grief filled his heart as he saw the world from her eyes. How selfish he had been—only thinking of his own ambitions, convincing himself he loved her, yet he hadn't even known the one thing that defined this relationship if he could even call it that.

Perhaps Adalind had been right all along. He would know Catriona, or so he thought, yet she would never know him, not the real him anyway. She just knew

Eoin of Accolon, King of Caledonia, who saves his damsel in distress, the love of his life, from a wicked wizard who wields dark arts and dragons to achieve his powerful ambition of being on the throne. He rolled his eyes at his own predictable storyline.

Catriona would never know that Valez, his best friend, was charming, reliable, and genuine. She would never know that Adalind was vain, delusional, and power-hungry. Every one of them in stark contrast to how they were written. Catriona would never truly know *him*. His face crumpled in despair.

Acutely feeling not only Catriona's loss in every regard but the loss of every possible future with her incited panic. Not even the sight of the sapling that now reached his knee could instill hope. He felt himself reverting back to the time before Catriona, back to how he felt with every other uninspiring reader before her.

He sensed Valez's presence behind him. He realized they were in the exact same place before, both staring at the plant—with only Valez seemingly unchanged. Eoin saw his eyes widen at the sight of the growth.

"There is something truly special about your young lady, Eoin. Look at what her light has done! There must be some sort of magic she exudes into our pages! I take back everything I've ever said about her and her unnatural hold on you." Valez chuckled and squeezed Eoin's shoulder.

Eoin wrenched himself free, feeling as if a dagger went straight through his heart. "What is it even about her that makes her so special? How is she any different than the hundreds of humans who have read our story!"

Was it all in his head? Was he elevating her because she was the first in decades? He paced back and forth ignoring Valez's growing concern.

"She isn't like those readers, Eoin. I believe you now. There is something different about her, I can't explain it fully, I can just feel something changing. Even our world is looking brighter and more vibrant—even when the darkness descends as she closes the book. Just look at this plant. If that isn't enough proof, then I don't know what is!"

Eoin could feel anger building inside of him—an

anger that he either couldn't or had no desire to stop. He felt like a fool for believing that he was in love with this reader or that she could possibly fall in love with him.

He was angry at Catriona's world for taking her mother away from her, for causing her so much sorrow with her father's ailing health, unruly brother, an unworthy man who broke her heart, and ultimately losing her dream in Paris.

Eoin clenched his fists by his sides. Neither of them could change the other's fate. It was hopeless—their worlds would remain broken, and a mere sapling wouldn't be able to change that.

"Eoin? What's the matter? I agree with you. Catriona is quite remarkable. Imagine how our world might change as she continues to read!" Valez's optimistic change of opinion of Catriona was the final push over the edge.

"Oh, is it? Is it truly because of this stupid plant that you finally believe?" Eoin stood over it and pushed his heel against its stalk. He heard Valez take a sharp inhale as if in pain, and he stopped.

Eoin bent down, "This isn't real. None of it is real! She isn't special; she's just another reader who, once she finishes our fictitious tale, will put us back on the shelf and forget we ever existed. She'll go back to her life, and we'll go back to no life whatsoever!" Eoin yanked the plant from its root and watched in satisfaction as Valez's face crumpled.

Eoin's regret was instantaneous as the plant withered in his hand, its bright hue fading along with the light that had been in both of their eyes since it first appeared. "Valez, I…I'm sorry, I shouldn't have done that—"

He couldn't finish his apology as Valez jumped on him and they began to roll down the mountain, leaving the crumpled sapling and all it had represented behind.

Chapter 13

Catriona

"Fairies are said to have roamed this land—from the Fairy Glen to the Fairy Pools—blurring the borders of our world into theirs until magic manipulates time and space to fulfill their fool-hearty fancies."

"Legend has it," my mother took my hand as we descended toward the pools, "a fiddler came to sit in the Glen so he could practice undisturbed. Whilst filling the land with such beautiful music, the fairies wanted him to enter their kingdom and entertain their festivities just for the night.

He agreed, but when he awoke the next morning, a century had passed, and he found that everyone he had ever loved was taken by the cruel passage of time.

But my favorite myth, Catriona, is the aura of magic that surrounds the crystalline waters of the Fairy Pools as they flicker between hues of sapphire and emerald.

I can imagine the selkies becoming so mesmerized by these waters that they change into their human forms at night and bathe in the light of the full moon, trying to recapture any youth lost as the passage of time steadily marches on."

I could still hear my mother's gentle voice echoing over the sound of distant fiddling. I shivered, not entirely from the cold, even though there was a light dusting of snow that swirled in the soft breeze as my boots kicked up their small flakes.

I left my rented crossover at the top of the road and walked down the small snow-covered path to the pools. In the spring and summer, this place was full of tourists and the buses that hauled them here lined the main road for miles.

Although it was winter and absolutely freezing, I was glad to be alone—to remember my mother's words as they traveled over the wind. It was as if time had stood still in this place.

It wasn't until my foot hit the ground and I was surrounded by the dark ridge, in contrast with the crystallized pools, that I could recall the full memory.

I was seven years old, and my eighth birthday was the next day. Mum wanted to take me "someplace that still holds true magic." Dad had to work, so it was a girls' weekend, to my absolute delight and Mum's unexpressed disappointment.

My father's absence wouldn't deter her, though, for this was her favorite place in Scotland. She had first visited the fairies, as she liked to say, on a class trip a few months before she met Dad.

The day we were there, she had a far-off look in her eyes as she absentmindedly stroked my hair. "The last time I was here was the loneliest I had ever been in my life."

She looked down with eyes that matched my own, still stroking my hair in a way that if she were to stop, I would vanish right in front of her. "I vowed right then and there that I would come back with someone I love and replace that memory."

Her eyes crinkled at the sides as her lips, which were always pink, even without makeup, ticked up. "I'm so glad it's with you, my darling."

She kissed the top of my head and rested her chin there for a long moment. Part of me knew she would have been happier if she could have replaced her lonely memory with both her husband and daughter. It was that day I began to resent my dad for inadvertently hurting her, and it only grew as time went on.

I hadn't fully understood what she had meant at the time, because my first time at the pools I was with my mum and happy. Now, I was alone and miserable—reversing the order in which my mother experienced this haunting place.

I sat down on the clearest perch—close enough in memory to where she and I had sat that day—and opened my book. This place didn't bode well for Eoin either—for here was where he would die.

***

Eoin

They had rolled down the entire ridge until Eoin's head was hanging on the side of the cleft where the Fairy Pools lay just below, with Valez astride, anchoring him in place.

As his face took on each blow from Valez's fists, the back of his head pounded on the sharp edge of the rock. Eoin let Valez carry on as long as he could endure the pain, knowing he deserved every last bit of it.

How could he have been so cruel? He only withstood the beating because of how numb he had become to everything around him. The loss of the sapling and all it had represented, and now Valez's friendship, along with his place in both his world and Catriona's, left him paralyzed.

He turned his head and looked at the trickling water below. He tried to will the magic said to be infused in these waters to wash over him but remembered that magic only existed in the real Fairy Pools… in Catriona's world, his was but a pale imitation to further mock his torment.

Valez's blows had slowed until Eoin no longer felt them or Valez's weight holding him, and he began to slip over the edge. He closed his eyes, hoping to feel the cool relief of the waters on the injuries he had sustained.

At the last second, Valez pulled him back and tossed him over to the dewed grass that gave him a fraction of relief the pools would have given.

"Do you realize what you have done!" Valez picked up Eoin's limp body and shook him as Eoin's head lolled back and forth with the inertia, unable to hold its weight against the onslaught of Valez's tide. "Answer me!" He waited with bated breath for Eoin's explanation.

"None of it is real. We are in a book. We're a story, Valez, that's it, we're characters someone created. It's not real…none of it is real." He let out a bitter laugh accompanied by blood as he echoed his own words to Adalind in what felt like a lifetime ago. He had gone back to the beginning, and all he could do was laugh.

A simmering growl escaped Valez's lips, one that Eoin had only heard when the book was open, one that was used only in the presence of the reader. He gulped in surprise as Valez tossed him against a rock. "You ruin everything! You act like a spoiled child as we coddle you until you deem yourself ready. The only reason we exist is because of you and yet you don't give a damn about anyone but yourself—that is until this reader arrived."

He spat out *reader* like it was poison in his mouth he needed to dispel. "And all of the sudden, after years of encouraging you as your friend to do something to make us relevant once more, you do it for her without a moment's hesitation!" Valez took a menacing step as Eoin peeled himself off the rock, seeing a part of his body now permanently sculpted into its cleft.

Eoin put up his hands to placate Valez's threatening advance. "Valez. Valez? Please hear me. I'm sorry for what I did. I have been a terrible friend to you, blinded by my own self-pity and loathing. Please forgive me, dear friend. It was unconsciously done."

For a moment, Eoin thought he had gotten through as Valez's tense shoulders relaxed and his eyes softened, but a fire Eoin had never seen appeared.

Valez roared in his pursuit, raising his staff high as if to conjure lightning from the sky as he did in this part of the story to conjure its magic. Since both men knew that could never happen, Valez swung it as a club, aiming for Eoin's head.

"Stop!" Eoin shielded his eyes as a white light appeared above. He was so relieved to see Catriona's face, knowing she was the only reason Valez stopped another wave of attacks until he realized what she was about to read: a fight between King Eoin of Accolon and Valez, the evil sorcerer—to the death.

***

Catriona

I scolded myself for reading ahead to Eoin's death, or what I presumed to be a cliffhanger—to throw the reader off and keep them reading to find out Eoin's fate—to see if he, in fact, lives. As I read from where the fight first began, I had forgotten about the cold, either completely numbed by it or I just couldn't care less as the lines between my world and Eoin's started to blur.

Eoin sidestepped every blast with deft precision, knowing just one blast would annihilate him. The only card Valez had to play was to duel him—staff against sword. I gasped at every physical blow Eoin received, knowing this battle wouldn't end well for him.

"Give up now, Your Majesty. Your kingdom, your people, your throne, even your queen are mine!"

Eoin spun against the side of the ridge, panting just to parry each of Valez's strikes.

"I'll die before I let you take my kingdom, and I'll go to

the depths of hell before I let you lay a finger on Adalind!"

My heart jumped at the fierceness with which he defended his true love. My heart stung, knowing I had no one in the entire world who felt that way about me. Even when I did, Henri never fought to keep me. I shook my head to dispel all thoughts of him and returned to the story.

"That," Valez said sadistically, "I can accommodate." He rammed Eoin repeatedly into a state of utter confusion, throwing him away from the ridge. Red lightning crackled around the top of Valez's staff. Thunder boomed as Valez raised it to the sky.

I was pulled out of the story as a clap of thunder and dark clouds covered the ridge. I jumped up, wanting to run on extinct, yet I couldn't tear my eyes away.

As lightning illuminated the blanket of clouds, I saw two figures facing one another. My cries of warning were drowned out in another roar of thunder.

I bit back a scream, but as the clouds lit up and the mist cleared, I saw a man staring at me—his eyes grew wider as they met mine. "Eoin?" I breathed in disbelief.

The red lightning and thunder that shook the ground set my feet to run the opposite way, straight to my car as torrential sleet stung my face.

After a couple of slips between panicked breathing—as if I were being chased—I jumped in the car and rested my head against the seat in an attempt to stop my racing heart. I squinted my eyes to see those two figures, one I swore I knew, who looked so shocked and afraid, who seemed to see me just as clearly as I saw him, but to no avail. The sleet and fog covered the entire landscape.

I took two shaky breaths. "In and out. In and out." I directed myself out loud as I remembered those piercing green eyes that seemed to bore into my soul.

I started the car and drove as quickly as the weather would allow—my mind rationalized that what I saw was a side effect of my overwhelming grief, but my heart kept whispering, *It was real.*

***

Eoin

Eoin and Valez stood frozen in place as they saw a woman through the mist. Eoin blinked once, twice as the mist continued to clear. He saw, he saw… *Catriona?* He knew those eyes too well for it not to be her—ones that were as dark as the ocean below while the sun shimmered on its surface.

For the first time, he could see her in her entirety. She was bundled up in a white coat, with a pink hat and matching gloves, blue trousers, and black boots.

She seemed to see him, too, as she visibly inhaled. *Eoin?* He couldn't help but beam at the overwhelming confirmation of her presence. He knew that voice. He knew the exact cadence in which she said his name—just as she had done a dozen times before.

To her, they went unheard, but now… he couldn't finish contemplating what this would mean to her, even what it meant to him as he snapped his head back to see Valez staring at a ball of red light atop his staff.

"Valez? What the bloody hell is that?" Eoin's whole body shook as he looked over and saw that Catriona was gone. Valez lifted his staff to the sky, as he had done thousands of times before, but this time was different. He looked different, like he… like he was *Valez, the evil sorcerer.*

Valez summoned a bolt of lightning and, in that moment, Eoin knew he was going to die, not just for the reader, but in his world too. There was a blinding light, the smell of charred wood, then nothing.

***

Catriona

Then nothing. I finished the chapter on the plane ride home just to have some closure and move on from what had happened at the Fairy Pools. *If anything did actually happen, that is.* I closed my eyes and audibly breathed in and out, ignoring what my flight companion possibly thought of me.

I gripped the seat handles hard and looked out the window. I watched in a meditated state as fluffy clumps of white clouds moved and molded themselves into different shapes until I saw Eoin's shocked expression looking back at me. I heard my name on his lips and shivered.

Even with shaking fingers, I shut the plastic shade with so much force that the balding middle-aged man beside me jumped and said, "Hey! What gives?" in his thick highland brogue.

"I'm sorry, I'm just…just in a bit of a state right now. I'll keep it to myself, don't worry. Don't want to be one of those passengers who spill their guts to a complete stranger."

I laughed, knowing I was unable to stop what was about to spill out. "Then she and that stranger talk the whole time until they realize that they have fallen in love with each other and forget the lives they were going to lead once the plane lands. I think that was the plot of a cheesy holiday movie that I watched once."

I looked over, and the man was looking at me as if I had grown three heads. "Don't worry; it's clear from your expression that you'd never fall for me and that shiny gold ring on your finger. So, how's the Mrs.? Why isn't she on this flight with ya?"

At that, he turned away from me as designed. I had transitioned into my mother's American accent and switched to an American's tendency to pry into others' personal lives without invitation. The first bit was me prattling on without control—my anxiety over what had just happened hijacked the wheel.

Once I was back in control, I shoved the book to the bottom of my carry-on, purposefully covering it with everything else I had packed that weekend for Gemma's engagement party, not for this spontaneous trip to Skye. I needed it to be as far away from me as possible, both mentally and physically.

Not properly dealing with my mother's grief was manifesting itself in the form of a story. In a world where she wasn't dead—that's why I saw Eoin. I imagined him in that place so I wouldn't be alone. That's all.

I knew sooner or later, I would have to confront my grief before I went insane, *or more insane*. In the meantime, I couldn't use Eoin's story as an escape or as a crutch. I needed time away from him. I just hoped that he would be okay without me. I rolled my eyes and shut them so I could escape my own delusional thinking that had gotten me into this mess.

***

Eoin

"Eoin? Eoin? What are ye playin' at man? Get up!" Eoin could barely hear who was calling him. His ears were ringing, and what little light came through the slits of his eyelids shot pain through his entire body. He sealed them shut so he could remember what happened without the interference of searing agony.

The vision of Catriona standing at the pool's edge, calling his name, alleviated every last ounce of misery that he imagined Valez's sudden blast of lightning caused. His eyes flew open, and a new wave of torment overtook him.

"Sire? Eoin!" He saw Sam's face hover over him; concern etched into every crease.

Ahh, yes, Eoin remembered. This was the part of the story where his brave first knight, Samuel, comes to find him mostly dead from Valez's blast of magic and takes him into hiding to nurse him back to health while divulging the state of the kingdom to him after Valez's underhanded coup.

Eoin listened for Catriona's voice to guide their actions as Sam was presently doing. He couldn't hear anything. He opened his eyes wider to see her face in the sky above him, but she wasn't there.

It was just Sam looking down at him with such uncertainty that Eoin realized what was written in the book was really happening. Sam's acting skills with a reader weren't at all this convincing, which only further confirmed Eoin's suspicions.

Eoin felt the edges of his vision darken, he would lose consciousness very soon, and without Sam's help, he could easily fade from existence.

"Sam, I know this is hard to believe, and I have little time to explain, but you have to carry on with how the book is written, even without the reader. You have to take me to the house and get the healer to nurse me back to health—for real, or I and our world will fade, do you understand? Valez is real. It's all becoming real; can't you feel it?" Eoin clung to Sam's chainmail, pulling him down so he would have to see the truth in Eoin's eyes.

"Aye, Eoin. I understand." Eoin trusted his written

best friend for the first time as darkness overtook him, and he fell limp in Sam's arms.

***

Catriona

After what felt like a tortuous travel itinerary, I made it home to a quiet house. I checked on Dad, who beamed at me and caressed my cheek. I forced a smile and moved out of his embrace.

I wasn't ready to continue our new-found relationship. I was still in that place where he disappointed Mum, leaving her to relive a memory she desired to have with him and abandoning me on my eighth birthday.

I moved into my bedroom and cracked the door. I had three missed calls from Jeremy and two short messages from him. "I came to pick you up at the train station, but you never showed. I assumed you had a great time with Gemma and decided to stay longer. I'm just at the pub with Liam and Ryan. See you when you get home. Dad's all taken care of."

I winced at the mention of Gemma. She had left

one text message. "Hope you made it back safe. We need to talk." I couldn't fix what I had done before I dealt with the reason it happened.

No matter how much it hurt to know she was upset, I had to confront the volcano of grief inside me that was threatening to erupt. I had to extinguish it before it could spew again at the wrong place and at the wrong time.

For the millionth time, I ignored Mum's last voice message, the one that was always there. The one my phone notified me was still there with its orange icon on top of the voicemail app every time I looked at my phone. I clicked my phone off and threw it on my bed.

I shuffled out of my room and lowered myself on the couch. Dad had the game on, as he always did, I never understood how he didn't get bored watching what seemed to be the same plays, teams, and predictable outcomes. I grabbed the remote on the arm of his chair and muted it. He turned his head surprised but softened as I began to talk.

"I went to Skye this weekend. The Fairy Pools to be

exact." I saw as understanding washed over him and I pressed on. "I could never understand how you could disappoint Mum like that, how you could disappoint me on my birthday! She wanted you there, Dad! She needed you there to erase a lonely memory she had. I needed you there with us! I think ever since then we've been disappointing one another, and we became sets of two: You and Mum or me and Mum. I think Jeremy gave Mum a way so that we all felt like one family instead of broken fractions. He allowed you to ignore me entirely, only inserting yourself if Mum forced your hand. I know that's why this broke you so much, Dad, why you're a hollow shell. Why I've had to take her place where it mattered most."

My throat burned as I swallowed a sob, as I was beginning to breach the walls I had carefully built and tear them down brick by brick. My dad's eyes glistened with unshed tears, but he was listening, he was hearing me, so I allowed myself to let it all go, holding nothing back.

"But I miss her too. I can't go on pretending I'm okay just so I can take care of you and Jeremy, just so you two can have someone strong to lean on whilst you all deal with your own grief. I'm not that strong! I yelled and left Gemma's party because I bottled it all up so tightly. I started seeing things that weren't there in Skye!"

I hyperventilated to stop myself from divulging that bit to my dad, he wouldn't understand. I barely understood what had happened at the Black Cuillin Ridge. I forced the image of Eoin's shocked face from my mind.

"Why did she die? What was the point? It doesn't make any sense to me. I keep thinking that if I just carry on with my life, help you and Jeremy get back to normal, I can just go back to Paris as if nothing ever happened. Leave the Scotland she's not in and keep the one she is in my heart forever. How am I… how am I supposed to do this without her?"

At that, my vision was blocked by an onslaught of never-ending tears. Hiccups clogged my voice, and my body convulsed with sobs.

After a few minutes of holding my own convulsing body, tucking every limb into myself just to feel a modicum of safety, I felt a hand on my shoulder gradually move up and down the length of my arm. "I'm so sorry, my darling girl." At the sound of his voice, a voice that was hoarse and strained, but his nevertheless, all my tears dried up, and I sprang up off the couch.

"Dad?" We looked at each other, shocked, before we moved to cry in each other's arms. I barely heard the front door open and close, but then I saw Jeremy's eyes widen before he lowered himself beside Dad and enveloped both of us with his long arms.

We were in this same position the first day I came home, the first day without Mum, but this time, Dad and I were laughing through our tears.

Jeremy poked his head up. "Hey! What's so funny? I thought we were having a moment together?"

"It's nothing, Son." Jeremy's eyes widened to the size of saucers, and Dad and I giggled even more, wiping at our eyes and noses. His voice was still strained, but with its second use, it had a bit more volume to it. Jeremy couldn't help but chuckle, and a tear ran down his cheek as well.

"Say something else, Dad! Come on!" Jeremy

cheered. Dad just smiled and beckoned us into another family hug.

This wasn't the end of our grief. Dad still had a long way to go before he could function independently, Jeremy hadn't been sober for long, and I still had to process mine a bit more. I also had so much to fix around me, but it was a start, and that was enough.

I went to bed for the first time since *that* day with a sense of contentment. My phone was waiting for me on my bed, as was Mum's voice message. It was time to listen to it, to know her final words to me.

My finger froze right above the screen. I prayed that it wasn't just a pocket dial, and all I would hear for a minute and a half was the inside of her purse.

My finger made contact as I hit play, and I took a sharp inhale at the sweet sound of her voice.

"Hi, honey. I'm sure I'm catching you on your way to the office for your first big day, but that's why I'm calling. Good luck today, my dear. I know you'll knock'em dead in there! Don't be afraid. You're the best daughter a mother could ever ask for. You've worked so hard for this. I love you so, so much.

Okay, I know, 'that's enough, Mum,' I can hear you say. I'm just popping 'round to the store for more supplies. I'm trying my hand at haggis. Did Jeremy tell you? He thinks I'm daft, but I've been in Scotland for over 20 years now, and I've cooked every Scottish dish and then some, but I've never made haggis, can you imagine? You'll have to try it once you're back! Okay, I love you. Have a great day. Ring me when you're free. I can't wait to hear all about your day!"

She made a kissing noise at the end, and I pressed to save the message and listened to it over and over again until it finally lulled me to sleep.

***

Eoin

Eoin felt hot then shivered in the cold as he heard a door open and close. He rolled his eyes back and forth, trying to find the strength to open them fully, only to be repeatedly succumbed by darkness.

Sweat pooled at the corners of his eyes until he felt a lukewarm cloth on his brow. He cracked his eyes open a little at a time until he saw Sam and Isla, the book's healer, hovering over him. He caught snippets of their conversation.

"He looks ghastly, Sam!" Isla's voice sounded alarmed.

"Aye, that's why I brought ye."

"I comes here every time Eoin seems dead in the story, but the book's not open, now, is it? I don't sees his pretty reader or her light."

"No, I don't know what's going on, but when I found him, smoke was billowing around him, every inch of his body blackened by soot, red scars covering every inch of him, as ye can see." Eoin became frightened and sprung up but groaned in agony and laid back on the wooden table.

"Ssh, ssh, Milord. There you goes, just breathes, that's it." She rubbed his shoulder in soothing circles. "I've cleaned and puts ointments on your wounds and wrapped thems in cloths.

"What do you know, Isla, you're not a true healer. Just written as one," Eoin cursed at her through his teeth.

"Aye, that's what I told Sam too, but when I gots

here, it's like I knew exactly whats to do, and my supplies have somehow attained their described treatments." She glowed with pride, but a twinge of fear past over her ruddy features. "What's going on, my King?"

"I could ask the same damn thing!" Sam stood up, discarding whatever spirit he was nursing. "Valez stormed into the castle, taking over everything with actual bloody lightning coming from his staff!" The inclusion of this last line was not scripted, although they all knew the book wasn't open and Catriona was not reading.

Eoin pinched the bridge of his nose as his head began to throb, presumably because of his fever, but also out of sheer annoyance. "The book is real—our world is slowly becoming real. The evil sorcerer Valez is written to be has inhabited him."

Eoin prayed he was right—that Valez wasn't behaving this way out of choice. He couldn't fathom the possibility that the real Valez almost obliterated him from existence.

"How can this be?" Sam came and stood over Eoin with a fresh tankard of whiskey by the smell of him.

"I don't know. I think it has something to do with Catriona…our reader." He added as he saw confusion written over the faces of both secondary characters. They obviously hadn't heard her name or cared too much to pay attention as he did.

He wouldn't share with them what he saw at the pools. He saw her. He saw Catriona. She was right there! He could have run to her and held her close—never letting go—if it hadn't been for Valez.

Eoin sucked in a breath, the sudden emergence of Valez's powers was startling, but it did mean something far more than he first realized—anything was possible.

A new wave of exhaustion and pain hit him, and he fell back into unconsciousness. His last thought was of Catriona. *Where is she? Why hasn't she returned to me?*

Chapter 14

Catriona

I took the next day off from the library—once again, Jonathan was more than gracious. I spent the day with my dad, and he spent the day talking my ear off—not that I minded; I had my dad back. Jeremy went off to school with the normal amount of complaining for a teenager. I also planned to call Gemma after she got off of work so I could metaphorically gravel at her feet.

All my things were still packed from the weekend, so I went to my room and cleared my case, mostly dirty clothes for the laundry and toiletries. Same for my carry-on—all except the book that stayed at the very bottom. Unable to do anything else, I just stared at it where it lay inside, almost too afraid to touch it. I finally dragged it out and held it with limp hands.

Confronting my grief head-on like that made me realize exactly what happened on Skye. At times, I felt like I could create something so powerful in my mind that it would almost become a vivid reality, like seeing Eoin in the mist. But it would pass as quickly as it came, as did

Eoin, and I would be left all alone.

I was alone at the Fairy Pools without Mum, just as she was her first time, so my mind must have envisioned someone—someone with whom I had the most recent interaction, someone I had connected with most during that time. *But he's not real. He's a fictional character.*

I chucked the book on the bed in disgust, mostly at myself for believing that the world beyond the cover was real—that Eoin was real and that it almost felt that he could care for me. The thought that he couldn't left me feeling hollow. I needed to return the book to the library, where it belonged.

I hadn't carried on with my fib of reading extra books just to hide this one. I needed to give it to Shona and explain why I took on more work voluntarily yet hadn't delivered on it. I could tell she was getting suspicious before I went away. This would be for the best for everyone involved. I would give the book back tomorrow, first thing.

I called Gemma after dinner. She picked up on the first ring, which I knew was a good sign.

"Hey, girl." Her tone was neither harsh nor was it

light. It was decisively neutral, and I understood why this was the approach she needed to take.

"Hey. Look, Gemma. I'm so sorry for the way I left. I'm sorry that I missed your toasts, a moment that I needed and wanted to be at to tell you how happy I am for you and Gabriel—that you found someone you absolutely deserve, who sees all of you and loves you unconditionally."

I inhaled with a shaky breath, waiting for her to jump in, but nothing. She needed more from me. "You were right; I hadn't dealt with my grief. I was holding it in—too afraid to confront it. Instead, I used my dad's health and Jeremy's behavior as an excuse. I even used your wedding as a way to not deal. I'm sorry that…that it boiled over at your celebrations—when it should have been about you and not me. I'm so sorry. Please forgive me, Gem."

This time, I held my breath and waited. I knew this was what both she and I needed. No more, no less. I wouldn't excuse my behavior as that would only negate the apology and her feelings, and anything less would reveal that I didn't care about how my grief affected her.

"Oh, Cat Attack. There is nothing to forgive. Are you okay?" I cried into the phone at the grace she showed me—that was Gemma, an empath to the core, which made her the greatest person I could have in my life and one I refused to ever lose.

"Yeah, I'm okay." I wiped my nose and cleared my throat so she could somewhat comprehend what I was saying. "I went to Skye to visit a memory of my mum, which helped me come home and confront my dad." I wasn't ready to tell her what I saw on Skye, even if it was a hallucination that stemmed from unresolved grief.

"How did that go? I know he couldn't answer you, but how do you feel?"

"Actually, after I got everything off my chest about our relationship, how I've not dealt with Mum's death, and just cried, he came over to comfort me, and…" I bit my lip, welling up again at the memory of hearing his voice for the first time in months. "He talked, Gem. His voice was cracked and dry, but it was there apologizing for every count I cited, even for ones I didn't voice."

"Oh my god! Catriona! That's amazing! Not only that he spoke, but that he listened to you and acknowledged how you have felt this entire time, and even apologized. I can't imagine how that must have felt from what you told me about your childhood. It seems like a lot to unpack, but you two did it!"

"I know, it almost feels like a dream. Like too good to be true. There's still a lot to talk about and work on, but it feels like we can have a fresh start and get to know one another and help each other heal."

"I'm so glad, Cat. You know, I was never really mad at you, not really. I was so worried how you ignored your pain and pushed it away like it didn't matter." I sniffled into the phone as she went on. "But you know, as your dad and Jeremy begin to heal and find their own way without your Mum, you might be free to do what you want, even come back to Paris!"

Paris. I had buried the hope of ever returning to Paris after Ludo told me he had given my position away, and life in Crieff forever cemented itself in place. When Dad spoke, my future seemed to be less certain, and because of that, I could take a tiny breath from suffocation.

Things were still uncertain, and thoughts of returning to Paris would have to wait, but at least those thoughts could come alive again.

"Yeah, we'll see. I want to make sure Dad and Jeremy are self-sufficient before I make any concrete plans, you know?" And, of course, she understood. We talked for hours before the tendrils of sleep forced us with several failed attempts to stop talking and hang up.

I plugged my phone up, setting the alarm for work in the morning, but paused as my hand hovered where the book normally resided, waiting for me to read it before I fell asleep. It wasn't there, it was in my satchel to be taken back to where I first found it—to be returned for its intended purpose before it fell back into my hands. Shona would study it, restore its pages and cover to her liking, then place it in a display case to be revered and marveled but never read.

A chill ran down my spine at the thought, but I was too afraid of what the book seemed to do to me every time I read it—what happened at the Fairy Pools. It would be best for everyone if it was back at the library. I extinguished the light, banishing all thoughts of Eoin's future, as well as my own until the morning.

***

Eoin

Darkness turned to faded light, but it was resolutely not Catriona's light that seeped through Eoin's vision. He felt nothing. The pain he once felt faded into nothingness. Neither could he conjure any feelings from within. He didn't feel fear, pain, or anger.

Part of him wanted to succumb to the advantages this could bring him until Catriona returned to restore every part of him once more. What he did want to feel and, therefore, refused to lose was how he felt about her, but even the thought of her didn't cause a fluttering in his heart as it once did.

He envisioned her face as it had been every time she opened the book, how she read his words, how she became so enraptured with his story. He tried to remember the misery he felt when he learned the truth of her circumstances, that her mother had died, that she had lost everything, and how he thought he had lost his grip on reality in that moment.

Then when he saw her through the mist—how he saw all of her sitting there at the Fairy Pools, speaking his name—a slow ember glowed in his heart, but its warmth was fleeting and it would not ignite.

He moved his attention to the harried whispers coming from his present caretakers. He could hear Sam pacing back and forth, surprisingly sober, which was not indicative of good news as he talked at Isla, "Normally, we are supposed to wait here as the action is being moved by the reader at the castle. They read about Valez's bloody usurpation, how he takes Adalind captive — all the while thinking Eoin is dead, yet the reader knows he's alive. Quite injured, but alive. However, said reader isn't reading. She hasn't opened the book at all!"

Eoin withered. *Catriona isn't reading?* He felt pain course through his heart and a tear escaped and ran down his cheek and neck. He could still feel, yet he wished to feel anything else, anything at all but her rejection of him.

"Eoin is always awake as the reader is in another part of the book. We chat and laugh and have a merry 'ole time. I don't understand." Sam's voice broke as he spoke through a suppressed sob. "He is getting worse; he's beginning to fade."

"He does looks awfully pale, doesn't he? I'm scared, Sam. This isn't supposed to be happening." Eoin heard Isla blow into her handkerchief. He could still picture its yellow daisies stitched along the edges as she cleared away her tears.

"You're right; this isn't supposed to be happening. We're fictional characters, for God's sake. This isn't real! No one should be able to fade from existence—our very existence is permanent, never changing." Sam's armor clanked loudly as he sat by the fire.

Eoin heard Isla move next to Sam's chair and place her hand on Sam's shoulder. "Aye, our purpose is to tell Eoin's story to the reader. I thinks his only chance is for Catriona to return and finish his story."

"For his sake, I pray she returns to him soon, or all will be lost."

What little Eoin could feel before all but evaporated, and he was nothing but a dry husk. He welcomed the inevitable, to fade away just as the dusk turns to dawn.

***

Catriona

I woke to dawn's first light—ten minutes before my alarm was set to go off. Even with Dad speaking and doing a few things for himself and Jeremy arriving and staying home at normal hours, I still set it to wake up and make breakfast, situate Dad in his chair, give him his medicine, and get Jeremy ready for school—right back in the routine I had started the day after Mum's funeral.

I padded out in my fleece pajamas and wool slippers to the kitchen to start the kettle for tea and make Jeremy's lunch. I rubbed at my crust-dusted eyes before my slippers hit the linoleum but jumped at the sight of my dad reading the paper with the hiss of bacon on the stove and the quiet whistle of the kettle before it blew full steam.

"Good morning, Catriona. Tea?" He smiled up

from his paper, stifling a chuckle from what was presumably shock written all over my face.

I gulped down tears and walked over to the table. He moved the paper and allowed me to hug him, half sitting on his knee in my pajamas like I was five years old again.

I kissed the top of his head and handed him the sports section. I moved to the refrigerator to make Jeremy's sandwich.

"I've already made Jer's lunch. It's in the door there." He pointed to the paper bag sitting on the shelf next to the milk. I pulled the milk out and fixed our tea – two spoonsful of sugar and a splash of milk. As I handed him his mug, I realized how much we had in common, but in our stubbornness never discovered.

We waited for Jeremy to wake up as Dad made us some bacon rolls. Jeremy smiled at the sight of us eating breakfast and talking about everything and nothing all at once. He descended quite naturally into the begrudging nature of having to go to school as Dad and I laughed at his expense.

I had nothing to do but enjoy my breakfast and get ready for work at a leisurely pace that I hadn't been used to since I had lived here—when Mum used to take care of us all. Now we were starting to take care of each other, intercepting one another's load without asking, and that was when I knew that we would be okay.

I still gave Dad his medicine before I left. He said he was going to try to go for a short walk, nothing too strenuous, just enough to gain some strength back in his legs.

I put my satchel on the passenger seat, knowing when I came home, it would no longer bear the weight of the book. My breath quickened as I pictured Jonathan's and even Shona's faces after I told them what I had done. I was more nervous about disappointing Jonathan than enduring Shona's wrath.

As I looked at the satchel, knowing every inch of the book without seeing it, I hesitated in the library's parking lot about what I was going to do. Every scenario I waded through had the same result: I would no longer possess the book, nor would it possess me. I would never know how Eoin's story ended.

Before I could talk myself out of my plan, I snatched the bag, ignoring the strain that tugged at my heart in what felt like a warning. A warning of what exactly? I had no idea.

The warmth of the library, along with Jonathan's welcoming smile, quelled the nagging in my soul, and I audibly sighed in comfort. I realized I wasn't ready to elicit Jonathan's judgment. I would give the book to Shona first so it would be safe in her care, and then I could explain myself to Jonathan while she fussed over the state that I had kept it in.

"Ah, good to have you back, Catriona!" Jonathan leaned in, lowering his voice. "It's been a bit dull around here without you." He laughed, cleaning the lenses of his glasses on the edge of his Aran knit jumper.

I lowered my voice in kind, "Shona's not the entertaining sort, is she?"

"No, always just business that one. I'm glad you were able to get away this weekend. Please don't hesitate if you need a day off for your family. How's your father?"

My smile pushed unshed tears to the surface at Jonathan's generosity. "He's much better; he started talking again and is slowly getting back to a routine." I paused at the image of my dad on his little walk around our house. "Thank you for asking and for your offer. I really appreciate it."

"Think nothing of it, my dear. Anything I can do to help? I'm just so happy you're here with us." He cleared his throat and placed his glasses on the bridge of his nose as his eyes magnified through the lenses. "Now, I won't keep you from your work. I know we're just a hair away from starting a database for the books, so I won't keep ya!"

I took the rare opportunity to quickly fulfill his request and not encourage his usual long morning chat. After placing my coat in the employee/storage room, I firmly tucked my satchel in my side and made my way upstairs.

Shona was at her usual case with a new antiquated book and her methods of repair and identification of old manuscripts.

Another cold shiver ran down my spine as I

pictured her invasive and even non-invasive methods of studying Eoin's story. It seemed somewhat callous to study it without also embracing the feelings his story evoked.

"Good morning. How was your holiday?" Shona said through tight lips without glancing away from her lighted magnifying glass.

I moved over to the case to take a closer look at the manuscript she was restoring. I must have surprised her as she almost knocked over the magnifying glass, which would have caused a domino effect for every piece of material she had laid out. I stifled a laugh and answered her initial question, "It was, umm, much needed, thanks."

"Good, is there something I can help you with, Ms. Lamont?" At the use of my surname, I could tell she was quite annoyed with me encroaching on her personal space, but I wanted to observe exactly what would happen once I gave her *The Adventures of Accolon.*

"What are you trying to do with this…?" I trailed off letting her fill in the title she was working on.

"*Treasure Island* by Robert Louis Stevenson. It's a

first edition." She caressed the cover gently with a gloved hand before going back to her sterile study.

"Wow, that's amazing! I loved reading *Treasure Island* in school. So, what was the first thing you did when you acquired it?"

She peered at me through her tiny glasses that sat at the end of her nose, sizing me up. "Well, I put on gloves so the oils from my fingers don't destroy any remaining pigment and ink. Then I handle it with great care as I go page by page, seeing what condition the words are in, even the illustrations if there are any. Then, I catalog what needs restoration and what type before I move on. The rest is rather complex, to say the least." She puffed her chest out, accompanied by a little snort at her own brilliance.

"So, what happens to it once the manuscript is restored?" I pressed my satchel further into my hip, desperately wanting to feel the hard surface of the book.

"Well, then it goes on display. I choose a page that has the most well-known passage, has historical relevance, or is just visually appealing. And every season, I rotate the displays, or in this case, I will rotate these books to display this new acquisition."

I gulped, thinking of Eoin's book forever on display on one page, hundreds of eyes reading and re-reading the same words without ever knowing this wonderful character who had captured my heart.

"Why the sudden interest? Did you find a book in your collection?" She preened and lowered her glasses, letting the gold chain catch them as they landed below her collarbone. I grabbed my satchel and then swung it behind my back.

"No, I was just curious. I see you every day with such careful elocution, I wanted to know exactly what was happening on your side of things." I edged back toward my rooms, and she went straight back to *Treasure Island* without a word.

The door creaked as I left it open just a sliver of a crack and slumped to the floor. I carefully removed the book, handling it with care just as Shona had with her manuscripts, and ran my fingers over it just as I had when I first found it.

I replayed Eoin's story in my mind's eye. When I

first met him at his foreboding castle, his struggle over his identity as king, his constant pursual of Adalind's love, his conflict with Valez's betrayal, then… I squeezed my eyes tight as the image of Eoin's face at the Black Cuillin Ridge bored into my soul, saying my name in a deep timber as he saw me too.

I stood up and shoved the book back in its hiding place — in the inner drawer of my roll-top desk. I wasn't ready for it to be poked and prodded by Shona, but I also wasn't ready to be immersed in his story. I wasn't ready to find out if Valez had truly killed him.

Is he still alive? He must be, but what condition is he in, and what will Valez do to his kingdom?

I was getting sucked in again. I was at my lowest point when I thought I saw Eoin. Now, things were going so well that I didn't want to go back to that mindset.

I needed to move forward with my life, and with the progress Dad and Jeremy were seeming to make, I could be back in Paris in a couple of months. That thought propelled me forward as I moved away from the desk and finished the last shelf of books before they were ready for their Dewey Decimal Classification.

As I left, I noticed that Shona had cleared her workstation and had already left. I let out a puff of air in relief. Jonathan was locking up his office and thanked me for staying later than usual. He didn't ask, but I wanted to make up for the days he had given me, and I felt confident Dad was able to take care of himself just this once.

I waved goodbye as Jonathan pulled out and I slid into the driver's seat. I placed my empty satchel on the seat next to me and stared at the way it moved and creased with ease. I threw the car in gear and sped as quickly as I could without looking in the rearview mirror.

The smell of pumpkin spice and the sound of gregarious laughter wafted out of the house as I walked up the drive. I came in through the kitchen door and found Jeremy at the stove and Dad at the table just as he was at breakfast.

"Hiya, Love, how was your day?" Dad said as I leaned in with an air kiss.

"Good. Sorry, I was late and couldn't give you your afternoon meds. Did you find them all right?" Before he could answer me, I checked the pill box myself.

"Yeah, I got it. I also walked up and down the lane, and I even talked to Old Man McGregor on the corner. He was so shocked to see me, he…" Both he and Jeremy broke out into laughter as Jeremy seemed to already know the story. "He missed the bottom step and landed clear on his arse."

"Oh my god, Dad, is he okay?" I couldn't help but laugh through my words.

"Oh, aye, I helped him up, and we had a nice wee chat. He asked how we were since Caroline." He faltered.

At the mention of her name, I grabbed his hand, terrified he would regress back to a functioning mute. "That was nice of him," I searched his eyes before turning my head. "What on earth are you making over there, Jer?" The smell distracted me, but it also let Dad come out of his reverie and back to the present.

"It's a creamy pumpkin soup. I got it from one of Mum's recipes." I turned my head to gauge Dad's reaction. "It's alright, Cat, it was Dad's idea." Jeremy lifted a wooden spoon I hadn't seen in anyone else's hands but

Mum's. Dad nodded and smiled with glistening eyes.

I was so worried about both of them with every mention of Mum that I forgot about how I was feeling about all of this. I smiled at just how fine they seemed now.

My face fell as I realized it was no longer them who needed me, but it was I who needed them.

They both saw my face, and Dad placed his hand on my arm while Jeremy divvied up a bowl of soup.

I ate through misty veiled tears that Dad and Jeremy gratefully let go unsaid and instead told me about their days, hitting some anecdotes with comedic flourishes just to try and make me laugh.

I wasn't exactly sure how I felt with our role reversals, but I knew it was necessary for all of us to move on. They knew it was my turn to mourn while they took care of me.

Still, I went to bed feeling rather empty. With all the reminders of Mum, and with Dad and Jeremy doing so well with their grief, I felt rather left behind in mine.

When I had thoughts like this swirling in my head seemingly without end, I would grab Eoin's story to quiet the storm in my mind—to escape.

I liked getting lost in fiction. Ironically, it could make my life feel more real. When I could compare a situation and frame it within a narrative, it gave my life more value—I felt less alone, *but at what cost?*

I remembered why I left the book back in the roll-top desk in the first place. I would definitely give it to Shona tomorrow. I shut off my lamp and stared at the moonlit ceiling.

My eyes stayed wide open as sleep refused to close them. I watched as the shadows of the tree branches danced together, as they cascaded along the walls and ceiling.

Loneliness seeped from inside me and ran throughout my body, down all my extremities, begging for some kind of release. But this release, this desperate need to feel something, would only propel me to do something stupid as it did numerous times in the past, like messaging Henri for phone sex, and I would regret it after two seconds of peace that release left me.

Before reaching for my phone, I imagined Eoin

feeling his hair—his soft, curly hair between my fingers that now flicked gently at first, just as I imagined his tongue would against my core.

I rubbed in circles until I felt my body contract and release in pleasure. *I need to get Eoin back.* I breathed and fell into a deep sleep.

Eoin was in my dreams like he had been every night since the very first day I found his book, but this dream felt different. Eoin looked pale and sick, lying in a dark hovel alone. His breath ragged as he gasped for air. He became almost translucent—he was fading.

I could see the bed through his chest until the outline of him suddenly vanished. I swiped at the empty air, wanting to feel him, the solidity of his body, but felt nothing. I screamed his name.

I bolted upright in a cold sweat, breathing just as heavily as when I was crying out his name, gulping the air around me. It was still dark. My phone screen read 4:30.

I need to get the book back. I need to find out what happens to Eoin.

***

Eoin

Warmth spread through his extremities, and a peace that could only come from the weightlessness of being picked up surrounded him. Then he felt the tender touch of Catriona's hand run down his chest.

Eoin lifted his hand to catch hers, but it dropped, and all he felt was the cold skin of his chest and a new level of emptiness as the room darkened even more.

The room filled with commotion, and he knew both Sam and Isla felt the weightlessness, but he doubted that they could feel Catriona's touch as he did. He heard Sam curse as darkness overtook them.

"God's death! Why didn't she open the goddamned book! She picked us up. Fuck!" Eoin heard Sam slam his fist on the table by the hearth.

"Calms down, Sam. We just needs to wait, she'll opens the book presently." Eoin opened his eyes to see Sam wrench himself from Isla's comforting caress.

"We don't have time to wait! I can see right through Eoin..." Sam glanced twice, clearly shocked to find Eoin staring at him.

Eoin tried to use his voice, but like every part of him, it was barely there. "Go… get… Valez" is all he could say. He still trusted that his friend was in there. Maybe without Catriona's light or magic, Valez's newfound powers were waning.

Even if they weren't, perhaps his magic could save Eoin's life. As he drifted back into unconsciousness, he heard the door close and tried to lift his lips in a smile at Sam's steadfast loyalty.

Within the void of unconsciousness, hues of purple, gold, and blue filled Eoin's mind. Then blurred shapes, his pupils moved back and forth in his slumber to pull his dream into focus.

He saw a white stone building nestled within dark green grass, surrounded by the purple heather of Scotland. The light of a full moon illuminated the landscape in an ethereal veil. He looked all around him. He had never seen this place before, yet somehow, he knew it.

A sharp light blinded his vision but he moved away just as quickly. As his eyes adjusted back to the light of the moon, he saw her, Catriona.

She got out of an odd-looking carriage with her hair plastered in different directions. She wore a flowing garment with baggy trousers that were stuffed in black riding boots.

This didn't seem like a dream. Catriona's eyes darted in every direction. She looked over her shoulder several times as she approached the white building. Her hands were shaking as she dug through a box.

Eoin heard her exhale as she found a key there. She never looked at him. He followed close behind, and she peered back once more as she unlocked the heavy wooden door.

She couldn't see him. He stood right behind her as she entered. She bounded up a flight of narrow stairs, and he followed. "I'm coming, Eoin." Eoin paused when he heard his name. He closed his eyes at the sound. It rang more clearly than when the pages stood between them, but it sounded hoarse and desperate.

He followed her into a room and saw her cradling a book, *his book*! The spine read *The Adventures of Accolon*. He had never seen it before, of course. It was a crimson red that looked to have faded over time, with golden clasp detailing on each corner. It had a triangular pattern that bordered a symmetrical floral pattern that covered the entire surface—it was exquisite.

Catriona clutched it to her heart. She was just a step away from an open desk. He felt his throat constrict, holding down a sob. *That's where she put me? Did she truly plan to leave me hidden—to fade away?*

Before a rush of anger could move throughout his body and forever harden his heart, he saw the flood of relief and fresh tears that filled Catriona's face. She sank to the floor and caressed the cover with the front and back of her hand.

He knelt beside her, wishing he could wipe away every tear with his thumbs as he cradled her head. He'd fold her into his embrace and quiet her fears—he was here, he was alive.

He looked up. She pressed her thumbs to the closed pages, ready to open the book. *Bang*. The vision of her blurred. *Bang*. Bursts of green and red filled his vision. *"Bloody hell!"* Finally, the familiar darkness returned as he heard Sam's voice.

He didn't dare open his eyes but held his breath to hear Valez's comforting voice wash over him in concern, but nothing came. Instead, it was Sam, sounding out of breath from running as he yelled, "Bloody hell! Valez, Valez!"

"Whats about Valez?" Isla demanded.

"He's taking this story way too seriously! The castle is operating just as it is described in the book for the reader, without a reader! He's sitting on the throne with his wand burning with red fire without consuming it. Everyone is behaving in their written roles; frightened eyes bored into mine, Isla. Adalind is really locked in the dungeon; I could hear her screaming her bloody head off!" Sam paused to catch his breath. "He thinks Eoin is truly dead and is never coming back."

"What?"

"Isla, I think our world is real. Valez is an evil sorcerer."

That was enough for Eoin. He finally wanted to go. To fade from existence. To no longer feel. Catriona wasn't coming. What he saw in the library was only a dream. He did believe she had put him back where she first found him, but she wasn't about to open his book and read. He was ready to go.

"Eoin, please, please don't go. Hold on for Catriona. She's coming, please, my King." Eoin didn't believe him.

Eoin felt the last threads of life pull tight…but then he felt one firmly anchor itself. One by one, he felt them tighten until he opened his eyes and saw a heavenly light and an angelic face come into view.

Warmth spread inside him until he felt it radiate out. He felt the light bask on his skin as if he were lying in the fields of purple heather with the sun high in the sky and Catriona's cheek pressed against his shoulder. He would wrap his arm around her waist and caress the soft skin under her breast with his fingers.

He looked up with clear eyes to see Catriona smiling at him. "You're alive," she breathed. "I'll never leave you again. I'll finish your story, I promise."

Eoin believed her, but he vowed right then and

there to find a way to be with her before his impending end. *If my world is becoming real, my happily ever after will not be with Adalind; it will be with Catriona.*

Catriona's face disappeared from view as she went to the castle to move the plot forward, but the light from her world still lingered.

Eoin sat up and looked at the bewildered faces of his comrades. "Right, tell me what I missed."

Chapter 15

Catriona

I sat on the puce carpet, staring at the open desk in disbelief, still cradling the book in my lap. My tears had dried as the vivid images of my dreams began to fade. Eoin was mostly alive and nursed back to health by his first knight, Samuel.

I breathed a sigh of relief as my body let go of its tense hold and relaxed into a state of total immersion.

I couldn't quite believe I was here and why. I had rushed out of my house, not worrying if I woke Dad and Jeremy, jumped in the car, and drove at full speed to get to the book—to save Eoin.

The whole time I was speeding toward the library, I prayed that Jonathan had left the spare key in the mailbox in case I ever needed to work after closing.

My fingers shook as they clasped around the cool metal. I had been afraid that I would be caught breaking and entering, yet here I sat, reading without any remaining feelings of fear.

I closed my eyes, remembering the feeling of

someone's presence behind me as I unlocked the door. *It was the same warmth that radiates from two people right before their bodies make contact—but no one was there.*

Even as I sat holding the book to my chest, I felt that same warmth envelop me. It left as I opened the book, yet I didn't feel alone. So, I kept reading. I read about Valez's coup, his cruel treatment of Eoin's subjects, and Adalind's imprisonment in the dark dungeons of the castle.

I don't know how long I sat reading, but I registered the light of a new day as my eyes adjusted to the rays of the sunrise that pierced through the windows. It wasn't until the sound of someone's voice clearing that forced me out of Eoin's world, and my head whipped in its direction.

Jonathan was standing at the door, his arms crossed and his face lined with concern. "Catriona? Why are you here so early, lass?" He looked down at the book still open in my lap.

I stood and gently placed the open book on my desk — for some reason, I was still afraid to close it or have it out of sight. "I'm sorry, Jonathan. I umm." My brain froze, unsure how to explain why I had let myself into the library in the middle of the night, why I was sitting on the floor of my workspace in my pajamas reading at the break of dawn.

The truth was the only way to explain it, or at least some version of the truth. "I..I found this book when I first started. It looks to be a first edition published in 1490. It's a story about a long-lost kingdom of Caledonia set in a fantastical medieval Scotland. I was so intrigued that I smuggled it out to read it."

Understanding passed through his eyes. "Aye…but that doesn't explain why you're here before the crack of dawn reading in your pajamas." Humor animated his face, and a small chuckle escaped his lips.

I couldn't help but laugh at the ridiculousness of the situation, too. "That's an excellent point. And well, I was feeling guilty about hiding it from Shona, so I brought it back yesterday to give it to her, but I still haven't finished it, and I couldn't sleep without knowing what happens."

I bit my lip. That wasn't the whole truth. I didn't

dare tell him about my visions or how Eoin's story was basically a coping mechanism for my ongoing grief—however, since Mum's death, I felt empty and alone, but once I found the book, I didn't feel so alone—I felt understood and complete.

"I understand if you need to tell Shona about this and have her take the book for her collection." I lowered my head, cautiously closed the book, and handed it to him.

He chuckled again and shook his head, "Well, this looks like a new book to me. It can't possibly be published in…1490!" He whistled as he indeed saw the handwritten inscription from the author, and his eyes lit up as he gently flipped through the ivory pages, somewhat yellowed with age. "I'd love to read it once you're finished. Just leave it on my desk once you're done, hmm?" He winked.

I smiled and nodded, holding the book once more to my chest. "I will. Thank you, Jonathan."

"Now, umm, why don't you go on home and get dressed and come back in an hour or so before lunch, eh?" Jonathan gestured to my floral pajama bottoms.

"Yes, I'll do that." I averted my gaze and gathered

my coat and keys. I silently handed him the spare key and darted to the car.

***

Eoin

By the fading light in the room, Eoin knew Catriona was in another part of the book. Her brief presence was enough to fully restore him. Eoin heard her voice move the story forward in his head, yet the story she was reading was really happening to him.

Eoin had Sam go over everything that transpired while he was in and out of consciousness, more accurately fading from existence.

Eoin remembered the look on Valez's face when he struck him seemingly dead, and from what Sam described at the castle, Valez was the wicked wizard he was written to be. If Eoin had not seen the murder in Valez's eyes, he would not have believed Sam's account.

He turned to Sam and Isla, who were patiently waiting as he mentally cataloged all this new information. "Okay, so we have to recall the story from now until the end to predict Valez's movements and still stay within our written world."

There were so many moving pieces now that Eoin could hardly keep them straight, let alone voice them aloud. Not only did he have to follow the action he heard Catriona read, but he had to keep the same mentality around Valez and, theoretically, every other character even when the book was closed. He was now Eoin of Accolon, King of Caledonia.

"Excuse me, Your Highness, but what story?" Sam looked at Isla and shrugged his shoulders.

Eoin took in their matching blank faces. *Do they no longer know what we are?* Only he knew the reality of their world—that they were fictional characters in a book. He shivered at the sudden implication. *I am all alone.*

"Never mind, Samuel." Sam's written character would find it odd if Eoin used the informal shortening of his name. "What is the status of the castle at present, First Knight?" Eoin recalled the words he said a thousand times before when the reader directed him. He half listened as Sam told him about the masquerade party Valez was throwing in honor of his self-imposed coronation — just as he would when they had a reader.

Although Eoin knew this change carried a promised whisper that he and Catriona could be together, he still didn't know what that meant for his world—or for his friends.

***

Catriona

I rushed home and finally saw my reflection. I blanched at the memory of Jonathan catching me reading in the library and standing in front of him like *this*. I took a shower, changed, and even dozed off for an hour before returning to work.

Jeremy was already at school. Part of me was glad both he and Dad took care of his sendoff, but another part of me wondered why I mildly missed taking care of them.

Dad was sitting in the living room, but he muted the news when I entered. "Where did you rush off to this morning?"

My footsteps faltered. "I…uh…well… Jonathan needed me in early to catalog some pieces that are being sent off to the Writer's Museum in Edinburgh." *What is it about this book that I can't seem to find the right words to explain the truth?*

"Oh, right, well, they're lucky to have you, I'd say. Is Jonathan still as likable as I remember?" His eyes moved from mine as he was undoubtedly remembering the day that he had met Mum.

"Yeah, he is. He's a lovely man and a great boss. I can see why you two were friends."

"Aye. I should give him a ring now that I'm a regular old chatterbox." We laughed, but the recent past still lingered in his sigh. "So, I'm thinking about going back to work." He looked me straight in the eye to gauge my reaction.

"Are you sure you're ready for that? I mean, it's been less than a week since you started talking." I moved to the couch and sat exactly where my overpouring grief collided with my dad's, which created one seemingly healing moment.

I could see the same recognition flit through his eyes, "Catriona, I don't think I'll ever get over the death of

Caroline...she was...she was the love of my life, but at some point, I'll have to move on... for my family." He grabbed my hand and smiled through unshed tears. "You never should have been forced to take on that role for us. I'm so sorry you had to put your life on hold because I wasn't strong enough to support us."

I placed my hand on top of his. I knew he wasn't just speaking of Mum's death but how he, at times, let life just pass by. "I know, Dad. Thank you for saying that. I still think it's too soon for you to go back, but umm why don't we make an appointment with your doctor and see what she thinks and even what Dr. Gayle thinks as well? I just don't want you to overdo it and relapse, you know?"

"Aye, whatever you think is best, my darling girl." He patted my hand and shifted his body back towards the Telly.

"Good." I stood and kissed the top of his head. "I'll call during my break, and I'll tell Jonathan hello for you. Love you."

"Love you," he turned and watched me go with glistening eyes.

My eyes glistened as well, but I averted my gaze and headed out before the tears could properly form. I never knew my dad and I would have this type of relationship. I never knew I would be able to be vulnerable or show emotion around him and equally receive it in return.

I went back to work as normal. Shona was completely unaware of what passed between Jonathan and me earlier this morning. He concealed a smile as he ducked into his office after a quick hello.

During my break, I called Dad's doctor and therapist and scheduled side-by-side appointments for this time next week. I requested that day off as Jonathan generously dismissed even the notion of formally asking and gave it to me.

Jeremy messaged me an hour before my shift was over that he and Dad were going out to dinner, stressing it was Delivino's—a nice Italian restaurant instead of opting to get drunk at their favorite pub, The Quaich, like last time, just in case I forgot—*as if I could forget.*

All I had planned for tonight was to read. My eyes

went to my satchel that contained the book. I wanted to keep it close to me from now on as the vision of Eoin fading continued to consume me.

When I got home, I ignored the stillness of the house without my guys. I ignored the sharp pang of not feeling needed anymore and the huge void it seemed to leave.

I grabbed the book from my satchel and sank into a chair, a chair I had been avoiding. *Her chair*. The one in the corner by the bay front windows that had the perfect view of Dad's.

As her chair embraced me, so did Eoin's story. The living room began to fade, and I was transported back to that dark room where Eoin lay badly injured from Valez's blast of magic on Gorgon's Mount.

I paused and closed my eyes, unable to fight the vivid image of that battle on Skye. I forced my eyes open before I could see the shock on Eoin's face before he could say my name and read on.

Isla, the village healer, whom some would call a witch under their breaths as she passed, nursed Eoin back to life. Samuel had infiltrated the castle and reported back that Valez was throwing a masquerade ball in celebration of his new reign.

"I grabbed my costume for you, Your Highness, and a lord's costume for me, as you instructed."

"Very good. No one can know we are there, Samuel. You will present yourself as Lord McGregor; no one knows what he looks like—the hermit that he is—and I will be your vassal knight—sworn to protect you at all costs."

"This will be interesting," Samuel stifled a laugh but straightened into position as Eoin's expression hardened.

"Valez thinks I'm dead, which will work to our advantage in assessing his powers, his hold on my people, and…to free Adalind." Eoin's voice broke, and his throat bobbed as he swallowed.

I re-read that description several times, trying to evoke the depth of their separation and Eoin's compounded sorrow in all he had lost in a short amount of time—his kingdom, his best friend, and his true love. I looked around the room to give myself a break from the swell of emotion that lifted off the page.

The living room looked much bigger from Mum's vantage point. She could see every angle of the house. She could sit here and read or sew and know exactly what her husband and children were doing at all times, which I hadn't realized until now was the source of her superpowers.

I shifted my eyes down to escape my own flood of emotions to read a somewhat lackluster description of Eoin and Samuel riding through the Highlands of Scotland, with Eoin only thinking of Adalind and trying not to imagine the condition in which Valez was keeping her.

As they entered the front gate—into the courtyard—they were stopped by guards as was protocol. Eoin wore a simple black tunic with sparse armor in case he needed to protect "his lord," donned with a matching silk mask. Samuel was dressed in a blue tunic with embroidered silver thread. His mask was a matching pale blue with shimmering silver and white beads.

Eoin noted the tension of the entire atmosphere as he entered in disguise. Everyone was on edge: the guards on post, the serfs who served at the behest of the noblemen and knights were all charged with fear and paranoia as they headed into the castle for the celebrations.

This wasn't a celebration; this was a show of force on Valez's part—an introduction of how things were going to be from now on.

I became so angry with Valez that I almost wanted to slam the book shut, but I kept reading just to find out exactly how Eoin would free his people from what was sure to be a cruel dictatorship and reunite with Adalind.

I read even faster so she would know he was alive and bask in the written details of their sexually charged reunion.

***

Eoin

Eoin put on a performance of a lifetime. The stakes were higher now. Not only was he acting for Catriona to keep her imagination alive through the now thinly layered veil that separated them, but he also had to act like a vassal knight to his lord to infiltrate Valez's self-congratulatory party. The story was moving on, but no one around him knew it. Only he could propel the plot forward, and that terrified him.

Samuel seamlessly passed muster as Lord McGregor. His written knight was much more capable than Sam ever was, but Eoin found that he missed Sam's carefree nature, his simplistic sense of humor, and overall jovialness in every situation. If he missed the old Sam this much, he dreaded what he was going to feel when confronted with the written Valez.

Eoin could still feel Catriona's eyes on him. He fought the urge to look up at her as he heard her voice in his head. Back at their safehouse, Samuel had asked why he kept looking up at the ceiling. So, he certainly didn't want to draw any unnecessary attention now. He just kept running through his plan of possibly making contact with Catriona to distract himself from her immediate presence.

Samuel nodded to him as they entered the Great Hall. They both spotted Valez sitting on Eoin's throne. A ball of red electricity sat above his staff, keeping those he wanted at bay and those he desired by his side—all fearfully compliant. Eoin signaled to Sam to split up so they could assess the situation.

Eoin still did as Catriona directed, but his eyes never left Valez, who wore a blood-red tunic with a matching flared mask that made him look like the devil himself. Eoin had seen him wear this costume ironically a thousand times, but this time, it was not the clothes that made Valez different; it was the fire in his eyes that Eoin had never seen before.

He swallowed the bile that had crept up his throat and burned on the way back down. He wanted to stay and listen to the conversation Valez seemed to be having with his forcefully rapt audience, but Catriona's voice led him to sneak out of the hall, down the long stone corridors and the uneven, rocky steps to the dungeons to save Adalind.

As he rounded the corner and hid in the shadows, his stomach turned at what he knew he had to do next. The guards who surrounded Adalind's cell wouldn't just "play dead" as Eoin pretended to knock them unconscious for the reader. He would have to use violence for the very first time in his life.

As he came upon the first guard, he closed his eyes and smashed down on the guard's helmet with the hilt of his sword. The others were alerted, and Eoin punched one unconscious and turned to the second, hitting his head just as the first.

He made to look for the keys to Adalind's cell on each guard, yet knowing the story, had Valez in possession of the keys.

As he caught his breath and checked on the well-being of each knight, he heard a slow clap coming from Adalind's cell. "Very impressive, Eoin. I didn't know you'd have it in you."

Eoin's eyes darted to the ceiling, and Adalind followed their direction. "Don't worry, she has paused to look elsewhere. I wouldn't compromise the story for your pretty little reader since she's all you seem to care about."

"Adalind? How are you still you? Everyone else…"

"Is how they were written to be? That our world has transformed into what it was created to mirror?" She brushed at her nails as though this was a regular occurrence.

Eoin stole another glance at Catriona. She was running her hands across the chair she was sitting in, her bright blue eyes glistening with unshed tears. He desperately wanted to know what was going through her head but was thankful to have a moment to figure out what the hell was going on.

He turned back to Adalind, who now gave him her full attention. "I think it has something to do with Catriona, combined with Valez's very real and palpable magic that has caused the book's world to come alive. What I don't understand is why you, of all people, were spared."

She swung back her long braid out of her face, "I don't know why either, and nor do I care. But since you apparently do, it could be simply because of her powerful imagination and her natural infinity for you and me."

Adalind wrapped her long, dainty fingers around the thick iron bars of her prison. "Perhaps I was spared because this is what I've always wanted. I've not kept it a secret that I want to be the queen I was written to be or have the romance you and I were destined to have… that you obstinately keep fighting." She pushed her hands out through the tiny openings, gesturing for his affections.

Eoin instinctively took a step back, "Yet that doesn't explain why I still retained the knowledge of our circumstances. I've made it very clear how much I despise my role in all of this."

"Oh, come off it, Eoin. You may have convinced yourself of that this entire time, running off like a child to play a brooding hermit, but somewhere deep inside, you've always wanted to be the king our author wrote you to be. Your heart warms when the book is closed, as some characters show you due honor and respect. Don't act like you're better than me—that's why I believe we were both spared."

Adalind let out a cackle that Eoin only imagined evil queens uttering when he suddenly felt her cold hands on his, realizing he had moved closer and wrapped his hands around the iron bars during her probing assessment of him.

"Hurry, my love!" She unconvincingly cried. "He's

coming to get me to 'entertain' for the party. He must not know that you're alive!" She grabbed Eoin's face and kissed him. He almost cursed her once she let go of his bottom lip with her teeth until he saw her wicked smile and eyebrows tick up—Catriona had resumed reading.

Eoin fought back, spitting Adalind's lingering taste out of his mouth as he resumed the act, "Keep strong, my love. I'll find a way to free you and my kingdom; I swear it." He forced himself to kiss her one more time as he bounded down the secret entrance that only he now knew existed. He heard Adalind play her part in who knocked out her guards so as not to raise suspicion of his presence.

He followed the passageway back to the kitchens, grabbing some food and ale as he went, ignoring the protests of the castle chefs, and headed back to the hall. As he took a bite of the soft bread roll, his stomach moved and made noises. This food was no longer just for pleasure but for hunger—for survival.

Eoin quickly forgot this new physical sensation as he saw Adalind sitting on Valez's lap, scantily clad, as he groped her revealing skin. Eoin could see the genuine fear in her eyes. He wanted to save her, just as his character would if the one that he loved was being assaulted right in front of him. No woman, not even Adalind, for that matter, deserved to be violated. It wasn't an act on his part as he charged the throne until he felt a strong grip on his arm.

Sam forced him into the shadows of the far wall. "I know, Sire, but you can't do anything about it now. You need to lie in wait until you can intercept Her Majesty on the way back to the dungeons, aye?" Sam let go of his strong hold as Eoin nodded his assent.

Eoin let out a puff of air. He prayed Adalind would be safe as she was the only one aware of the reality of their situation. Eoin still didn't know how she, of all people, was spared the magic that emanated in their world, sealing everyone else's written fate.

He briefly thought about Grant, the horse master, and Beatrice and wondered if he was happy now that she was finally his true wife. Not that they would remember the time before anyhow, but part of him wished them both happiness. Their world being real wouldn't be like that for everyone.

Although there was some truth in what Adalind had said, he didn't like the feudal system that was no doubt in place at the time of his writing, how the state of one's prosperity or suffering was based entirely on the chance of one's birth. How the elite few convinced themselves, it was the will of God to rule and be richly served by the people who, in turn, suffered.

To be how we are written forever? Valez, no longer my friend, but my enemy? Catriona finishing the book and leaving me all alone in this world that she created with only Adalind as my sole confidant?

The thought of Adalind having that level of agency still bothered him. He always thought she was like Sam—one dimensional—not wanting to stray too far from their destiny, just glad to exist and go around each time with the reader.

Why wasn't Valez spared? Eoin wanted to punch something. He felt so lost and uncertain until he heard Catriona's voice. She was still reading. She was almost at the end of the chapter, where he knew she would possibly end for the night.

If everything was changing around him, then it was possible the barrier between her and him had changed, as well. This was his last chance to find out. The chapter would end with his imprisonment right alongside Adalind. If he was going to find some connection to Catriona, it was now or never.

Eoin knew the action was not on him. The story had Catriona squarely on Adalind refusing to dance for Valez and his court, Valez striking her face and sending her back to the dungeons.

Eoin winced, knowing the blow she had received was real—that Adalind was in very real pain. He hid behind a statue of one of his supposed ancestors that possessed its own archway high up within the stone wall. He was ready not only to ambush Adalind's captors but to touch the slanted ceiling where he knew Catriona's hand would come to rest before she turned to the next chapter.

As Eoin saw a black boot come into view and Catriona's hand on the page, he lifted his hand to hers and felt the smooth plain of her palm on his. It was warm, and a spark shot down his entire body. He wanted to lace his fingers with hers, but the sensation was gone as the figure below came into view.

"Hello, Eoin." Valez stood alone, without Adalind or the guards. The light of the corridor flashed back and forth as Catriona flipped the page back and forth, over and over again until the castle shook from the sheer force of her slamming the book shut.

Eoin closed his eyes and sighed. *She felt me, too.*

When he opened his eyes, Valez's staff stared him squarely in the face—in the exact same way it had at the Black Cuillin Ridge. "We need to talk. Now!"

Chapter 16

Catriona

I flipped the page back and forth. Why did I just feel a spark as if I was holding someone's hand? My imagination had gone too far. How could I possibly feel the physical effects of my fictional crush?!

I slammed the book shut to quell this ridiculous tension. I had never felt this way about any fictional character, not even Mr. Darcy! I had read my fair share of books, but none in which I felt the touch of a human hand.

Detaching myself from Mum's winged-back chair, I noticed the imprints of my fingers still lingered on the blue upholstery.

I went straight to my room and slammed the door just as I had the book, leaving it behind in the living room. Why was the incarnation of Eoin haunting me in this way?

I tossed and turned all night. At one point, I vaguely heard Dad and Jeremy return from dinner; no sounds of slurring words, thumps from imbalance, just some good-hearted chuckles and the quiet click of Jeremy's door.

I heard my door crack open a hair and closed my eyes as I saw Dad's shadow on the carpet. When it was dark once more, I opened my eyes and was surprised when a few hot tears spilled out. Mum had always checked on me before she went to bed. My dad had never done that.

In the wake of this change, I never knew how much I needed my father's love and affection, how much that left a void in my heart, how it affected every subsequent relationship I had with a man.

A few teardrops turned into a torrential downpour as I thought of the ways in which I had allowed Henri to take advantage of me, how I was so desperate for his affirmation that I endured the constant bad just to get a taste of the meager good.

I did the same thing growing up with Dad until I could no longer hold onto the indifference just to get his notice, so I ignored him altogether and him me.

The void in my heart created by time shrunk with every tender moment Dad and I had together, but the thought that it had to take Mum's untimely death just to have it… *I don't think that will ever go away.*

I knew I would have to stop dwelling on what-could-have-been because that was a reality I could never access. A very real reality was now that my dad and I were moving toward a healthy father-daughter relationship, there was hope that I could eventually have a healthy romantic relationship.

My hand tingled at the thought of what I believed to be Eoin holding my hand. I squeezed it shut and drifted off with the feeling of butterflies dancing over the teardrops on my hand.

***

Eoin

Valez seemingly timed his entrance so as not to change the prose, but Eoin didn't know how much agency Valez had in his choices or if he was still aware of Catriona's existence.

Eoin held up his hands and moved out from behind the ivory statue. Valez was still poised to blast Eoin if he made one false move and mirrored Eoin's every step. He adjusted his staff as Eoin jumped down from the relatively high height of the in-wall figure.

"So, you survived?" Valez cackled but kept his offensive stance.

Eoin held his hands aloft and searched his friend's eyes. "I did. Either you didn't truly mean to kill me, or your powers failed you." Eoin had to choose each word carefully, straddling the line between fact and fiction.

Valez's smirk never faltered, even with Eoin's bait that challenged the validity of his powers. "I held nothing back, Eoin of Accolon. You're either stronger than you appear, or you had someone just as powerful as me bring you back to life."

Eoin thought of Catriona and her light. He knew it was her who restored him from fading from existence, and for just a moment, he dreaded the possibility that Valez was also referring to her—but that would mean he was fully cognizant of what he had done to Eoin.

No, this still felt fundamental to the written Valez. *He's referring to Isla as the story dictates. She is, in fact, more than the village healer—that she herself has a level of magic to counter Valez's that saves Eoin of Accolon.*

"It doesn't matter now, does it? I'm alive, and this is my kingdom. If you leave quietly, I swear I'll do everything in my power to *save you.*" Eoin knew what was about to happen, but he meant what he said. He would find a way to save Valez from the unwilling fate that seized him.

"That is very gracious of you, Your Highness, very gracious indeed…but I'm afraid it is you who does not appreciate the severity of the situation." Four black knights flanked Valez's sides. Eoin blinked to adjust his vision.

These were not Eoin's castle guards—they weren't the two "oafs" that were written to capture him, lock him up, and then secretly aid him in defeating Valez.

"You conjured your own knights?!" Eoin swallowed the fear that riddled his entire being. A translucent black smoke continually billowed off their sleek armor. As one grabbed his arm, a chill ran down his spine—*these guards are not human.*

The lightning on Valez's staff moved in time with his sardonic laugh. "That's not all I conjured." He moved his staff forward, "Lock him up." The soulless guards followed his staff. Eoin felt paralyzed, unable to move in the tight clutches of these supernatural knights.

Panic gripped Eoin's heart like a vice. "Valez, wait!" Valez turned, and his glittering red cape wafted behind him, giving the illusion of fire dancing behind him. "This isn't you. You're my friend, my best friend. Remember?" Eoin's voice broke. He didn't care what he was jeopardizing; what Valez had done and what he could now do frightened him to death.

Valez moved as if he were floating and stopped mere inches from Eoin's face, "I was never your friend." His voice was so vehement that it brought fresh tears to Eoin's eyes.

No part of Eoin's body could move, only the tears that freely flowed down his face. Valez turned away and Eoin heard him return to his guests as the life of the party.

The guards dragged Eoin to his entrapment that Valez had made special for him. It had the same consistency as the dark knights. There were no doors, no locks, just an iron cage that extended from the floor to the ceiling.

They pushed him in through the bars, and he landed hard on the stone floor. He jumped to his feet and moved to pass through the cell but clanged against cold metal squares, ones in which not even all his fingers could fit through. Valez had created an inescapable prison that had only one key—Valez himself.

Eoin moved to the far corner of his new prison and curled into a ball. His cries carried to earless walls. For the first time in his existence, he didn't know what was going to happen, which was something he had always longed for, but, at this moment, terrified him beyond imagination.

When he opened his swollen eyes, he saw the palm of his hand, the one that held Catriona's. He gripped it to his chest and dreamed only of her.

***

Catriona

The visceral way in which Valez told Eoin he was never his friend—his advisor—that it was all an act for this one shot at power tore right through me. Eoin must have felt the utter betrayal, even though it had been foreshadowed for the reader since the beginning.

On top of that, Valez took Adalind from Eoin's adjoining cell to relocate her to Gorgon's Mount so she could be guarded by a ferocious dragon. This book really dated itself with that plot device, but I found myself enthralled, nevertheless.

I looked up to take a little break from the story. I was sitting in the waiting room of Dr. Gayle's office while Dad had his session to assess his readiness to return to work.

I had an hour to kill as I waited in a wholesome patient room that tried its hardest to resemble a living space but, because of budget restraints, failed in every way that mattered most.

My eyes flitted down to the open book in my lap. The first time I met Eoin and was introduced to his story, it was in similar surroundings.

I was able to escape to another world while I waited for my dad in a world where he was helpless, where he had hurt himself, in a world that was crumbling around me. At present, I was waiting as my dad was getting better, where my world was healing, but where Eoin's world was falling apart.

The separation of Eoin and Adalind caused such a stirring within me, a strong yearning to experience such a dire situation for myself.

Adalind's own suffering and delirium while in the entrapment of Valez, believing beyond a shadow of a doubt that Eoin would rescue her, was awful, yet it had me turning the pages so quickly that I missed a few prepositions here and there just to get to their romantic reunion.

No one in real life wants to be separated from their true love. No one desires to be imprisoned by a power-hungry psychopath awaiting to be saved while in constant torture.

A climax of this multitude is desired in a good story. The reader can experience these dangers within the pages of a book and still lead a safe and happy life.

But when that same darkness escapes the pages of a book, there is no great narrative or some great reason for tragedy. My mum's death certainly did not make for a great story in my life for some greater destiny or fate—it was senseless.

I closed the book, letting my hand be pressed against the pages. I let it linger and anticipated the feeling of a strong, inviting hand instead of the flat, crisp page beneath. After a minute, I slid my hand out and rested it against my forehead as the book closed completely.

My view of reality and fiction was precarious, to say the least, as Eoin, his presence, and these characters felt more real with each passing hour. *Maybe I should book an appointment with Dr. Gayle, too.*

As if conjured by my thoughts, Dr. Gayle came out holding the door for my dad. They laughed at some shared joke just before the door opened. Dad shook his hand and came to stand by me.

"So, what's the prognosis?" I directed my question to both men, waiting to land my focus on whoever answered first.

Dr. Gayle cleared his throat, "Walter has improved greatly from when I first saw him. There is still a lot to work through, but I think he's ready to return to work. I do recommend starting with part-time hours and taking on more as you see fit. I've noted that in your papers to give to your employer." He handed Dad a stack of papers and gave both of us a winning smile.

"That's great news!" I flung myself in Dad's arms as they wrapped around me, crinkling Dr. Gayle's notes against my back.

"Aye, it is. I can't thank ye enough, Peter. And Catriona, here, has been my lifeline." We beamed at each other.

"That's wonderful, and if you ever want to book regular sessions, or even you, Catriona in what you've been through and even now as your role of caretaker is less needed, you can come to me, or I'll be happy to recommend someone…"

"Thanks, I appreciate that. I'll definitely think about it." Dad shot me a hard look at my harsh interruption.

"I'll give you a call, Peter. Thank you for everything." They shook hands one more time as I gathered my book and purse from the neighboring chair and headed for the exit.

We drove back in silence. I could tell Dad was still mad about my obvious dismissal of Dr. Gayle's offer.

It became almost too deafening, and I began to fear that he would clam up like he had before until he said my name without directing his head toward mine, "You know, Catriona, I don't think it'd be the worst idea if you wanted to talk to a professional like Peter."

"Dad…"

"Let me finish. You don't have to see him if you don't want to. Maybe a female therapist would make you more comfortable, but I fear if you leave everything you've been through unchecked, well… I just don't want you to forget about you. So, you can move forward and live the life that you want to live."

I had pulled into the driveway, so his last few words were said face-to-face. It was true; I did have a hard time admitting that I needed help, and I tended to pull away when others noticed what I tried so hard to conceal.

This time was no different, but I wasn't quite ready to see Dr. Gayle or anyone else for that matter. It seemed like a waste of time, especially if it was something I could work out for myself.

I could feel my almost filled void at the center of my heart open a stitch as his last few words flung me squarely into the past.

"Oh, so now you want me to live the life I want to live? Where was that attitude when I got my job in Paris right out of uni or my promotion last year? You couldn't even jump on the phone to congratulate me when Mum offered!"

Dad turned his face away and looked out his window, but the void continued to open stitch by stitch, and I couldn't stop myself, "Just because you decided to be my dad after Mum died doesn't mean you get to tell me what to do! Or think of yourself as an expert on who I am!"

I climbed out of the car and went straight to my room. My heart ached as instant regret consumed me. I ignored the image of my dad's face creased by guilt and pain.

I landed on my bed and pressed my face into my pillow. I didn't know what I was going to do. Dr. Gayle was right; I was no longer needed as the caretaker of my family, and I was afraid of where that left me.

I didn't have a plan for my future, and that's what worried my dad. It worried me, too, but I felt too paralyzed to move forward in this world alone.

***

Eoin

Eoin could see Catriona's hand covering the ceiling of his confinement. He wept for joy at its meaning. She had felt him and was longing to feel him again.

His tears turned to sorrow the longer her hand lingered, unable to touch it. He was so far away from it, until it slowly slipped from view and was replaced by dark stone.

Just as Catriona had read, the guards came and collected Adalind from her cell across from his. What Catriona had not read was that the guards were the four soulless knights who exuded death and destruction.

Adalind's eyes doubled in size as Eoin saw fear crack at the edges of her delicately poised face for the first time since they were written.

"Eoin? Eoin, what's going on? Please, please don't let them take me!" Eoin knew this wasn't an act on Adalind's part, even though she was aware that Catriona was still reading.

Eoin wasn't acting for Catriona either, "Adalind, it's okay. It'll be alright. Look at me. Do what he says. I'll come for you. I promise."

Understanding passed over Adalind's frightened face. She looked like a scared little girl, and every part of him wanted to protect her.

Although he was alone, he could still hear Adalind's haunting cries as she struggled against the death-like hold of the inhuman knights that took her to a fate unscripted. He threw his fists against the wall, feeling utterly helpless to save those he was sworn to protect.

Eoin sunk on his heels and leaned on the iron bars. He didn't have a plan to escape his imprisonment and save Adalind as the story dictated. He had no idea how to restore his world back to a book and continue the story for Catriona.

It wasn't until he saw Catriona's light and her face

come into view from above that he realized maybe he didn't want it to go back. Maybe this was all happening for a reason—if his world was becoming real, maybe he could just walk out of his world and into hers as easily as traveling from one village to the next.

As she was now in full view, Eoin noticed that she was outside. The sky was so blue, and the plants around her as green as the sapling that had grown on Gorgon's Mount, but she wasn't alone.

His heart stopped as he heard a man's voice, but it quickly fell back into its normal rhythm as he knew it to be the soft Scottish lilt of her father.

"You left it in the car," her father said barely above a whisper.

"Thanks." Eoin noted how she turned her face down to his book in remorse. How puffy and red her eyes were from crying. He'd escape right this minute to rescue her if this man made her cry; he didn't care if it was her own father.

"I'll leave you to it then."

"Dad!" She sounded scared at the prospect of him

leaving.

"Yes, love?"

"Thank you for bringing me my book," she tilted it up so Eoin could see everything from her vantage point. He laid eyes on the man she called father for the first time.

The father's eyes seemed to match Catriona's in more ways than one—he had her distinct round eyes that were dark blue, but they too were red and puffy, with a hint of tears resting at the corners.

He brushed back his graying hair not knowing what to say to his precious daughter, "I thought you'd like to have it. It's not often I see you without having it somewhere near you, just so you can read it at any time…must be something really special."

Her father's shoulders flinched as if to move toward her, but he stopped himself short. "I'm making dinner; I'll call when it's ready."

Catriona just nodded and she turned back to Eoin and squeezed her eyes shut. Eoin surmised something had just happened between them, but he hadn't been present for it.

Once he figured out how to get out of his world, he would be there to comfort her no matter the circumstance in which she needed it.

"Why are you looking up at the ceiling again, Sire?" Eoin jumped back against the stone wall in surprise. Samuel's voice was lined with concern at his king's strange behavior, but it was quickly replaced with dread at the sight of Eoin's unnatural cell.

"Nothing, Samuel." Eoin tried to subtly look up again. She still wasn't reading. "What is it?"

"A single carriage left the castle at the crack of dawn with the Queen inside flanked by two of Valez's men."

Eoin heard Catriona's voice as she began to read. "Did you have your men follow her?"

"Aye, they sent a scout back. It appears he's taking her to the Black Cuillin Ridge, back to where you…"

"I remember, Samuel… I'm glad you were there to save me."

"Aye, me too, Your Highness."

The two men paused thinking about what to do

next. Eoin knew how the story was supposed to go, but he didn't know how he was going to escape—it was no longer easily written for him.

"How are we going to get you out? There are no doors on this cell!" Samuel slammed his chest into the solid iron bars.

"I think Valez is the key. Did he leave with the Queen's carriage?"

"No, he's still in the tower doing God only knows. Every once in a while, the castle shakes, and a piercing light blasts out from the tower window."

Eoin sprang off the wall with an idea, "Samuel! You brilliant bastard! You have to steal his staff."

"What? That's a death sentence, Your Majesty."

"It's the only way!" Eoin lowered his voice in recognition of what he was asking of his loyal first knight, "I know, Samuel, but it is the only way I'll get out of here to save Adalind and our kingdom from this evil."

Eoin still wasn't comfortable referring to Valez as evil. He still believed that the goodness of his friend was still inside. "But first, bring me parchment, a quill, and some ink. I have something for your man to deliver to Adalind."

"Yes, Milord." Samuel bowed deeply, then bounded for the stairs.

"And Samuel? I trust you with my life."

"And mine with yours."

Eoin's eyes glistened as Sam sprinted out of the dungeon. He finally felt like a deserving leader but hated the very real stakes that surrounded it. He feared for Sam's life at the hands of who he knew Valez was written to be.

Eoin looked back up as Catriona was reading about whatever Valez was doing, Eoin no longer knew, and subsequently Sam's actions in stealthily retrieving his requested parchment, quill, and ink.

Samuel came back and rolled the parchment so that it fit through a tiny square hole of his cell along with the quill and ink bottle. He told Eoin how he planned to steal Valez's staff. Eoin listened with concern but agreed as this was their only chance.

Once alone, Eoin began to write. He wasn't entirely alone. Catriona was still reading, so he could look up at her as much as he desired. With the events of the book made real, he would have to actually write his letter and poem to Adalind.

He wrote to inform her of his plan to be released and come save her. He assured her that no matter what, he would protect her, and he meant it.

Eoin then looked up at Catriona's dark blue eyes. They reminded him of the depths and mysteries that the waters of Loch Ness held.

He turned the parchment over and dabbed his quill in fresh ink.

Right now, you're just a hand, a hand in mine
Right now, you're just two eyes, two eyes that guide
Right now, you're just a face, a face that shines

Right now, I know I am truly not alone
Right now, I long to know every part of you
Right now, I wait….

A line of ink scratched across the page as Eoin spun

in his dungeon and it suddenly darkened. He landed hard on the cobbled floor.

Once his world stilled, he stood and shouted to the ceiling above, "No, Catriona, it's not what you think. It was for you! It has always been for you."

Knowing his shouted protests went unheard, he ended the poem aloud, *"…until our hearts become one."*

He sunk back to the floor and let the stones dig into his back as he continued to look up, but he felt a slow smile form as warmth spread throughout his heart. *She wants to be with me too—ha, to think she was jealous of Adalind.*

"Don't worry, my love, there is nothing to be jealous of. We'll speak to each other soon enough." Eoin placed his hands behind his head—Valez's staff would free him in more ways than one.

***

Catriona

Eoin may not have felt alone, although he was physically alone, but I did. He was writing the most beautiful poem to a woman he loved in earnest because of their separation.

The idea of Adalind affecting Eoin so acutely and totally unbeknownst to her was so lovely that it left me breathless and completely empty.

I had once resented Henri for never painting me—that he was never so overcome by his love that just the sight of me caused him to commit it to memory by recreating my image with something he loved for someone he loved—*but he never loved me.*

Even before I finished that thought, I knew it wasn't Henri who caused me to react to Eoin's words in that way. It was Eoin. He had always been there when I needed him. He was there every time I opened his book—just waiting for me.

When I thought I had felt his hand, something shifted, but his poem to Adalind was a startling reminder that it was only in my imagination. Eoin had no conscious thought for me, or at all for that matter. He was fictional, printed, never changing beyond the pages that were written for him.

This thought left me so desolate that I started to no

longer feel any pain, which had been my constant state of being as of late. I felt so vacuous and cold as I went inside and heard Jeremy's shouts for dinner.

Dad and I didn't say a word to each other, barely made eye contact, and just went through the perfunctory mechanics of eating.

Jeremy tried to spark conversation but quickly noticed the tension and dropped it, adopting our same demeanor. After I felt adequately full, I washed my dishes and went straight to my room.

As I sat in my chair, I opened the book, just as I would any other—to finish a good story.

Before I could get even one word read, Gemma called.

"Hiya, Gemma."

"Hey, sweetie. Everything okay?"

I looked down at the book in my lap. I sighed and put it on my bed still face open. "Yeah, I'm alright. What's going?"

"Just wanted to see how your new year was starting out and sort of, kind of… wanted to talk about the wedding…if that's all right of course?"

I gulped. I hated that I had made Gemma feel like she needed to walk on eggshells around me about the best day of her life. "Of course, it is, Gem. Never hold back again about it, ever. This is your day, and I'll be the best maid of honor! I promise."

My heart lightened as the weight of that left her, and she could just be excited about every little detail that made it *her* day, which she summed up as a checklist: "April wedding, gold and blush color scheme, elegant minimalism and trendy infusion theme, peonies for the bouquets, and it will be at The Rodin Museum in Paris."

I sucked in a sharp breath at the thought of returning to Paris. It felt like a past life. Gemma didn't notice and kept ticking items off her list, "I think we'll do one full week of wedding stuff: shower, stag and hen night, rehearsal dinner, and then the wedding!" She squealed so loudly that I had to remove my ear from the phone. "Can you get away for a week?"

"Yes… yes, of course I can. I don't know where I'll be in three months, but I wouldn't miss any of it for the world, Gemma. Who knows, I might be back in Paris by then." I paused to see if I could mentally picture that possibility, but I couldn't quite grasp it. "I'll start planning the hen night!"

"Fab! Okay, well, I'll let you go; I know it's getting late there. Love you." She made a kiss noise into the phone and waited to hear my "love you too" before she hung up.

I sighed and placed my phone on the dresser. I sat back in my chair, staring at the blank side of my door. How I envied Gemma and her future—how certain it was for her.

My future was unknown and fraught with so many moving variables that I couldn't get to stay still long enough to come up with a definite course of action. Gemma's wedding was the only solid future I had, and I needed to plan a killer hen night because she deserved it.

Knowing my door would never answer my deep-seated questions about my future, I turned and grabbed my book.

Once it was in my lap and I was ready to dive back into the story, the words began to scramble—letters hopping over each other as if they were deciphering a hidden code—and then they blurred until both pages were completely blank.

My heart jumped up into my throat. *What did I do? Shona's going to kill me!* I flipped the book over, looking at the cover, then back to the blank pages.

A line of words slowly formed in the middle of the page, as if an invisible quill was writing, "Will you be taking me to the wedding, then?"

It took me a second to register what was happening. I dropped the book and ran out of my room, slamming the door to create whatever barricade I needed.

I pressed my back against my bedroom door with my eyes closed, breathing in and out. *Is the book alive? Could Eoin be real?*

When I opened my eyes, both Dad and Jeremy were staring at me with their mouths agape.

"You alright, Cat?" Jeremy finally asked. I nodded my head. I couldn't voice what had happened aloud.

Either I was going crazy… or the book really was alive, but both explanations didn't incite much confidence in my sanity, so I just stayed silent.

***

Eoin

It worked! Eoin couldn't believe it. He talked to her! He talked to Catriona! He wasn't exactly thrilled in the way she reacted, however understandable.

Samuel was able to lure Valez from his incantation room by inciting a possible break-in as there appeared to be a giant hole in the east-side wall, indicating insurrection and upheaval to Valez's reign.

At Samuel's urgent persistence, Valez hastily followed—flanked by his ghostly knights, as a few loyalists who were standing by stole his staff to free Eoin.

As soon as the staff was in Eoin's hand, the doorless prison vanished, and that is when he spoke those words to Catriona.

He held the staff aloft, and after overhearing her conversation with Gemma—well, only Catriona's responses and, at one point, Gemma's squeals—he knew what he would say, the only thing that would convey that he was real, that he could hear everything she said.

When Eoin clocked her reaction, and she let go of him, seemingly out of view, Eoin braced himself for impact, for his world to shake and turn over, but nothing happened. He looked at Valez's staff in wonder. Another change in his world that he couldn't explain.

Samuel had managed to double back before Valez could reach the perfectly intact stone wall and was now urging Eoin to move quickly—to escape the castle, to escape Valez's clutches, because without his staff, Valez was almost powerless and he would stop at nothing to get it back, but Eoin wouldn't dare leave the staff. He wouldn't give up the one thing that seemed to allow him to finally connect with Catriona.

He slung his bag over his shoulder, the one Samuel packed provisions in, and hoisted Valez's staff with his other hand.

Eoin and Samuel escaped the castle walls through the secret passages that the author had created for him. Never would he imagine that they would be used in a real life-and-death situation.

They journeyed back to the safe house where Eoin almost faded from existence. Isla was no longer there, and he sent Samuel out to scout the perimeter and stand guard, but his safety was the last thing on his mind. He wanted to be alone so he could use the staff and contact Catriona again.

"Catriona? Catriona, are you there? I'm so sorry I scared you before. It's me, Eoin. Eoin of Accolon." He looked up at a dimly lit ceiling. "I know it may be hard to believe, but I can explain everything. If you'll allow me."

He lowered his head and stared at the staff that now glowed with a soft purple glow instead of the crackling red when in the hands of Valez.

"Eoin?" He heard her sweet voice that was barely a whisper. He closed his eyes as inescapable tears filled within until he could no longer hold them there.

Eoin looked up, and there she was—just as beautiful and enchanting as the first day she had opened his book and begun to read.

Part III

Chapter 17

Catriona

"So, Catriona. Why are you here today?"

"Umm, my mum passed away in a car accident five months ago." I no longer had to do the math in my head. She died in October, and the calendar on the therapist's wall reminded me that we were well into March.

"I'm sorry to hear that. How have you been feeling since then?" I just stared at Dr. McClatchie. I fixated on her brown bun that sat perfectly perched high on top of her head.

Her question prompted my memories to flash in front of me at warp speed—from the day I got the call from Dad that changed my entire life to seeing and talking to a fictional character.

"Catriona?" She reached her hand across our shared space and touched my wrist.

I didn't move away from the contact, and neither did she as I continued, "Honestly, I didn't. I didn't allow myself to feel. When I first heard that she had…died, I did…I did cry, but once I arrived home and had to plan her funeral, I just sort of stepped into her place and began taking care of my family… the way she would have… I guess I put their surmounting grief first so I wouldn't have to deal with my own."

Dr. McClatchie let my words sit there for a moment so I could fully register them for myself before she took her hand away and sat back with sympathetic eyes. "That must have been hard."

"Yeah, yeah, it was."

"And now? Have you acknowledged her death and put your grief first?"

"I have, at least, that's what I'm working on. I actually exploded in the wrong place and at the wrong time, at my best friend's engagement party, but I've been trying to work through it—and my dad and brother have given me the space and time to focus on myself instead of having to worry about them." I chewed my bottom lip, not sure how much I should divulge in my first session.

"How do you feel? That is, how do you feel about your family moving on?"

"Catriona? Catriona. How do you feel about all this?

About me being real, that is?" Eoin's words to me echoed through my mind until I could think of nothing else but him.

"Catriona? Are you sure you're okay to move on? You seem distracted," I heard Dr. McClatchie's voice break through my reverie.

"Hmm? Oh, I'm sorry. Yeah, I am a little bit."

"Is it something you want to talk about with me?" Dr. McClatchie, or Fiona, as she continually insisted that I call her, leaned forward again.

"No, not right now. I'm still trying to figure it out…what I'm supposed to do now, that is." I looked down at my empty purse.

"I understand. Maybe that is something you and I can discuss next week. Think about where you see yourself. Make a list of what options are available to you that you may not realize at the moment, hmm?"

"Sounds good. Yes, I'll do that. Thank you so much, Fiona."

My mind wasn't fully cognizant of the present as I left her office or as I caught a bus back home. Instead, it took me back to *that* night—the night Eoin first spoke to me. When everything seemed to click into place, as I found the courage to reenter my room only a couple of months ago…

"Eoin?" I crossed the room and knelt on the floor to see the pages, to see what he was writing to me, but I was still too afraid to touch the book—*to touch him.*

"Catriona? Catriona! I'm so sorry I scared you before. I uhh...I actually don't know quite what to say. How are you feeling? I mean, how do you feel about all this? About me being real, that is?"

"I…I don't know." I honestly didn't know how I felt. I had moved from frightened to ecstatic to relief, then back to frightened, all in one beat of my heart.

"It's understandable. I suppose I have had a bit of a head start. I've been able to hear and see you since the first day you opened my book."

"Really? You saw everything?" I wracked my brain to when I first opened Eoin's story. When he would have had the chance to see me. I blushed, realizing the magnitude of what I had been holding in my hands all this time.

The words described a breathy laugh before they appeared. "*Dinna fash.* Don't worry, I didn't see anything you wouldn't wish anyone else to see. If I did have the vantage point in times of privacy, I turned my gaze away."

I laughed in turn, trying to hide the heat rising to my face. "I suppose some things that were written about you are true then, like how you are a man of honor."

But how am I to know that for sure? Surely, I'm not his first reader—maybe this happened to others? Maybe he's lying—that he really did take advantage of seeing everything while remaining unseen.

"Eoin? Am I the first reader you've ever spoken to since you were written?"

"Aye. You are. I've had countless readers since my inception, but you were the first in…decades. And in that time, I had lost all hope of a reader ever opening my book. I had even convinced myself that was what I wanted—to be left alone and quietly fade from existence."

The words he spoke faded as he paused before a new sentence began writing itself. "But when I first felt the weightlessness of being picked up—when I felt your touch—I knew I had been lying to myself. You renewed my spirit, Catriona, and even if that's all we share, I will always be grateful to you for that."

My fingers traced every word that formed on the page, absorbing everything Eoin was saying. I held back tears that seemed to form with this knowledge—that this whole time, I hadn't been alone. Someone cared for me, needed me, just as I needed them.

"I feel the exact same way," I laughed through the tears I could no longer hold back and dashed them away. "Your story, Eoin, well, it gave me a voice on things that would normally go unheard…ever since…" I choked on a sob, feeling so overwhelmed by it all.

"Aye, I know. I'm so sorry about your mother, Catriona. I wish I could be there to comfort you. To wipe away every tear from your sweet face."

I placed my hand on my cheek, causing tears to spread across the expanse of my face. "I keep forgetting you can see me, because I can't see you," I laughed at just how natural it felt, but I imagined how odd it would look to see me speaking aloud to an empty room waiting for words to appear in an already written book.

"You know what I look like, how the book describes me."

"Yeah, but I can't see your expression when we're talking, can't interpret what you're thinking. You definitely have the advantage." I let out a nervous laugh. How I longed to see him in real time—to see the way he looked at me—to know the feeling behind his words.

"Perhaps but know that I *am* here with you. We can talk for as long as we want. Just as you used to read through the night, now you can read what I think about you, about me… about us."

All I could do was nod and wait for his next words, "Place your hand on the page, Catriona." I did as he said and felt his hand. It was rough and warm, filling the entire page, fitting perfectly against mine.

"I can feel you," I breathed. "I felt you that night…"

"Aye, I felt your hand just as real as I do now. Things are happening in here, things are changing,

Catriona. I've never been able to touch or, as you now know, even speak to a reader. You're different."

"Really? You haven't connected with any other reader in the past six centuries?" My heart ached just thinking about that loneliness—to have to exist in that reality.

"No, no one. I mean, I could see them just as I do you, when they would open the book to read, but they just read, and my fellow characters and I moved the plot along. Once they finished the story, we would go back to the beginning to do it all over again."

Although I couldn't hear his voice, I felt the gloom and almost despair in reliving the same fate, the same life over and over again, with nothing to hope for—nothing to dream.

It's almost exactly how I felt moments before his words appeared on the page. I felt like I had no future, no hope in moving forward in this life—in this life that fate had cruelly dealt with—until Eoin spoke to me.

I closed my eyes to picture him, the way the book described him, but also how his face might look as it formed with each emotion when he spoke.

My eyes opened wide as I remembered, as I remembered actually seeing him—how terrified his eyes looked as they locked onto mine.

"You were at the Fairy Pools…in Skye, weren't you? Did I really see you there, Eoin?"

"Aye, I saw you bundled in your wee jacket and how I found myself looking into eyes that I've somehow known all my life. I also saw you that night at the library. The night I almost…the night I almost faded from existence."

"I saw you too, almost ghost-like lying in your bed, but I thought I was dreaming. Is that what Valez did to you on the mountain when red lightning struck? Could you feel anything?' My heartbeat quickened as I waited for his answer, not sure how mortality worked for him—within his world.

"Aye, Valez struck me for the first time since we were written. The moment I saw you through the mist with your bonnie golden hair flowing around you, his powers became real, he became the villain he was written to be, and he struck me, just as the story dictates."

I waited for him to continue, but the page remained blank for so long that fear began to infiltrate my heart. *He can't fade away from me again.* "Eoin? Eoin, are you still there?"

"I felt so cold, Catriona," he continued as though he didn't hear me. "When I saw my friend leave and someone else take his place. Everything went dark at first, but then there was this peace that washed over me when I finally realized the very real pain and trouble would soon be over, but fear terrorized me when I thought I'd never see you again."

He paused once more. He was reliving that moment in his mind, processing everything that had happened and trying to put it into words for me. "Of course, I never made it past the light, *ye ken*? I saw your light instead. It was your light, Catriona, and your face that brought me back."

My hands were clasped over my mouth as I read. I was acutely aware of the reality of his words as they sunk in—that the battle against Valez really happened, that the story within his book was never real, that is, until I started reading, and that he had almost died…because of me.

"I can't believe I almost let that happen! To think I was so afraid of what I saw on Skye… that I almost gave you up." A loud sob rolled up my throat and out of my mouth. My hands absorbed the ones that continued without a clear sign of stopping.

"Ssh, ssh. Do not cry, *mo chridhe.* How could you possibly have known this was real—that I was real and in peril?"

Mo chridhe, "my heart" in Gaelic, and my heart swelled at his term of endearment for me.

"Was it real? Your story and the characters around you?" The fluttering in my heart vanished as I left out the one person that I really wanted to know was real or not, the one person the book said was Eoin's true love.

"No, none of it was real. We all lived separate lives from what the author wrote us to be. I'm not in love with Adalind, Catriona."

"How did you know?"

"It is written all over your face, love. I hate to tell

you this, but everything you're thinking is told through your eyes."

"That explains a lot, actually." I thought about all the arguments I had lost against Gemma, Jeremy, and even Mum over the years. "So, who is Adalind when the book is closed?"

"If you could only see me rolling my eyes, you'd understand. She wants her and me to be how we are written, but not because of any true feelings of love, but for the status of being queen and the easiness that comes with following a written path."

I smiled, letting him know I was pleased with that information about Adalind, that he seemed to only want me. My smile faltered, "Eoin. You said, 'We all lived separate lives.' Has that changed?"

"Aye, ever since that moment at the Pools, all the characters around me have forgotten who they are and have become who they were written to be. They don't know that we're in a book, that we have a reader and a purpose; my world has become real, Catriona."

"What does that mean? You're all alone in this?"

"I am, and the one person I could always count on—the one person I could confide everything in is now gone. Valez was a dear friend to me, Catriona. Quite the opposite of his written character. He had no evil bone in his body. He had no powers—he was kind, wise, and even silly, at times."

I waited to let Eoin remember his friend, who, in essence, was gone. "I'm so sorry, Eoin. I feel as if I took him away from you."

"No, it might have started when you began reading, but everything that has happened and what is happening between you and me…I don't know if I'd change it for the world."

Eoin's voice was so gentle and caring that it made me feel electrified with anticipation of what this all meant. *His voice? I can hear his voice?!*

"Eoin! Say something, I think I heard your voice in my head before your words even finished forming on the page!"

"Umm, well in saying that I hope that we can find a way to restore Valez and everyone else, and to have you by my side while we figure it out…together. Did you hear me that time, love?"

"Yes! Your voice is so soft and deep, I can hardly believe it!"

"That I'm real?" He chuckled and I let the warm playfulness of it echo in my mind.

"Yes, and that any of this is happening, that another world exists in this one, that it's you and me against the world… or worlds. Are there other characters alive in other books?" My mind went to the vast array of books in the library—in Shona's collection—then to all the books that ever existed and still exist today.

Eoin laughed in wonder, "I don't know, it's certainly possible, aye?"

I realized that in the course of our conversation, I had moved from the floor to my bed and was now tucked under the covers with the book propped up against the other pillow.

As our conversation came to a comfortable lull, I imagined this scenario if it wasn't just a book next to me in my bed, but if it was actually Eoin—his magnificent form languidly stretched out next to me—talking to me and caressing me into the wee hours of the night.

"Are you alright, Catriona? You look startled all of a sudden."

"Yes, just got a bit nervous." I looked at the bed again and crossed my arms. I began to rub them to rid my body of the cold that a familiar shiver caused. Eoin thought he was assisting in dispelling my nerves with his gentle concern, but it only caused the shivers to increase.

"Aye, I understand. Catriona, I want you to be as comfortable as possible. I want you to feel safe and secure in my presence."

I blushed and broke eye contact from the book because the feeling was too intense. The fact that I was acutely aware of my presence and his right beside me left a tingling knot at the base of my chest.

I realized that although he was in the form of a book, he was still a man—a man I barely knew, yet I felt such a strong connection to him.

Being alone with Eoin for this long perplexed me. He made me want to give my all to him and I briefly wondered if he felt the same way.

We talked for hours, with one part of me always touching the book. He told me everything about his past, every detail since he was written, and I talked about my past until the day I found him.

We slowly began to paint a picture of a future that we each desired to see, but before I could fully grasp it, I was lulled to sleep by Eoin's sweet Highlander brogue, whispering sweet nothings until glittering stars lined my dreams.

***

Eoin

Eoin watched as Catriona fell into a deep sleep. He continued to whisper the story of when she first picked up his book—every feeling he had then and continued to feel whenever she opened him, even his feelings of emptiness and dread when she was gone for long stretches at a time.

He had no idea how much she heard or comprehended, nor did it matter. What mattered was that they were now connected. She knew he was real—that he was more than just a fictional character within the pages of a book. She could get to know the real him, the one that always existed but was only known to Valez but never to the reader.

He didn't know what made Catriona different from the others, nor did he care. All that mattered was that it was her that he was able to connect with after all this time. After a few centuries, Eoin began to hate his written fate, but somehow, this connection with Catriona felt destined. But he hated to think that it took her mother's death for her to find him. Yet, when he thought about the centuries of readers before her—it was difficult to explain it as anything else. If it was fate that brought them together, then he knew that they would have found each other no matter what happened.

As Eoin stared at Catriona's sleeping form, a purple light from Valez's staff that was still clutched in his hand caught his eye.

He set it down, and the light dissipated. He looked up to still see Catriona, but he doubted that she could hear him without the staff. *That's something we'll have to test when she awakes.*

The front door of his safehouse swung open, and he grabbed the staff in defense, pointing it at whoever came through. When he saw Sam's muted, brown hair that squarely framed his face, he lowered it.

Sam lifted one of his bushy brows. "Not becoming the warlock you've sworn to kill, are you, Milord?" Humor seeped from his voice, but it also held a slight edge of unease.

"No, just a reflex, I suppose. I was in deep thought about what to do with it right before you busted in." He lined his voice with the same humor, trying to dispel all worry from Sam's oblong face.

"Speaking of, I've just gotten word that the evil sorcerer has sent out his knights that spread nothing but death and destruction wherever they go to ensure the return of his staff and Your Majesty, no matter the cost."

"Do you know their location at present?"

"Aye, they're tearing through every village from the castle to Gorgon's Mount, which means we need to leave here, now!"

Eoin stole a glance at Catriona, ignoring Sam's objection once again. "Let's go. We have to keep this staff from them at all costs."

Sam nodded and went out to prepare the horses.

Eoin grabbed the staff and twirled it in his hand. He realized that he had never held the staff before, the story never prompted him to steal it or possess it, but it seemed this was the only thing that allowed him and Catriona to speak, and he'd be damned to let out of his sight.

Maybe the magic in the staff was the only way to fix his world and finally be with Catriona in person—in her world. This also meant that Valez would hunt him over the face of their new world to get it back.

Whatever fate this new story seemed to hold, Eoin would do whatever it took to be with Catriona. After this night, he knew nothing would keep him from her ever again.

***

Catriona

The very next morning, I awoke to the sound of rain, as was Scottish fashion, and found the book face open, still resting on the pillow beside me. I picked it up and hesitated for the briefest of moments. *Maybe it was just a dream. A wish I made in the absence of hope.*

I felt my cheeks burn as I heard Eoin's familiar voice, the one I most definitely heard both in and out of my dreams. "Good morning, *mo cridhe.*"

We reminisced about our first night together, and I revealed how much I cherished the comforting balm he left on my heart.

Eoin and I shared a small exchange every day, and every day, I felt his kindness grow into a tenderness that I could not shake.

As with all my exchanges with men though, I could be reading way too much into the situation and be incredibly wrong about his intentions.

Whenever dating and romance are suggested, well, in that department, I am truly lost. I can barely think of a future for myself, let alone factoring in another person, a fictional one trapped inside a book, at that!

However, I would tuck in a secret smile every time we exchanged pleasantries.

Winter passed by with a gradual quickness, but the darkness and cold that characterized the months of January and February in Scotland only prolonged my inner turmoil.

All I wanted to do was cry every time I spoke to Eoin. I wanted to cry from the never-ending pit that was my loneliness. It sat on my chest, as the pages that separated us were a constant reminder of what I could never have yet wanted with every fiber of my being—I wanted him here with me.

Can one person know they'll end up with another before the other realizes it? If so, it is a very lonely existence until that hopeful ending comes true, if it ever comes true.

After that first night, I realized Eoin was more than just an escape—there was a connection there beyond the circumstantial. Our long conversations became a time of healing for both of us, and the scars we had both attained were healed every time we came together.

My reverie came to an abrupt stop along with the bus. I blushed in embarrassment as Greg, the bus driver, had to call out my stop.

"Cheers, Greg," I waved sheepishly before I hopped off and ran down the narrow street to my house.

I ignored my neighbors' faces as I jogged past in my flowing pink skirt and tan Mary-Jane wedges. All I wanted to do was be home and talk to Eoin about my day.

Although I was convinced Eoin was real, I couldn't ignore the other parts of me that were still reeling from my mum's death and the uncertainty of a future without her or without my guys.

I pushed past those feelings just as I did the front door. Dad startled a little in his chair but sagged back in his comfortable position and back to his book that I lent for him from the library. When he saw how much I loved my book, he wanted to get back into reading. He said anything historical, so I found a book in my section on the Battle of Culloden.

"Hiya, pet." He inched his reading glasses down to the tip of his nose to look up at me. "You all right?"

Ever since that day in the car, when he had softly mentioned that I should consider therapy and I blew up at him, we had tiptoed around each other, especially around the subject of therapy.

It wasn't until winter had passed and Eoin and I had been talking for a few months that I mentioned giving therapy a try. Dad didn't say anything, but I saw him let out a quiet breath of relief.

Jeremy also seemed relieved when I told him—I think he was just as tired of walking on eggshells around me, not just me, but Dad and me together. I guess he had forgotten that's exactly how he grew up, but a part of me was glad he didn't have to live like that anymore.

I tried to rush by his chair as I responded to his question. "I'm fine. The session was fine. Just have to work on how I envision my future, that's all…that's my homework." I shifted my weight once more to head to my room, but Dad didn't pick up on my cue.

"Oh yes, I always have a homework assignment from Peter as well. This week, I need to work on opening up to others with whom I have a thirty-second or longer interaction. I tell you, sometimes I think it's all quackery, but then when I think of…" He took off his glasses, hiding half his face with his hand to remove some tears. I set aside my hurry and sat on the arm of his recliner and rubbed his shoulder.

He ran his hand down the rest of his face and put his glasses back on. "Don't fuss over me, darling. I was right in the middle of the massacre of our ancestors, *eeshk*. I learned this in school of course, but this historian doesn't mind getting his hands dirty, if you know what I mean." I smiled down at him and rubbed his shoulder one more time. "Seriously, go on, now. I know you were in a hurry to read your own book."

I kissed him on the head and ran to my room.

When I was at the door, I heard my dad yell, "You'd think you'd be finished with it by now with how much you read it!" He chuckled, but I stayed frozen.

Of course, it was taking me forever. I wasn't really reading the book; I was talking to its main character.

Although my pride was somewhat wounded, as Dad knew that I was a quick and avid reader, I would rather him think I was taking forever to finish reading than the alternative—he would certainly send me to a psychiatric hospital if he knew the truth.

The thought of speaking to Eoin dispelled all my worries. I would normally wait until both Dad and Jeremy were fast asleep before Eoin and I would talk for hours, but I couldn't wait—I wanted to tell him about my session and tell him resolutely I knew he was real, that what he and I had was real.

***

Eoin

Eoin lived for his conversations with Catriona. Every night, when her father and brother went to sleep, she would open his book, and they would spend the rest of the night talking.

Sometimes, she would open the book during the day just to wave or say a quick hello, but this arrangement seemed to suit him just as well with his current circumstances.

At night, Sam volunteered to patrol their perimeter

and keep watch while he thought Eoin slept, but Eoin didn't sleep. He would use Valez's staff to talk to Catriona all night.

Eoin and Catriona tested his theory. When the staff was not in his hand with its glowing purple ember atop, she could not hear him, nor did his words appear on the page as they did when they first conversed.

As most of Eoin and Sam's hiding places were outside, he would have to cover the staff with his cloak so as not to signal their location to Valez or his dark knights. He also didn't want to frighten Sam with his constant use of "sorcery."

It had been a few months since he and Sam escaped the castle with Valez's staff. They had been on the run and in hiding as Valez's knights tore and pillaged every village in search of him. His heart swelled with pride when he heard of his people's loyalty, but it also pained him to know what Valez was putting them through to find him.

Sam and Eoin wouldn't stay with anyone, no matter how much they insisted. He wouldn't allow them to endure torture on his behalf if Valez got wind of anyone assisting and abetting the crown's traitor, which was just so ironic. Eoin almost laughed at the ridiculousness of their new reality as only he was aware of how life used to be like—save for Adalind.

When Catriona would slowly drift off to sleep, Eoin would then use the staff to contact Adalind, periodically updating one another on their wellbeing.

"Do you have a plan to overthrow Valez yet?" Adalind's biting voice came through the staff, but it also carried a well-traced tremor.

"I'm working on it. I'm not sure 'overthrowing' is the answer. I want to restore him back to…himself…and everyone else for that matter."

Eoin couldn't admit he had no idea how he was going to do that, nor did he tell her that he and Catriona had connected and were in some sort of relationship between the pages and that part of his plan involved being with Catriona.

"Just do whatever is the quickest, Eoin. If that means killing Valez so we can get to the ending, just do it!"

Eoin ignored her insensitivity, knowing she was terrified. "How are you fairing?"

"I'm relatively comfortable in Gorgon's Mount. I don't know why so many came here during the reader hiatus—it's so cold and dirty, Eoin! Gorgon isn't the gracious host I heard he used to be, either."

It saddened Eoin to learn that Gorgon had tripled in size and was now the ferocious fire-breathing, treasure-loving dragon he was written to be. She said as long as she was quiet, he stayed sound asleep emersed by his mountain of gold and jewels.

In his last conversation with her, Adalind told him that meals had been few and far between. Valez's men only brought her a chunk of bread every other day. She bemoaned how they had never felt hunger before, never needed food to sustain life.

At the thought of Adalind's allotment of bread, Eoin's stomach growled and echoed through the forest. They were on the move again to find any signs of life. Sam turned around and looked down at him. Sam was already halfway up the hill.

Eoin noticed how sunken Sam's eyes looked and the dark rings that began to encircle them. He was just as tired and hungry as Eoin.

Valez's dead knights were sapping the life out of everything around them. Vegetation had turned to ash, and streams and rivers had all dried up, along with their wildlife.

The grass around the campsite began to turn yellow and then brown. Sam spotted Valez's knights searching the forest around them, coming too close for his liking.

It made Eoin think of his makeshift camp before Catriona had found him, how different that life had been. Tears pricked the corner of his eyes—how beautiful his surroundings used to be, and how he had taken it for granted, comparing it to the real world for centuries.

Seeing what Valez's magic was doing to it…it made him sick to think how others were surviving in what Eoin could only describe what he saw as a drought.

For months, they followed the land untouched by black magic—scavenging, hunting, and drinking what water was left.

Eoin was about to stagger up the hill to catch up with Sam when he saw Catriona's sweet face in the sky above. Only Eoin could hear and see her, and her melodic hello was enough motivation to run up the hill and pass Sam.

I can't use the staff here, not in front of Sam.

"Eoin? Are you there?" She sounded worried. He had intentionally kept his dire circumstances from her—how he and Sam were so close to starvation, their movements had slowed, and delirium was just about to set in.

He turned back to Sam who had just made it up, strenuously catching his breath. "I think I can smell a stream from here, why don't you head there first and get some water and see if there are any fish we can eat, hmm?"

"Un-bloody-likely. Even so, it's not safe for you to be left alone, Your Highness."

Catriona's face began to strain with worry. Eoin wanted to talk to her. He knew she had had her therapy session today to confirm to herself she wasn't going mad by talking to him.

As she explained to him what exactly therapy was, he found the notion brilliant in concept—to think, if he had someone to talk to in that manner over the centuries, would he have felt so lost and confused about himself and his life?

"I'll be fine, Samuel. I just need to catch my breath for a second."

"Aye, you ran up the hill faster than a red stag." Sam moved past him, his mouth watering at his own mention of a deer along with Eoin's promise of fresh water and fish.

When he was finally out of view, Eoin removed the staff from under his cloak, and with his first word, it ignited with a soft glow.

"I'm here, Catriona!" He just caught her as she started to lower the cover.

"Is everything all right? I waited for a bit, but you didn't answer as you normally do." She bit her bottom lip in concern.

"I'm all right, love. I'm sorry I couldn't talk. Sam and I were heading over a hill to follow the stream. How was your day?" He lightened his voice so she wouldn't focus too much on his well-being—so she would know that he was only thinking about her.

"It was good. I'm glad to have the space and someone who didn't know my mum to talk about her. And about my future."

Eoin knew exactly how she felt. Like her, he had no idea what his future looked like. He had no idea what to do or what he wanted, but he knew, just as she did, he would have to figure it out sooner rather than later.

"Aye, I understand. Did you talk about me and, well, us?" He meant it to sound—how had she put it?—flirty? But it came out more as an interrogation than not.

"No, because I know you're real, and what we have, complicated as it is, is true." She took her hand to her lips, kissed it, and blew it. Eoin wished he could kiss her soft, puckered lips with his own—dry as they were.

He closed his eyes with her declaration and absolute certainty in their connection. "I'm so happy to hear you say that, mo chridhe. I am, and we are."

"I know. My therapist wants me to think about the future and where I want to be, and I don't know how yet, but I want it to be with you, Eoin."

Eoin closed his eyes, and tears he didn't know were even there were set free. He no longer had to figure out his future—it was Catriona. Of course, he had no idea what the journey looked like to get there, but that was something they could both figure out together. That thought alone dried all of his tears, and he was ready to embark on their future together—as soon as possible.

Before he could express to her his sheer, unadulterated joy, he heard, "Catriona?" from her side, and then he heard, "Eoin?" from his. They had both been caught. Catriona's brother had walked in on her, talking to her book, and Sam saw Eoin wielding Valez's staff with its lavender glow.

Eoin locked eyes with Catriona, who looked embarrassed and frightened. They both stayed frozen, unsure of what to say or do next.

Catriona placed her hand on the book and whispered, "Stay with me?"

Eoin wished he could climb the nearest tree to rest his hand on hers. Instead, his last words with the bright, glowing ember on top of the staff were, "I promise."

Chapter 18

Catriona

"Catriona?" I heard Jeremy's voice crack behind me.

I froze in place and closed my eyes. I briefly looked down at the book and whispered to Eoin, "Stay with me?"

"I promise" were the last words I heard Eoin say before I turned around to the anticipated look of bewilderment on Jeremy's face.

"Hiya, Jeremy! All right?" My voice squeaked as I waited on edge for Jeremy to disclose what he had just witnessed.

"Umm, why were you just talking to your book?" He knew a laugh should have followed from the both of us, but as I remained silent, his face fell.

"Please, Jer. It's not what you think. It can't possibly be what you think." This time I chuckled—hoping Eoin was laughing as well at what could only be our shared inside joke.

"I'm trying really hard not to think you've cracked, Cat. And don't laugh. I'm as serious as you seemed to be when talking to that book of yours."

"I haven't 'cracked'!" You don't have to worry about me."

"How can I not, Cat? You've only just started therapy after months of denial about Mum, and then I walk in on you declaring your undying love to a book as if you thought someone was listening!"

"Well, when you put it like that, it does sound like I've gone mental." The look in Jeremy's eyes told me that I wouldn't be able to convince him of my sanity with anything but the truth. "Jer, please give me the benefit of the doubt when I tell you this."

Jeremy crossed his arms but nodded in agreement.

I had been holding the book open tight against my stomach. I lowered it, hoping Eoin was still with me—just as he promised.

"I found this book when I first started at the library, and ever since then, I've felt connected to the story and the characters, the main one in particular." I felt my cheeks burn in a familiar way.

"So? Dorks…I mean readers, like yourself, feel that

way all the time…or so I hear." His face had lightened, but doubt still lined his voice.

"I thought that too, but when I went to Skye after Gemma's party, I was reading about a battle in the same place, at the Fairy Pools," I paused to make sure Jeremy was tracking all of this. "Then what I was reading happened right in front of me! I saw him, I saw Eoin of Accolon!" I showed Jeremy the title page.

He still didn't say anything, just watched me, following the slightest move I made with his eyes.

"Then, a few months ago, the pages that were full of words, *the story*, disappeared, and Eoin spoke to me! His words formed on the page as he spoke. He said my name, and, after I freaked out, like you're about to do, I answered, and he answered me until I heard his voice in my head...and we've been talking ever since."

I saw Jeremy's foot inch back, about to fly out of my room to tell our dad that I needed to be confined in a psychiatric hospital or something. I grabbed him and pushed him into my chair, ignoring the panic-stricken look in his eyes before it could paralyze my resolve.

"I can prove it, Jer!" I sat on the arm beside him and held the book so Jeremy could see the pages. The book retained its normal text as the pages would only go blank when Eoin spoke.

I had almost forgotten this facet of the book when Eoin first spoke to me—ever since I heard Eoin's voice in my head, I never felt the need to read his words that would appear on the page.

"Eoin? Are you there? Please say something to my brother, Jeremy and show him that you are, in fact, real." The smugness I felt that no doubt registered on my face began to dissolve as the book remained the same. *He promised me.*

"Eoin?" My voice cracked as tears obscured my vision.

Something must have happened to him. Valez or Gorgon or someone must have taken him or he's defending his life. He wouldn't leave me. He wouldn't break his promise.

I felt Jeremy's arms encircle me to bring me down beside him in the chair. "Cat, it's okay. Don't cry. Mum's passing really hurt all of us…and I'm sorry I was such a little shit and didn't even consider asking you how you were holding up—that you felt like you had to create an imaginary friend just to cope."

My eyes went bone dry. "He's not imaginary! I thought my grief had conjured what I was seeing, *at first,* but he's real, Jer! The world he's in has been made real…because of me." I whispered half to myself. "Something must have happened to him." I searched the book again as Jeremy tore himself from my side.

"I think…I think I need to tell Dad what's happening to you, Cat. So, we can get you some real help."

"I don't need help! I'm already seeing Dr. McClatchie, aren't I? Jer, please, please don't tell Dad yet. I'll make you a deal. If I can't prove that Eoin is real before I leave for Gemma's wedding, then you two can do whatever you like, even if that means that I can't be at my best friend's wedding—that's how sure I am. Deal?" I held out my hand for a "gentleman's agreement"—a silly gesture of agreement I initiated when he was little, just to make him laugh.

"This isn't a game, Catriona. I'm seriously worried

about you...but against my better judgment, I also trust you. So, deal." He didn't shake my hand, but the fear that had encompassed his entire frame lifted just a bit, enough to know that I had saved myself and Eoin some time. He gently closed my bedroom door as he left.

I ran over to the book and sank deep into my chair, but it still displayed its original text. "Where are you, my love?" I ran my hand across the pages and closed my eyes, anticipating his deep voice to reverberate in my mind all the way down to my heart.

After a few minutes, my heart stung with the unknown. "I'll wait for you. Please let me know, any way you can that you're unhurt, that you're safe and well."

I closed the book, and for the first time since Eoin came into my life, I felt uncertain and alone. I felt like a compass tirelessly spinning in circles—unable to find its destination.

***

Eoin

Sam grabbed the staff from Eoin's hand. Eoin had

just promised Catriona that he would stay with her as she tried to explain to her brother what was going on—why she was talking to a book, *his book,* and not only talking to it but conversing intimately with it.

He looked up to the sky. It was so dark that he half expected to see stars dotted across its expanse, but it was just the color of her tunic. She was pressing the book against her.

A shiver ran down his body as he imagined how she'd feel pressed tightly against him—how he'd wrap his hands around her hips and pull her hard against him—but his reverie was cut short as he heard shuffling from the brush beside him, and then the undeniable sound of nesting birds fleeing toward the sky.

Eoin jumped into a defensive stance, ready for an attack. As the brush remained still and quiet, he looked back at Sam. His hand that had only moments before held the staff was now empty. Sam had thrown it in the shrubbery next to them.

As Eoin made to retrieve it, Sam blocked his path with his sword, "Not so fast, Your Highness."

"Sam…it's not what you think. Please let me explain," he heard the panic seeping into his voice as the sky brightened, and he could overhear Catriona's conversation with her brother. How she pleaded with him to believe her, how he threatened to have her locked away for what her brother perceived was for her own safety.

Eoin knew it was only a matter of time before Catriona called on him to speak to them. What would she think if he was not there to answer the moment that she needed him? He could not bear to hurt her—for her to think that he had broken his promise.

The two men circled one another. Eoin raised his hands and splayed his fingers in surrender as Sam continued to point his broad sword at him, "Why were you using the sorcerer's staff and talking to someone unseen?"

"It's too difficult to explain right now, Sam, but you have to trust me!" Eoin tried to focus hard on his words to placate his First Knight, but Catriona's voice broke through, and all he could hear was her.

"Eoin? Are you there? Please say something to my brother, Jeremy, and show him that you are, in fact, real."

Eoin looked up to the sky. Catriona's lovely face began to crumble as her voice choked on a sob, "Eoin?"

Eoin's eyes filled with tears, and he looked over at the brush that camouflaged the staff. "Please, Sam, please let me have the staff. It's the only way to defeat Valez—to make everything right again."

Catriona's sweet voice filled the air around him, "Where are you, my love?" He saw her hand move up and down, waiting for him.

His heart stung, imagining how she must be feeling—confused, betrayed, hurt, angry, and finally concerned as she said, "I'll wait for you. Please let me know any way you can that you're unhurt, that you're safe and well."

Catriona's light slowly dimmed, as did his world, as did his heart.

"Stop looking up! You've been looking above every chance you get, reacting as if someone was there! I know my king, and you, sir, are not him."

"What do you mean, Sam? I'm still your king…I'm still your friend."

"That's another thing, you keep calling me Sam. You used to always call me Samuel!"

Eoin was at a loss for words. He couldn't explain to the book's version of Sam how they were before. Not only had he lost Sam, but he also knew, beyond a shadow of a doubt, that he was about to lose Samuel, as well.

"I think Valez's magic has taken over you, corrupted you, Milord. And I'm going to make sure that you've been purged of his influence once and for all!" Sam trudged over and disentangled the staff from the shrub's extensive foliage.

Eoin's heart jumped into his throat, "What are you going to do with it?"

"Exactly what has to be done. It must be destroyed." Sam darted into the forest, quicker than Eoin had ever seen him run.

Utter shock paralyzed Eoin from head to toe, and a thousand thoughts whirled in his mind, but the one that triumphed, the one that got his feet racing toward Sam and the staff, was Catriona.

Nothing would stop him from being with her. He

wouldn't allow her to feel abandoned or alone for much longer. Knowing that, together, they would never feel this way again.

***

Catriona

I always notice that in romance novels or movies, no matter where the main character is—whether in a big city like London or Paris or in a small village like mine—her love interest will show up unexpectedly: either they will run into one another around town, or he will just show up at her front door. Afterward, they will ride off into the sunset and live happily ever after. That doesn't happen in real life, but the expectation that it sets becomes a disillusionment—making any hope that the love of my life will show up out of the blue obsolete.

The longer I went without hearing from Eoin, the more lifeless I felt, and bitterness seeped in and reverberated out until my heart felt as hard as stone.

For two weeks, the color that my world once held was now dimmed and gray. The light that Eoin had brought into my life with his first spoken words was completely gone, and my outlook was as dark as Eoin's castle walls.

The faster Gemma's wedding week approached; the more Jeremy avoided eye contact with me—he pretty much avoided any form of contact with me.

We both knew our deal was coming to an end, and he would have to tell Dad what he believed to be insanity and get me help right away.

The more certain that future seemed to be, the more I seemed to welcome it. I knew I wasn't crazy. I knew Eoin was real, but what terrified me to my core was the possibility that he no longer existed—that Valez had killed him, that he faded from existence just as he almost did before. Only this time, there was nothing I could do to save him.

From what Eoin told me, his world was changing, and whatever magic or healing I once brought as a reader no longer mattered. So, being in a safe place to grieve his loss and rest without having to worry about the meager mechanics of living seemed suitable.

I packed for either Gemma's wedding or whatever

psychiatric hospital Dad checked me into. I still wanted to have faith that Eoin would return to me and prove that he was real to Jeremy.

I wanted to believe with all of my heart that he had overheard our gentlemen's agreement, even if unexplainable circumstances kept Eoin from speaking, but a cold shudder ran through me at the thought of him never returning. I couldn't fathom the feeling of never hearing his voice again.

I remembered when I first found Eoin's book and had little time to read—how the circumstances of my life at the time kept me from him. Eoin told me exactly how he felt—he felt nothing but hopelessness and devastation. The tables had decidedly turned as it was me who felt hopeless and so cold without the warmth I had only briefly known.

What had kept me going was just the whisper of a wish that Eoin was alive—that it was his circumstances that prevented him from speaking—just as mine had kept me from reading when I first found him.

Ever since Jeremy caught me talking to Eoin, I had kept the book open to the same page, and every day, I checked those two pages and waited with steadfast anticipation for Eoin's voice.

With every passing day, that hope dimmed until a bottomless pit took its place. I had stopped checking, and I had stopped listening.

A few more days went by until that fateful day in April. All my things were packed, for what, I was no longer certain, but I was ready to go, nevertheless.

I peeled myself off my bed and moved toward my bedroom door—resigned to hand over my fate to Jeremy's discretion. As I placed my hand on the cool metal of the doorknob, a tiny voice popped into my head. A voice that was not my own. *Eoin?*

"Catriona! Are you there?"

I sprang to the open book on my bed. "Eoin? Where have you been?! Are you okay?" I searched the blank pages as if I would be able to find him, to see his face.

His words appeared in whisps on the blank page at the same time I heard them in my head, "Aye, love. I'm not physically harmed in any way."

"Then why the hell haven't you answered me?! My

brother thinks I'm mental. I was just about to tell him I was ready to go to hospital!" My hands shook the book as I held it up, and hot tears streamed down my face in both fury and relief.

"I'm so sorry, *mo chridhe.* Samuel took the only means by which I could speak to you—he took Valez's staff when we were simultaneously caught speaking to each other."

My mind went back to that day when I knew I had been caught, but I had no idea that he had also been caught by his closest friend, who thought him to be as crazy as me.

"I had to hunt him down, Catriona. He somehow managed to stay one step ahead of me until we reached the Fairy Rings. He stood over them, threatening to drop the staff in the middle of the dotted-stone rings so it could be lost to another land, to another time."

Eoin told me the full extent of what was happening to his world. How Valez's dark knights zapped any and all life from the land that they trod. His land was left dry and barren—any morsel of food and water was gone.

He said he didn't want me to worry about his

increasing hunger, how close to starvation he and Samuel had come, how they were following the land that was untouched to stay alive and hidden.

I began to cry at the misery and silent suffering Eoin was enduring. I cursed myself for being so selfish, thinking I was the one who was suffering more. *Hell, I'm the one who caused all of this!* Before I came along, Eoin lived the same quiet and comfortable life for centuries.

"Eoin, it's my fault your world is real, that you and your people are suffering—that your best friend is now evil, and the only person supporting you has betrayed you." I couldn't help but sob freely at the enormity of it all. Not knowing where he and I were to go from here.

"It's not your fault, Catriona." His voice felt like a soothing caress up and down my back. "What you don't know is, I was slowly fading before you found me. We all were. The ending was fading, leaving dark voids. Without a reader, without you, *mo chridhe,* we'd be gone."

"What are we going to do, Eoin?" I grabbed a tissue and wiped away the buildup of snot and tears, no longer giving a second thought to looking or sounding a certain way—I realized that I could be myself and feel safe in Eoin's presence.

"We fix your world first. Go and get your brother."

***

Eoin

Eoin stood alone amongst the rings of the fairies with Valez's staff clutched tightly in his hands. Suppressed tears broke through their well-guarded walls as he saw the familiar purple hue that he now only associated with Catriona's voice.

When he had barely snatched the staff from falling into the fairy world below, he whipped it at Sam and blue electricity sparked from its end. Eoin wanted to scare Sam, to send him away before either one became a threat to the other.

"You're right, Samuel. I have tasted the magic Valez's staff has to offer. If you're not going to join me, I suggest you run." Eoin thrusted the staff forward, sending fraying sparks that stopped just short of its target.

"I said I'd die for my king when I took my oath as First Knight of the King of Caledonia." Eoin felt a flood of relief fill his

body until Sam turned his face away and whispered, "But you are no longer my king."

Eoin kept his stance, fighting back a hot flood of tears until Sam's forlorn figure disappeared behind the sloping green hills and protruding boulders.

The staff softened and turned to lavender as his shock wore off, and he remembered his purpose. "Catriona! Are you there?"

Eoin couldn't allow himself to think about what his long absence had done to her. If he had, he would have been immobilized. He thought of one thing and one thing only—take Valez's staff back at all costs.

The short stretch of time without Catriona felt like an eternity, but the moment he caught Sam, the moment he saw her face, the tortured time apart dissolved into an unremembered past.

Eoin waited for her to fetch her brother so he could speak to him, forbidding him from locking her up in an insane asylum or threatening anything of the sort ever again.

Eoin saw Catriona hovering over him as she

adjusted the book to face Jeremy. The lad was very tall but still a whisp of a boy. He had light brown thin hair that stood up in place, a style fashionable for his time, Eoin could only conclude.

"Eoin, are you there?" Catriona winked at him.

"Aye, love, I'm here. Good to finally meet you, lad."

"Holy fuck, he's real!" Jeremy's head whipped out of view, and Eoin heard a series of crashing noises.

"My, my Catriona, your brother sure has quite the mouth on him, doesn't he?"

Catriona laughed and knelt beside Jeremy to show him what Eoin had said. Jeremy offered up a nervous laugh, but when Eoin saw Jeremy register how natural and free Catriona seemed, he was confident that her brother understood.

Eoin breathed out the ball of anxiety he had been holding in for weeks. "Now, does that mean you're done threatening Catriona's wellbeing?"

"Uhh, yes... yes sir, of course," Jeremy straightened himself and stood.

Catriona followed, switching her gaze from Eoin to Jeremy, "Please don't tell Dad or anyone for that matter. There's still a lot that Eoin and I need to figure out before I let everyone know that a fictional character really exists." Catriona searched Jeremy's face with pleading eyes.

"Of course, I won't tell anyone." Brother and sister shared mirroring smiles. Jeremy suddenly broke it and grabbed at his watch. "We need to get you to the airport now, or you'll be late for Gemma's shower!"

Jeremy was no longer in view, but Eoin could still hear him bustling about in Catriona's chambers.

"I can't go! Eoin's in danger in the book. We have to figure out how to restore it or get him out of there!"

Eoin's heart jumped. *She wants me to be with her? In her world?* The wide smile that plastered his face fell when he saw how torn she looked at the prospect of missing her best friend's wedding.

He knew she would do anything to save him, so he resolved to hold on as long as he could so she could be there for Gemma. "You should go, love."

"What?" Catriona's head snapped back to the book

as she lowered herself onto her bed.

"You need to go, *mo chridhe.* I'll be fine. I can hold on as long as I'm with you." He saw that she still needed convincing. Her concern for him needed to be alleviated. Eoin cleared his throat, "Mademoiselle Lamont, it would give me the greatest pleasure to be bestowed as your escort to your best friend's wedding if you'll have me. I'm on one knee, so you may know the sincerity of my heart."

Catriona still didn't look convinced, but she wiped a few tears from her cheeks and smiled sweetly at him, "Of course, I'll have you. But please, please don't leave again. Please don't hide from me any danger you may be in. Promise?"

"As long as I'm alive, I promise I will never leave you. Now, let's get to Paris!" Eoin heard Catriona squeal in delight as Jeremy hastened her out the door.

Eoin would keep his promise to Catriona—they would never be separated again.

Until they could be united, he decided to hide away and wait for Catriona to introduce him to all her world had to offer…in Paris.

Chapter 19

Catriona

I wished I could have seen the look on Eoin's face as he laid his eyes on the cloud-streaked sky from the airplane window for the very first time. The pure wonder in his voice was enough to take away every anxiety I had about returning to Paris.

He drowned out the other voices in my head—the ones that would cripple me if I let them. The one that reminded me of life before Mum died, the one that said I didn't deserve to be in the City of Lights…to be an editor at a large and successful publishing house. The one that said I wasn't pretty enough to be with a guy like Henri, and now possibly a man like Eoin.

As the plane touched down on Paris' soil, those voices no longer plagued me, even when I had to close the book and be apart from Eoin. I knew I wasn't the same person I was six months ago, and I felt myself lighten at that thought.

I felt even lighter at the thought of sharing Paris with Eoin and maybe begin to replace some of those bad memories with him.

When I was finally able to open the book again, I appeared to be a woman just reading in the back of a taxi, but in my mind, I was a woman sitting beside her boyfriend as he excitedly pointed out Paris' most famous monuments. Even leaning across me to see the ones on my side.

At least, that's what I pictured from the lilt in Eoin's voice as we rode along. I couldn't help but laugh at his childlike curiosity, "What is that arch one called, *mo chridhe?"*.

"The Arc de Triomphe." I spoke aloud the names of each one we passed, and the taxi driver hummed in agreement to who he thought was his millionth tourist. *Eoin definitely fits that description.*

When we pulled up to the address that Gemma gave me for Gabriel's mother's home, I waved goodbye to Eoin and closed the book.

The taxi driver waved to me in confusion after I handed him the fare and a tip. Having a relationship with a character in a book was proving to be its own brand of comedic relief, but I had a sneaking suspicion that humor wouldn't be able to sustain me and Eoin for much longer.

Eoin knew my itinerary, but I felt a wave of unease every time I closed the cover. His present circumstances and the state of his world gave me pause about leaving him on his own and enjoying myself.

His strong, reassuring voice kept replaying in my head, *"Catriona, dinna fash about me. Have a grand time with Gemma!"*

Nerves filled my lungs, taking away what little air remained when I walked into the grand parlor room where Josephine, Gabriel's mother, and his sister, Emily, were throwing the bridal shower.

An attendant took my present and put it on the mountain of gold and white wrapped gifts, with my green gift bag sticking out like a sore thumb next to what was clearly a mandated color scheme. *I guess I was more checked out these past few weeks than I thought.*

When I heard a familiar squeal fill the room, my whole body relaxed as Gemma came running over and squished me into her signature hug.

"Ahh! Caty, it's so good to hold you, so good to see you!" We swayed in our embrace for a few seconds before she pulled away, as we both saw Josephine approaching us.

"Catriona, how lovely to see you again," She grabbed both my hands and kissed my cheeks. "Now, let me steal you so we can let Gemma get back to her party guests, hmm?"

Gemma took the hint, but not before giving me a lopsided grin. I stifled a laugh. Josephine came from old money and was very posh, more so than Gemma's parents, and we both understood that appearances at this level still had to be regarded.

Josephine placed my arm in hers as we strolled side-by-side until we reached a circle of women. My eyes locked onto a familiar, warm face. Patricia gave me a big smile and waited patiently until I was introduced to everyone. When that formality was over, she came around and gave me the same warm hug as her daughter, "Hello, my darling. You're looking well." She rubbed my shoulder, and I understood what she was referencing.

The last time she saw me, I was drunk, and my face was puffy from crying. I had just blown up her daughter's engagement party, but none of that resided in her kind eyes.

"Thank you, Patricia. It's so good to see you again." I lowered my voice so only she could hear me. "I'm so sorry about the party…."

She stuck her hand up and brushed her smooth hand across my face, "No need to apologize. I could see the pain that gripped you, but I'm happy to see that is it almost faded."

"Almost?"

She nodded, "That kind of pain never truly goes away. It will always be a part of you, but how it lives in you is up to you." She patted my hands in what felt like a shared understanding. "Now, let's get you some tea and those delicious mini cucumber sandwiches."

The rest of the shower was lovely. We all drank high tea, each at our own little round tables with white lace tablecloths. Since I was in the bridal party, I sat with Gemma, Patricia, Josephine, and Emily, whom I was glad to catch up with again, but with much more time do so.

She asked about Jeremy, and I was happy to share with her how I had the best brother in the world. Emily smiled warmly at my glowing depiction of Jeremy—*I'll have to introduce them one day.*

As Gemma opened each present from the Mount Everest of gifts, thanking her family and friends, I reached under the table for my purse, for my book—for Eoin.

I stroked the spine, hoping Eoin could still feel me. Even though we couldn't speak, I wanted him to know I was thinking about him, that no matter what, our connection was still as strong as ever.

My mind also went to what I had planned for tomorrow's hen night. This bachelorette party had "Gemma" written all over it.

After dinner and a show at Moulin Rouge, we hit a few nightclubs that weren't as touristy, but securing a reservation at Moulin Rouge was something two Brits like Gemma and I always wanted, but for the rest of the bridal party, Gemma's French friends, it wasn't a novelty.

So, the last club we hit was just what we needed.

After several club hops of dancing and drinking, we wanted to decompress. We secured a corner booth to enjoy a final round of drinks, which meant that gossip about men naturally followed, along with the dirty details of Gemma and Gabriel's honeymoon in Bora Bora.

When every sexual innuendo for the wedding night was exhausted, and every woman described their "perfect" partner, the attention I hadn't been volunteering was now on me.

Gemma opened her mouth to save me from having to explain why I wasn't dating, but with all the liquid courage coursing through me, I interrupted her. "I am seeing someone, actually," my tongue swirled, trying to find the giant straw in my tropical cocktail.

Gemma whipped her head towards me, "What? Who?" She sounded almost hurt that I hadn't told her, but her inebriation made her giddy in wanting to know more as she bounced closer to me.

"I can't say yet, but he's kind, honorable…and an old soul, I guess you could say." I smiled into my drink as I thought about Eoin and took a sip as I finally secured the straw in place between my lips.

Gemma was about to press for more details until a couple came too close to our booth, and by the way they were dancing, they would have been better off going home to do whatever they were doing in the privacy of their own home.

We all did our best to avert our gazes, but when it became obvious that they weren't going to leave any time soon, and as we all felt too drunk to last much longer, we knew it was time to call it a night.

Gemma and the girls went to the toilets before we all left to hail a taxi. I decided to wait outside and check in with Eoin, but to the rest to the world, I was reading.

I wobbled down to a quiet spot toward the end of the building and cracked open the book. "Hey, baby," I cooed.

"Hiya, beautiful," I heard him laugh. "Having a good time?"

"Yes…I told them about you, you know."

"You did?! You must really be steamin'. What did Gemma say, then?"

"I'm not drunk," I laughed and swayed forward. "I only told her I was seeing someone kind and handsome."

"Oh, did you now? Did you also tell them…"

"Catriona?" A high-pitched male's voice interrupted Eoin's question. I whipped around and just blinked at the stumbling form coming toward me.

"Henri?" I felt suddenly very sober as he staggered toward me.

I kept the book open, splayed across my hands. "*Henri?* Catriona, are you all right?" I nodded down to Eoin but found it hard to swallow.

With one look at Henri's ratty, white T-shirt, I realized he was the disgusting man dancing too close to our booth.

When Henri finally made it to me, he tried to kiss my cheek, but the size of Eoin's book prevented him, and I sighed in relief.

"What are you doing back in Paris, basby." Henri slurred the word "baby," as he always did when we were dating, but now it wasn't so cute. He placed his hand on the building's wall to hold himself up and simultaneously lean into me.

"It's none of your business after you cheated on me, now, is it?"

"Aww, don't be like that. We used to have a lot of fun. We still could while you're here, *mon petite."*

He tried to slide a seductive finger down my cheek and over my lips, but I side-stepped the gesture, and he vaulted forward, almost landing face-first into the brick wall.

"Catriona, just walk away. Please get away from him now!" Eoin pleaded in my mind. He had never met Henri. He didn't know if he was a danger or not. I never thought of Henri as a threat, but being alone with him, drunk as he was, and with Eoin's quiet pleas, I began to feel uneasy.

Before Henri could attempt another embrace, a sickly-sweet voice sang his name. A tall woman with raven black hair and smeared red lipstick that resembled the Joker waddled over to us.

"Baby, come on. Let's go home and fuck." She

stuck an unlit cigarette in her mouth.

"Just a minute, Lou-Lou." He slung his gangly arm around her shoulder. "Catriona, you know where to find me if you ever, you know, want to be painted." His attempt at seduction finished in a pointed sneer.

Lou-Lou's eyes widened, but she kept quiet. Understanding of who each other was dawned on the both of us, but I felt nothing. As he clutched her arm, barely keeping himself upright, I felt the tiniest hint of sympathy for her.

Eoin cleared his throat but was interrupted again as Gemma and the rest of her bridal party spilled out of the club.

"Catriona? You, all right?" Gemma said as I made it back toward the entrance. "You look like you've seen a ghost."

"You know that disgusting guy we saw dancing near our table? It was Henri. He just stopped to chat—him and Lou-Lou."

"What the actual fuck? That son-of-a-bitch!" She looked down the street. She seemed to sober too at the name of my good-for-nothing ex as if she was ready to kick his ass if she spotted him.

I brushed my hand against the page and closed the book. I grabbed Gemma by the shoulders and hugged her. "It's fine. Come on, it's off to Bedfordshire. You need to be well-rested before you get married!"

She tried to swat my arm, but when she missed, I took her hand and linked our arms as we hailed a taxi. I was relieved when the other three insisted on taking their own.

When Gemma was dropped off at her and Gabriel's flat, Gabriel came out to guide her in. I rode the rest of the way back to my hotel with the book on my lap and Eoin's voice in my head.

Gemma's parents booked me a room in the same hotel they were staying. With three drinks in tonight, Gemma disclosed that their room was right next to mine. It took me four drinks to admit to myself that it felt nice to be looked after by a maternal figure again.

When I entered my hotel room, I took my smeared makeup off, slipped into my pajamas, and under the covers of the plush, king-size bed. I opened the book to speak to the man who meant more to me than Henri ever could.

Seeing him tonight and knowing what I had with Eoin made me realize how I truly saw myself less than a year ago. How little thought I gave to Henri's poor treatment of me and just accepted it.

With Eoin's sweet affirmations, I knew I would never have to settle for less-than ever again.

***

Eoin

Eoin wanted to be there, in Catriona's room. He wanted to cradle her back against him as his hand ran down the length of her smooth arm. He wanted to move the hair away from her face as she let go of the dark memories that still haunted her in Paris. He wanted to show her exactly how precious she was to him.

The way Henri spoke to her, the way he tried to put his hands on her, Eoin wanted to rip out of the pages and throttle him to an inch of his miserable life, but the way

Catriona reacted, and stepped out of reach, Eoin knew she felt nothing for the scum, and that eased his anger, if only for a moment.

Being with her in her room as she gazed lovingly at him, Eoin needed to express to her exactly what she was worth and how she deserved to be treated for the rest of her life.

"When a man loves a woman, *mon chridhe,* he shows her with his actions." Eoin sucked in a nervous breath as he prepared himself for what he was about to admit, "I choose you, Catriona. I choose to love you every day. It's an active choice to have you in my life forever. It's not an invisible force that is out of our control. It's not a flame of desire that is fleeting and can be snuffed out—it's constant, never wavering."

Catriona knitted her eyebrows together, her eyes darting side-to-side as if she was piecing something together from what Eoin said to her past, "You know, I didn't tell Henri everything I believed or wanted in fear that I'd lose him—that he'd slip through my fingers at any moment if I disagreed or had any strong opinion—and I have strong opinions to give, as you know."

"Aye, I do at that, but that upsets me quite a bit—to think that you felt that you had to censor yourself or mold yourself to be someone you thought a man wanted. Henri never deserved you." Eoin inhaled again and locked onto her searching eyes, wishing she could see the sincerity in his, "I love you, Catriona…all of you, everything that makes you so wonderfully you."

Eoin exhaled, waiting for his words to register. He didn't expect her to say that she loved him back. He would gladly give her all of him without any expectation, but his heart swelled in the anticipation—in the joy of hearing those words from her sweet lips.

"Thank you, Eoin. I never dared to dream of anyone feeling that way about me. Desiring even the darkest, oddest parts of me." She stifled a yawn, and Eoin could see in her eyes that she wasn't ready to tell him that she loved him.

"Get some sleep, *mo chridhe*. I'll be here when you awake."

"Good night," she blew him a kiss and

extinguished the light in her room, but she kept the book open on the next pillow, just as she did every night.

Eoin sat back down by the fire he had labored over for hours—he never had to build a fire before. If it was written, it was there, but it could never emanate the same warmth that the real thing provided.

He sat just outside a small cave that he had found to take cover while Catriona was away. It was a hidden cleft in the mounts of Glen Etive—a valley untouched by Valez's magic.

It still held vibrant shades of green and yellow, with a flowing crystal stream full of fish and the songs of birds cascading throughout the trees.

It was enough to keep him going physically—but it was the constant thought of being united with Catriona that kept him going mentally. *If she wants us to be, that is.*

Eoin felt exhausted by all that he had seen since Catriona took him to Paris—flying high above the clouds, pointing out every historical monument from the taxi.

He also felt overwhelmed with not knowing how she truly felt about him and what his future and the future of his book would hold.

***

Catriona

I awoke with an insistent pounding inside my head, and I knew it wasn't from my hangover. Eoin told me that he loved me last night! And I couldn't say it back.

The truth was, after seeing Henri, and as drunk as I was, I didn't want that to be the first time we said those words to one another, nor was I in the proper head space to convey exactly how I felt.

I winced when I imagined how Eoin must have felt at the dismissal of his feelings. I tried to ignore Eoin's pain, along with a wave of nausea that came over me—two terrible reminders of last night.

I rolled over and said a quick good morning to Eoin. I told him I had a busy day and that Gemma's rehearsal dinner was tonight. He said that he understood as I gently closed the book.

As soon as the cover hit the page, I sprinted to the bathroom and threw up last night's celebrations, barely making it to the toilet. After I was certain everything had been expelled, I crawled back into bed and stayed there until the very last minute before I needed to get ready for Gemma's rehearsal dinner.

Hard as I tried, I couldn't think of anything else but Eoin the entire night. I only registered every detail, everyone I spoke to, as a blur.

The one thing I would be present for, the one thing I needed to make up to Gemma from her engagement party, was my toast. When the time was right, I dinged my crystal champagne glass and waited for silence to fill the room. Before I began, I glued my eyes on only one person, my best friend, who was getting married.

"I am eternally grateful, not only to be called Gemma's best friend but that I can be her maid of honor on the most important day of her life. I don't know anyone more deserving, more loving than she is to not only have found the love of her life but to marry a man who is her friend, her confidant, and her equal. A man who sees her—sees all her wonderful qualities, sees what she keeps deep down. A man who sees everything that makes Gemma the woman we all know and love."

Everyone cooed, and Gemma smiled through fresh tears as I continued, "I couldn't imagine this life without her own special brand that makes it all worthwhile. Gabriel, you're a good man who is totally and absolutely in love with my best friend, and I couldn't imagine letting her go to anyone less deserving." I raised my glass before both Gemma and I cried a river in this ornate dining hall, "To Gemma and Gabriel and the beautiful life that they will build together!"

"To Gemma and Gabriel!" Everyone echoed as their shimmering glasses were raised, clinked, and then sipped.

After I gave my heart out to Gemma, I reverted inward, and my mind went straight to Eoin. I had left the book back in the hotel room, but after what I said about Gabriel and Gemma, every word resonated with me and Eoin. I wanted him by my side as my friends declared their love for one another in front of the entire world tomorrow, but my heart sank, knowing that was impossible.

The big day finally came, and there were

absolutely no words to describe my best friend's wedding to her best friend in any other way but perfection. It was like a fairytale, and I felt honored just to be a part of their happily ever after.

Gemma seemed to float on clouds to the altar with her dad by her side. Her wedding dress, which was pure white silk, brushed the purple and white rose petals as she walked down the floral-lined grass aisle.

When her eyes magnetized on Gabriel's face, he saw her at the exact same moment, and they were both glowing.

There was not a dry eye as the bride and groom exchanged their vows, followed by the immortal words from the priest, "I now pronounce you man and wife. You may kiss the bride."

Gabriel dipped and kissed Gemma in one elegant move. Their friends and family stood and applauded as they walked back down the aisle together in wedding bliss.

After countless photographs were taken, being placed here and there—posing with Gemma and Gabriel, Gemma and the bridesmaids, then the whole wedding party—we finally made it to the reception.

The same outdoor space was now littered with thinly veiled white tents so the sun and then later the stars could shine through.

When Gemma and Gabriel were announced, and they had their first dance, my breath left my chest as I watched how fulfilled they each looked. I reached down and pulled out my book and opened it, just to know I wasn't alone in a crowd. I tried not to look like I was bored and therefore reading, so I looked around, spoke to a few people at my table, drank the champagne that kept flowing, and finally took a bite of the first course.

As I found myself lost in Eoin's words, yet unable to respond, I felt a light tap on my shoulder, "May I have this dance?" Ludo stood in front of me with his hand outstretched.

"Of course!" I took his hand as I stood. I gave Eoin one last look and covered the book with a napkin.

Ludo and I danced in comfortable silence to a mid-tempo song for a few moments before he cleared his throat, "I wanted to apologize for the last time I saw you,

Catriona."

"No, I'm sorry I left so abruptly and didn't have the courage to return your phone calls." I looked down at my feet, making sure they went forward as he stepped back, then back as he stepped forward.

"Well, then, let's leave it at that because I have an offer for you, if you're interested?" He held in a chuckle as my head shot up and met his crinkled eyes.

"You do?"

"Oui. Acquisitions editor of fiction is yours…if you want it." He looked away, letting me think about his overly generous offer.

Acquisitions editor of fiction was my dream job—I would decide what manuscripts B&P Livre Publishers published!

As I let the idea form in my head, I found that it did not evoke the same feelings of excitement it would have six months ago. The faces of my dad and Jeremy flashed across my mind, and the thought of Scotland filled my heart with warmth, and then Eoin encompassed the rest.

"Could I think about it, Ludo? Just so I can talk it over with my family first."

"Of course, take all the time you need," Ludo spun me out, then spun me back in as the song ended.

Part of me knew I wouldn't be taking the job, but I wanted at least one good memory with my boss and mentor.

After group dancing with Gemma and Gabriel and after so many slices of cake and glasses of champagne that I lost count, I found myself back at the bridal table with Eoin.

The book was still open on the table, strategically hidden by a floral centerpiece, napkins, and my hands, but I left enough space so he could still see me.

The night was winding down, and only a few stragglers remained. Normally, the bride and groom would have been long gone, but Gemma and Gabriel were lost in each other's arms as only the flutes and violins softly played their song.

I sat transfixed on the love that they emanated from the first moment they met to the moment they became husband and wife.

From Eoin's whispered words, I knew he could read everything I was thinking, and I began to cry. I wanted him to be physically beside me. I wanted to him to offer me his hand and lead me out onto the dance floor, pull me close, enfold me into his chest, and softly kiss me whenever I looked up. Then, I would rest my head once more against his strong chest, as we stayed safely in each other's arms.

We both knew something had felt off between us the night he told me he loved me, and I couldn't say it back. It was because something had shifted between us, and I couldn't figure out how to fix it.

Eoin's voice overtook my thoughts, as if he could read them, "Our feelings for each other haven't changed, *mo chridhe*. Only the desire of our circumstances and how they can be expressed has."

I looked up at the single form of Gabriel and Gemma as they swayed gently to a song that only they could hear.

My heart no longer hurt in the uncertainty of

having Eoin, it hurt in the certain anticipation of it.

The pain of past hurt and distrust of men that had once imprisoned my heart dissolved and I was ready to let Eoin in—to have all of me.

I looked around to make sure no one was nearby. "Eoin?" I whispered. "I love you. I love you with all my heart…and I want you here, by my side, forever."

***

Eoin

"Our feelings for each other haven't changed, mo chridhe. Only the desire of our circumstances and how they can be expressed has."

Eoin put the staff down, unsure if Catriona would be able to speak to him as a few guests still remained around her at the wedding.

She had risked enough by bringing out his book at the table. He knew that she didn't want to take away from Gemma's wedding with such odd behavior or get caught again as she did with her brother.

He settled comfortably on the ground, lying flat on

his back with his hands behind his head, as he gazed up at Catriona. She looked so bonnie with her braided updo and lavender gown. It reminded him of the staff's glow whenever they spoke.

He closed his eyes for just a second, but then he heard her voice whispering softly in the breeze, "Eoin? I love you. I love you with all my heart…and I want you here, by my side, forever."

Eoin's eyes shot open, and he jumped to his feet. "I love you, Catriona! Do you mean that? You want us to be together? Without the book?"

"I do. Can you do that?" Catriona said through misty eyes.

Before Eoin could answer that he didn't know for sure but that he would figure it out if his life depended on it, he saw the staff leaning against the cave wall—not a single glow emanated from its end.

He didn't realize he wasn't holding it when he declared his love for Catriona. It seemed that they no longer needed whatever magic it possessed to communicate.

"Catriona, if you'll have me, I believe I know a way to leave the book and enter your world."

She began to cry and nodded her head, pressing her hand against her mouth so she wouldn't draw too much attention to herself from the muffled sounds of joy that could still be heard from between her fingers.

He closed his eyes and let a few tears fall freely at the thought of being united with Catriona—*with his heart.*

Eoin grabbed the staff and twirled it in his hands. *You'll be the key to my freedom one last time.* He looked back up at Catriona and knew those words to be true.

Chapter 20

Catriona

While whisking Gemma and Gabriel off to their honeymoon down a row of sparklers, I couldn't help but feel that my heart looked the exact same way as the crackling light that I held in my hand. I loved Eoin, and he loved me, and he was coming out of his world, out of the book, to be with me!

I felt a pair of arms wrap around me as a nearby observer took the sparkler from my hand. Gemma pulled back and winked at me, "See you in a couple of weeks!"

"Go on, now, get out here. I'll be seeing you." My eyes felt misty, realizing how happy it made me that she stopped to say one last goodbye.

She blew me a kiss as she ran back to Gabriel's waiting hand. They jumped into their ornamented limo, and as it sped away, Gemma jumped through the moonroof to give one last wave to those of us who lasted this late.

I waved and tucked in a smile. *When she comes back, I'll have someone very special to introduce her to.*

I moved my hand down to my purse that contained the book—soon, nothing would be able to separate us. If Eoin were here with me after we said "I love you" to one another, we would rush back to my hotel room, hastily removing each other's clothes without breaking our frantic kisses.

As I felt that familiar tingle between my legs back in my hotel room, I leaned the book against the vanity. I wanted to look at my reflection to know exactly what Eoin was seeing. My breath caught in my throat as I saw a soft blush rise from my neck to my cheeks and I suddenly did not know how to proceed.

"Are you all right, Catriona?" I heard Eoin say. I exhaled and imagined him coming up behind me and caressing my bare shoulders, our eyes meeting in the reflection.

"Yes, just a bit nervous, that's all." I looked at the book and then back at the bed. I kept my arms crossed and began to rub them to rid my body of the cold that a familiar shiver caused.

"Aye, I understand. I'm a bit nervous myself, but I

want you to be as comfortable as possible. I want you to always feel safe and secure with me. We will only go where you want. I'll follow you no matter what, now and for the rest of my life."

My heart flipped and the ache between my legs swelled. My hands found the zipper of my dress and as it slipped from my body, I heard Eoin's sharp inhale. "Would you come behind me and unzip my dress until it pooled on the floor like this?" He groaned. He knew what I was doing and what we would have to do next to be together.

Our words and what he could see of me were all we had, but in my head, Eoin moved from behind me, and his eyes traveled to my white-lace bra. He cupped the bra in his hands and swiped his thumbs over the ridges of the lace almost reverently. I took a sharp breath. I doubted that he had ever seen modern lingerie before. I let out a soft moan as my nipples hardened under his thumbs.

He smirked at my obvious pleasure and eventually lifted my breasts within it and kissed them. He rubbed my breasts with his palms from outside the bra, all while kissing my lips and neck, "God, you're so beautiful, Catriona." His breath tickled my neck. He lifted his head and looked into my eyes. "From the moment I first saw you, you were a vision in the clouds." He brought one hand up and held my cheek, his thumb rubbing near the corner of my eye as he searched my face.

I directed his hands downward to take off my matching underwear. He moved us to the bed all the while rubbing my ass. I felt the coolness of the comforter on my back and the warmth from Eoin's body on top of me. He kissed my stomach as he slowly slid the remainder of my underwear down my legs.

"Oh, god," I moaned as I sat up and pulled him back to my lips. I unclasped my bra without breaking our kiss and my breasts fell out freely.

I heard Eoin curse with a guttural groan as he broke the kiss and took one of my nipples into his mouth. I bit my lip on a moan and hugged his head tightly to my chest running my hands over his soft curls. His head traveled down my body and between my legs. His soft, curly hair between my fingers moved as he did. I brushed his hair involuntarily, "I love you, Eoin of Accolon." He was there. I could see his beautiful head of hair at my most precious spot. I felt his hum of acknowledgment vibrate against me. I could tell that he didn't want to stop his devotion as he swirled his tongue in rhythmic circles, stopping only to suck and then swirl it in an unwavering pattern that left me panting and crying out his name. He stuck in and out two…three fingers in time with his tongue.

I couldn't recall what exploded first, the stars behind my eyes or my heart that felt like it would beat out of my chest. All I remembered was hearing the low rumbling of Eoin's pleased laughter as my breathing slowed and my body felt limp and satiated.

"What are you thinking, *mo chridhe.*" Eoin's voice was husky as he was still trying to catch his breath.

"A lot of things." I turned on my side and lifted the book so Eoin could see all of me, letting the thinly veiled sheets hug every curve of my body. My cheeks burned imagining Eoin's eyes running up and down the length of me.

"Me too. Especially how I canna wait to run my hands up and down every curve of your body," he let out a groan, but then chuckled. "You're thinking of something else though, aren't you?"

I was still riding a wave of pleasure, and it was given new life with Eoin's intentional observation of me. "You can read me like a book, can't you?" I was delighted when I heard his rich laughter at my terrible pun. "I was just thinking about what I'm going to do once I get home—how to plan a life for us."

"You don't have to do that alone anymore, love. I'm here, and soon I'll be right there beside you. Not just for…what just happened between us…but for everyday life."

"I appreciate that, but I want to make sure you have a safe place to land and decompress. You are entering into a new world, after all. A different time." I chuckled at the prospect of seeing Eoin's face when he would soon take on my world and all that the 21st century had to offer.

"You have some idea forming, don't you? I can see it dancing in your eyes, love."

"Ugh, I can't wait until you're here so I can read your expression too!" I covered my eyes and listened as the harmony of our laughter filled the room.

"I await that day, more than you know, Catriona." His laughter tapered, as did mine.

"I do have an idea, about the future."

"Aye? Tell me." The deep timbre of his voice resounded between my thighs.

"I want us to stay in Scotland, so, it's less of transition for you. And, after this year, I don't want to be too far from my dad and Jeremy."

"You don't want to take your dream job here in Paris? I support you, of course, but you dinna need to fash about me. I'll be happy wherever you are, *mo chridhe.*"

"No, Scotland is my home. It's where my family is and will be. It's where my heart belongs."

"Aye, whatever your heart wants, my love, it's yours."

"Well, then, that settles it. I'm going to see if there are any editorial jobs in Edinburgh or Glasgow, and we can go from there!"

"Aye. If that's what you want, it's yours. I shall need to venture back to the castle to talk to Valez about my world and what needs to be done before I depart it."

My heart tightened at the thought of Eoin being in Valez's presence after their last encounter at the Black Cuillin Ridge—when I saw the sky fill with red lightning, knowing now that it was Valez striking Eoin and leaving him for dead.

Eoin's reassuring voice released the iron grip around my heart and then lulled me into a deep sleep—into a dreamland of a life spent with him, forever.

A few days later, as I was sitting in Mum's chair searching for editorial jobs in Edinburgh and a few in Glasgow, my eyes grew wide when I saw a familiar publisher—Luath Press in Edinburgh.

I had interned there during my last semester at uni, and looking back, I loved the independent feel—being able to publish books based on heart rather than solely on marketability.

I clicked on the advertisement for editor, and began filling out their online application, uploading my

CV and covering letter. The book sat open on my lap so Eoin could be a part of this process—a part of a future we were building together.

As soon as I submitted my application, I lifted the book so Eoin could see the screen when Dad walked in. He did a double-take, either at where I was sitting or at the book I seemed to be holding backwards as the pages faced my laptop.

"Whatcha doing, pet?" He lifted one brow.

I settled the book back in a natural position. "Just applying to a job in Edinburgh."

My dad tried to hide his relief and pure elation at the prospect of his daughter staying close by, but he cleared his throat, "Are you sure? You're not just staying for me and Jeremy, because if you really want to go back to Paris, I support you. Jeremy and I will be just fine, don't you worry."

"It's okay, Dad. It's what I want," I gave him a reassuring smile. "In fact, I just applied for an editor's position at my old internship."

"That's exciting! You'll be a shoo-in." Dad came

over and gave me a light kiss on the head, then settled back in his chair.

"I'm glad you and your father are speaking again, *mo chridhe.* He's listening to you and showing his support."

"He is."

"Hmm? What'd you say, dear?" Dad looked up from the paper.

"Nothing," I laughed along with Eoin in my head, as Jeremy came into the room.

He clocked me laughing at the book that sat open on my lap and gave a little salute to Eoin as he passed.

"I'm starting to really like the lad—I can't wait to properly meet him!"

I just nodded and smiled, not wanting to confuse my dad more than I already had.

Later that week, as my shift ended at the library, my phone pinged—there in my inbox sat an email inviting me to interview for the editor's position at Luath Press on Monday.

My heart leapt and thumped rapidly, but then a quiet calmness fell over me—a feeling that everything would work out.

My feeling was correct. After the interview, the editorial manager remembered me from uni and offered me the job outright—I accepted.

On the way back down the very steep hill to the Waverley train station, I phoned Ludo about his most generous offer, but that I sadly had to decline it.

"I completely understand, Catriona. I'm so happy for you, and that you'll be closer to your family. Please don't hesitate to contact me if you need anything or to just give a quick update."

"Thank you, Ludo, for everything."

Once comfortably seated by the train's window, I closed my eyes on the journey back to Crieff. Next, I would have to tell Jonathan that I was leaving the library—leaving the place that helped me rebuild a new life from the ashes of loss and gave me an unbelievable story that I would never forget.

A story that was still being written—one where Eoin and I could take the pen and write our story together.

***

Eoin

Eoin did his best to keep his pace to match Catriona's timeline. Although the thought of finally being with Catriona, in the real world, was all-encompassing, he was also thankful that her process of getting there took some time.

After their improvised lovemaking in Catriona's hotel room, which still left him breathless, all he could do was picture her standing there bare before him. He could still hear her soft voice telling him what she wanted him to do to her. He growled and told her all the ways he would touch her with his hands, his mouth, his tongue…

Eoin wasted no time packing so he could make his words a reality and fulfill Catriona with more than just his voice from a book. He grabbed the staff and left what was likely the last green patch in Caledonia—in his world.

As he made his way back to what was once his home for six centuries, he found himself weeping at the state of it. The land around him was only dust—gray and black as far as the eye could see.

Even when his world was just a story, it still had

some variation of colors that mimicked the world it strived to portray. It was not as vibrant as the real world, but it was still a comforting place they could all call home.

Eoin shuddered at the real-life implications that his world now possessed. He didn't know how to provide for his people without killing the source of their turmoil—Valez.

Deep down, Eoin knew his friend still resided inside the evil sorcerer, yet he didn't know how to bring him back. All he knew was that he could never bring himself to kill Valez.

As Eoin kept to what used to be the borders of his book—that was once just a long dark void—he remembered how he felt right before Catriona found him, how Valez sent him on a quest to patrol their borders and observe the ending for any changes—for any fading.

He remembered how tempted he was to jump into the void, either to be cascaded into the real world, where he longed to be even before he met Catriona or to be put out of his infinite misery of waiting for a reader he did not believe would come.

What he didn't know at the time was that the ending had, indeed, changed, that it had faded right before Catriona found him.

She was the reason he saw the disappearing path that he and Adalind would always walk down to their "happily-ever-after" before the reader closed the book for the very last time.

Eoin knew with all his heart that he and Catriona were never meant to make it to that ending and part ways. What they had planned was the ending to their new beginning.

Before that could happen, Eoin needed to do right by his people, and restore their world. He needed to ensure their safety and happiness before he could experience his.

After an arduous journey, Eoin made it to a clearing he knew all too well. To the left lied his makeshift camp—a place he once called home. He hadn't realized it was his purgatory—but it was one that was entirely in his control.

To the right, was the foreboding castle—a place that once represented a prison, a life he had no say in, a life dictated to him for centuries.

As he approached his camp, a ray of light from the heavens began to illuminate it, and Catriona's face lit up the overcast sky.

"Eoin! Guess what?"

"Ha! I have so many guesses, but go on, tell me, *mo chridhe*."

"Dad and I found a flat that is perfect for you and me in Edinburgh!"

"That's fantastic news! And as soon as I find employment, I'll pay back restitution for all you've done for us, Catriona."

"Don't worry about that, Eoin. We'll figure it out together. All you have to do is get out of there."

"It's in hand, my love. Just give me the signal, and I'll be there, I promise. I love you."

"I love you too. Speak soon, there's so much to do!" The joy emanating from Catriona's squeal stirred so much in Eoin that he needed to sit down, as the clouds no longer contained her light.

Although his campsite had clearly been ransacked

by Valez's knights while he was on the run, his favorite and well-placed log was still there, resting on the bank overlooking the loch. Eoin sat down on "Old Faithful" and rested his face in his hands.

As the idea of leaving—finally entering Catriona's world—was becoming more real, an unfamiliar feeling overtook him. He suddenly became self-conscious. *Will Catriona accept me? She's never laid eyes on me. I may not be to her liking.*

The unrecognizable reflection that looked back at him from the water's surface startled him. He touched the greasy ends of his hair that now reached past his shoulders.

He grabbed at the coarse hair around his face. He knew it was there, and it itched like hell, but to see how long and scraggly it looked filling the surface of his face, he blanched. He was never able to grow hair before. This would not do for a woman so deserving of the king she had read about for months.

Eoin stripped down and jumped into the cold and refreshing water. It was not how he remembered it at all when he was merely a fictional character. Though it was dark and lifeless from the presence of Valez's knights, he was thankful it still retained water. Perhaps it was too deep and vast for their dark magic to suck it up entirely.

He washed his body and hair. Then, once out of the water, he took his knife to his beard and sheared off as much as he could, only nicking his face a few times near the top of his jaw and once on his chin. He cut his hair as best he could to where it hung before—curling just below his ears.

After a rudimentary search, he was able to find a clean outfit from a chest untouched from the ransack—a billowing, white tunic with brown trousers and boots. As he put on his gray cloak, tucking the staff underneath, he faced the castle. It was time to seal everyone's fate once and for all.

Eoin reached the castle walls, where two soulless knights stood watch. They didn't say anything when they spotted him below, just inclined their heads in question.

"I'm King Eoin of Accolon, and I wish to speak to your leader."

The knights looked at one another, nodded, and lifted the gate as four more came through flanking Eoin on both sides. Eoin braced for the bone-chilling sensation that he knew would run up and down his spine from their forceful hold.

As they dragged him through the courtyard, Eoin noticed how empty and deserted it looked. He saw a few ash-sunken faces, including the solemn faces of Grant, the horse master, and his wife Beatrice, peeking out of the windows—fearfully curious.

Eoin kept a brave face for his people, indicating that everything would be alright, that he would set it all straight—he would see to their safety and wellbeing before his departure.

When they made it to the great hall, the knights threw Eoin across the expanse, until he fell hard onto the stone floor before Valez on *his* throne.

Eoin looked around to catch the breath that had been knocked out of him. His eyes had a hard time adjusting to the degree of darkness that filled the hall as wooden boards fully covered the colorful stain-glass windows—not allowing an ounce of light to create tiny rainbows throughout the room.

Eoin remembered how the hall was used in celebration as they would all await each new reader who cracked open their book and began their story.

Eoin subtly clutched the staff close to his body underneath his cloak, reminding himself that he had the upper hand to reverse any and all damage Valez had enacted on his people, on his land. So, perhaps they could all start anew.

When Eoin stood and met Valez's eyes, all he could see was infinite darkness that replaced the bright gold irises of his once dear friend.

"Hello, Eoin," Valez sneered. "Welcome back."

"Valez. We need to talk." Eoin's words echoed what Valez had said to him the night of the masquerade party, the night Valez imprisoned him in an inescapable cell—when his story became unwritten, and he thought all hope was lost.

Eoin stood in the same place his story would always begin, only this time, it would have a different beginning, one where it would be told only once—by him and Catriona.

He looked up in the same posture he would always await her as she began to read—only this time, he awaited Catriona's call for him to join her, forever.

Chapter 21

Catriona

My last day at the library was only a half-day—Jonathan wouldn't hear any of my protests of working a full shift, urging me to get to Edinburgh as fast as I could. With his persistence, I didn't insist any further as I was eager to settle into my new flat and welcome Eoin into my world.

After the last book was put into the Library of Innerpeffray's brand-new, fully operational database that I had spent the last few months creating, I looked around at the two rooms that had been my workspace for over half a year. I felt immensely proud knowing the small part I had played in reviving this magical Highland library for generations to come.

Before I left, I turned around and pictured what this room looked like on my very first day—books and boxes littered the floor, so much so that I couldn't even see the puce-colored carpet below. The white built-in bookcases had a thin layer of dust, making them seem almost gray in color. I also remembered the day I found

Eoin's book—*The Adventures of Accolon.*

I ran my hand gently along my satchel, where I felt the hard surface of the book inside. I could never have imagined what I found at the bottom of a long-forgotten box. As I sat on the floor that lonesome night, I felt as if my life no longer had any meaning—but what I didn't know then was that I was holding my entire future in my hands.

I spun on my heel, holding back tears that I knew were bound to come after my goodbye to Jonathan. He was stuffed behind his giant desk in his tiny office, just as he had been during my interview.

When he spotted me, his eyes went wide, and he dashed out of his office as fast as he could, squeezing out of the tight space, "So, you off to the big city then?"

"I am. Thank you, Jonathan for taking a chance on me, and letting me be a part of such a special place."

"Ach, no. It is I who am thankful that you stumbled onto my doorstep that day. Because of you, we'll have lenders next week who will be able to check out books from our newest collection—and give these old stories some fresh eyes!" He gestured to the centuries-old manuscripts on display in their glass confinements.

I stopped my mind from picturing how close Eoin came to that same fate because of me. I also pushed past the idea that these other books were alive, just like Eoin, and were trapped in one place without a reader to give their stories a purpose. "It was nothing, I'm just glad I could help."

"Are you joking? If it hadn't been for you, it would have taken Shona and me years to get it fully operational. Even then, it wouldn't have had your unique touch," he winked.

My heart filled with warmth at Jonathan's appraisal of my work, and I darted forward to give him a small hug. He was startled at first, but then he sighed and gave me two light pats on my shoulders.

"Get going now. I will not keep you any longer, lass." He dashed a few tears away from underneath his glasses that I pretended not to see for his sake.

I made it to the front door when I heard him call out, "Catriona. Did you ever finish that book I was meant to read after you?"

My entire body froze, and I dropped my hand to my satchel. I turned around to see Jonathan in the doorway of his office. "No, I haven't. I'm almost finished. Is… is it alright if I bring it back the next time, I'm in town? I doubt it'll be that long—I'll be homesick before I know it," I gave a nervous laugh then held my breath, waiting for his reply.

"Of course, my dear. No hurry at all." The jovialness of his voice allowed me to breathe easy as I gave one last wave on my way out the door.

I was glad when Jonathan mentioned that Shona would not be coming in until later—hopefully after I was long gone. I placed my satchel in the front seat beside me. I was just about to open the book and give Eoin an update when Shona pulled up right beside me. I quickly tucked it back in my satchel and climbed out as Shona came around her car to mine.

"Catriona, I'm so glad I caught you. I just wanted to say…good job. Your section of the library looks presentable for new lenders," she gave me a tight-lipped smile.

I stood beside my car and leaned against the open

door that stood as a barrier between us. "Thank you, Shona. I'm glad I could have contributed."

Shona opened her mouth to speak, but it turned into a widening gap as her eyes darted to the book peeking out of my satchel.

"Catriona, what book is that?"

"Umm. Just a book I found in my section that Jonathan is letting me check out. I'm our first lender, isn't that funny?"

She ignored my attempted diversion. "It looks older than your books, it should belong in my collection. If I'm not mistaken, from what I can see…no, it can't be!"

The humor dropped from my face at her tone of astonishment. "What?"

"Is that…? It can't be…"

When I didn't answer, she started to make her way to the passenger side. I jumped back behind the wheel and put it into gear before she could get reach the door handle.

I sped backward, making sure that I didn't hit her as she shouted at my car window, "Stop, Catriona! You don't understand! That book could be the key to unlocking

Scotland's entire history, even our future!"

I spun the car forward and out of the parking lot until I was too far out of reach to hear her shouted pleas. I tried to ignore what she was shouting about Eoin's book, along with her look of utter shock. Was she about to say *The Adventures of Accolon?* How could she have automatically known its title without fully seeing it?

I let out a shaky breath—we were leaving for Edinburgh today. Dad and Jeremy were loading everything while I was at the library. I found myself even more anxious to get on the road as Shona's determining voice still rang in my head—unsure how far she would go to get her hands on *my* book.

The sooner we got there, the sooner I could be assured of Eoin's safety. After that, I would gladly hand off his book to Jonathan and by extension, Shona for whatever she wanted to do with it.

Until Eoin is here with me, I won't stop fighting for him. There are some things in life that can't be forced, but this isn't one of them. Eoin and I will determine our own future together. I'll be damned if anyone tries to take that from us.

As I pulled into our driveway, seeing my guys ready to go, I felt a wave of relief—Eoin and I were only one step away from finally living our dream.

***

Eoin

"Well? What are you waiting for, Eoin? What is it that you and I need to talk about before I throw you back into your doorless cell?" Valez laughed at his own wittiness, prompting forced laughter from the rest of his court.

"You've done it, Valez. You've proven yourself to be a worthy adversary," Eoin paused, and the laughter ended as Valez's posture grew rigid. Eoin continued, "For reasons you cannot comprehend, I don't have it in my heart to kill you, nor do I think we can both exist in Caledonia."

"Are you proposing something, Eoin? It seems to me that I'm the only one with the upper hand and I am in no mood to negotiate. I could kill you with a wave of my…"

"Staff?" Eoin removed his cloak with a flourish, brandishing it in front of him.

"Guards! Get him!" Five supernatural guards flanked each side of the hall and marched toward Eoin.

"Ah, ah, ah. Have them stop right there, Valez, or I'll snap your precious staff in half." Eoin wrapped his hands around the stem, bending it until it creaked against his forceful strain.

"Halt," Valez's face burned in anger, but he quickly adopted a look of good humor when he realized what cards Eoin possessed. "Alright, Eoin. I'll play. What do you suggest, then?"

Eoin tried to push past the memory of Valez having the same candor right before a friendly game of chess as they discussed everything under the sun, but that felt like a lifetime ago—something Eoin knew he would never get back.

"My kingdom, my people, and this staff are all yours, Valez."

"What a generous offer, Your Highness, but besides my staff, I have all of those things," Valez's voice was confident, yet fear flashed across his eyes. He knew he wouldn't be able to control the people of Caledonia for much longer without his staff, without his magic.

Once the people realized he was virtually powerless, they would rise up against him and overthrow his reign of terror, and reestablish Eoin as their true monarch.

"Ahh, but we both know that one greatly outweighs all the others," Eoin waved the staff tauntingly in his hand, eliciting a growl from Valez.

"All right, Eoin. What do you want?"

"You are a very talented sorcerer, Valez. So, I know that with this staff and just a few words spoken, you can transport me anywhere…to another world even."

Valez laughed mockingly, "And I assume there are certain terms you wish to establish before you return my staff and I send you to this unknown world?"

"I don't need you to believe me, but yes. In exchange for your staff and my freedom, I also demand that the people and their land be restored to their full health and glory—to live out the rest of their lives in peace and comfort and that you become the benevolent leader that they deserve."

Valez didn't laugh this time. He narrowed his eyes at Eoin. He knew that Valez would do anything to have his powers back, even acquiescing to the terms Eoin set before him.

"Those are steep terms, Eoin. It does make me wonder, however, what or, more accurately, who is waiting for you in this brand-new world that would tempt you to trust me to keep these terms, not only that but to leave your friends and even your darling queen behind?" At Valez's gesture, a knight opened the side door and Sam, Isla, and finally Adalind filed out in heavy iron chains.

"Let them go, Valez, and you'll have your staff, your magic, and this kingdom—we can both get what we want!"

A soft light filtered through the dingy hall, as Catriona came into glorious view. "Eoin? It's time, baby…it's time to come home."

Panic filled Eoin's entire chest, "Let them go Valez, and the staff is yours."

Valez snapped his fingers, and the guards unlocked each and every shackle. As the chains fell to the stone floor, time seemed to stand still. When the ringing of each chain ceased, Isla ran to the far-end of the wall with the others, but Sam and Adalind stayed and stared at Eoin.

"Eoin, you fool, you can't leave us! That's not how this works! If you leave us for Catriona, what will happen to the rest of us?" Adalind's voice rose an octave as each word was lined with despair.

Catriona called his name again, and he closed his eyes to focus only on her voice. "It'll be alright, Adda. I'm doing this for all of you," Eoin held out the staff to Valez.

As Valez floated down and took the staff, Eoin saw Sam turn his head with a look of utter shame. Eoin's heart burned in the pain that no one, save Adalind, could remember what or who they were, nor fully comprehend what he was doing. To them, it looked as if their beloved king no longer cared for them—that he was so cavalier and heartless as to gamble their lives away to an evil sorcerer for something seemingly unreal.

Eoin tried to push those haunting thoughts out of

his mind and instead, he looked up at Catriona. She didn't look worried, only hopeful at his promised arrival. "You got what you wanted, Valez. Now send me to 21st-century Edinburgh—to Catriona."

Eoin closed his eyes, ignoring the shocked gasps and judgmental murmurs of his people that reverberated throughout the hall.

As a blinding light filtered through Eoin's closed eyes, he flung them open. The last thing he saw was that familiar light from Valez's staff and Catriona's lovely face.

***

Catriona

Almost everything I ever owned and needed was in my new flat. My guys did an amazing job bringing heavy furniture, boxes, and all the rest up four narrow flights of steps.

Once my bedroom side table was in place, I tucked the book safely in the drawer until everything was ready for Eoin to come out.

Dad rushed back down, claiming he forgot one last

thing, leaving Jeremy and I alone in the living area surrounded by boxes.

"So, what's the plan, Cat?"

I blushed knowing exactly what he was asking. "Well, once you two get out of here, I'll make sure everything is ready, open the book, and let Eoin know that it's time."

"It's still so weird to think about—that a fictional character in a book is real…but I can't wait to meet him in person…to make sure he's good enough to be with my sister. You know the drill."

"Who's not good enough to be with who now?" We heard Dad's voice in the doorway, but we only saw a chair and his legs.

"Dad? What are you doing? Is that...?" He maneuvered Mum's chair until it fit through the threshold, and he sat it down in the middle of the room.

"Aye, I thought you'd want a reminder of her. A soft place to read and write. So, a part of her will always be in your life…no matter where it takes you."

I flung myself in his arms as tears hit his shoulder

and darkened his gray t-shirt. I felt Jeremy enfold us both. Although this habit had only come from Mum's death, it was one that solidified our shared bond, our shared grief—that made us a family.

"I'm so proud of you, Catriona, and I know that your Mum would have been as well," Dad leaned back as Jeremy and I detached ourselves.

"Thanks, Dad," I flicked away a single tear that still rested at the corner of my eye.

"All right, well, that's all of it. We'll let you get settled. Phone us if you need anything, love," my dad said, kissing me on the head and starting for the door. "Lock this when we leave."

"Yes, Sir," I laughed as Jeremy slung one arm around my shoulder and pulled me into a side hug.

"I'll come visit in a week or so, and we can all go out," he winked at me.

My smile widened as I couldn't wait to get drinks with Jeremy and Eoin together. "Sounds good. Love you both."

"Love you," my guys said in unison as I shut the

door. I locked it, just as my dad instructed, but I began to find that I felt safer as I was now on my own for the very first time. I was further comforted knowing that Eoin would be here soon and would protect me forever.

I wanted to make sure everything was ready for him to make his transition as seamless as possible. It would be naive to think there wouldn't be some sort of culture shock, or was there such a thing as a world-traveling shock? *Similar to time traveling, I imagine.*

After a quick run to the store, I had bags full of food, a couple of bottles of whiskey, extra pillows for a safe landing, and a first aid kit—just in case. I laughed at this assortment of items and what they represented, but still, I had no idea what to expect.

The butterflies that had resided in my stomach since I felt Eoin's hand through the pages were fluttering rapidly. I pulled the book out of my drawer and set it open on the bed as I settled my nerves.

I stared at the blocks of text—Eoin's original story. "Eoin? It's time, baby." I looked around my flat—*soon to be our flat*. "It's time to come home." I waited, knowing what was at stake in his world, that it might take some time.

When a half an hour passed, and the words remained the same, I called his name again. I kept my mind away from the memories of when he was gone before—from every scenario that could involve Valez.

As I stood from the bed and turned the book towards me, the blocks of text faded, and cursive words in red ink began to form. A chill ran down my spine as I didn't hear Eoin's voice in my head.

"Hello, Catriona. It's an honor to finally meet you."

"Who are you? Where's Eoin?!"

"Well, that's really up to you, Catriona. His fate is in your hands now."

I swallowed what felt like molten lava. I knew exactly who I was speaking to. "What do you want, Valez?"

"Ah, clever girl, I can see why Eoin is so taken with you—why he's so determined to risk the lives of his people for *you*."

"Just tell me what I have to do to be with Eoin and I'll do it."

"You two are quite the pair, aren't you? Well, then, when you're ready, touch the pages of the book, and I'll bring you to him."

I looked around my flat. What was meant to be Eoin's and my future, our home, felt empty and cold.

Part of me knew that I couldn't trust Valez, but I also knew that he would never let Eoin leave the book now. He took Eoin, knowing I would do anything to be with him. Valez wanted me in the book, for what reason, I did not know, nor did it matter.

I wrote a quick letter to Jeremy and left it on my bed, explaining as best I could where I had gone, and to take care of the book—to take care of me—until Eoin and I could return.

After wiping away the tears that had formed, I tried hard not to think about what my disappearance would do to my dad, to Jeremy, to Gemma.

As I approached the open book, where Valez's last words remained in blood-red ink, I closed my eyes and paused for just a second.

After I finish a book, I hold it tight against my chest,

absorbing every part of the story, reminiscing the feelings that had struck a chord within me. There is satisfaction in finishing a book—it's the feeling of completing a hard day's work—but there is also this terrible void, a sadness, like having to say goodbye to old friends, not knowing when you will see each other again, yet reassuring one another that it is just "so long," instead of knowing deep down that this is the end.

When that feeling would hit me with any other book, I would quickly categorize it on the shelf, slowly leaving a world immersed back into my own. This time, as I picked up *The Adventures of Accolon,* I would not be saying goodbye—this would not be the end of the story. Instead, I would be a part of it.

As red lightning blinded my vision and what felt like pins and needles pricking my entire body, all I could think about was Eoin—that no matter what world we might be in, we would finally be together.

Acknowledgments

The Enchanted Reader is a love letter to you, my dear reader. Catriona and Eoin's story began with what every reader desires—what if the magic of reading didn't wear off? What if the reader affected the characters of a book just as the characters affect the reader? There are little details we all do while reading a book that you will certainly catch.

This book would not be possible without so many people around me who had an equal part in making my lifelong dream come true that my words of gratitude feel somewhat inadequate.

I will be forever grateful to my publisher, Steve Cawte, who took a chance on me and was so patient as he listened to my questions, concerns, and suggestions to bring my vision to life. Being a part of the publishing process with him was a rare opportunity that not many authors get. I am thankful that he personally advocates for authors and their work.

I want to thank Justin Wiggins, who introduced me

to Steve and endorsed my manuscript. He has provided me with so much support as a fellow author who has been through this process multiple times. And none of this would be possible without my college friend, Caroline Myer, who came across my posts and introduced me to Justin.

Before it could make it to Steve's desk, Peyton Garland, a brilliant editor, author, and friend, sat down with me week after week to give me edits and feedback for each and every chapter. Establishing that schedule drove me to produce the best content I could and meet my word count. She introduced me to writers' conferences, walked me through agent submissions and pitches, and blurbed my book! Most importantly, she gave me the confidence that I could be a published author. I can't even begin to repay her for her invaluable contribution.

In turn, I have a friend whom I've known since high school, who listened as I told her about this story over our weekly dinners; not only that, but Jaime Ballew Zerbe gave me plot ideas, character development, and read a huge portion of my manuscript alongside her wedding planning! During many of our dinners, her black Labrador Retriever, Savannah Grace, joined us and became a huge inspiration for Gorgon the Dragon's puppy-like demeanor.

I want to thank a few people who read my manuscript and gave me so much feedback and encouragement. Justine Mclatchie not only read my book, but she was the first one to ever hear this story. On a train to Edinburgh during our master's publishing course, I had just met Justine, yet she shared with me stories she had written and others that she had in the works, and that's when I shared with her the idea for *The Enchanted Reader.* After that, a beautiful, transcontinental friendship was formed. A huge thanks to Amanda Jester and my father, Roger Law, for reading a very early and unpolished version of my manuscript!

I owe the world to the greatest friend a girl can have! Kayla Koslosky not only encouraged me, but she took it upon herself to be my social media manager. Before I could even ask, she drew up a marketing plan, showed me how to optimize social media platforms, and played a huge part in envisioning the book cover's design. Beyond her expertise, she provided me with so much emotional support that I'm not sure how she coped, but I am indescribably thankful for her.

Lastly, I want to thank my loving family, who have been with me through every step of the process, knowing that this has been my dream since childhood. To my mother, Brenda Law, my sister, Sarah Law, and her dog, Dallas, who also inspired Gorgon; to my sister, Jessica Fosdick, my brother-in-law, Matthew Fosdick, and my beautiful niece, Evie, thank you all for being there for me and believing in me. And to my grandma, Anna Demory, thank you for never giving up hope, even when, at times, I did.

Thank you all for making *The Enchanted Reader* a reality!

ABOUT THE AUTHOR

Molly discovered a lifelong love for Scotland and its tragic history and craggy mountains during her master's program in publishing studies at the University of Stirling, where she studied and lived for a year.

She is fascinated by fairytale retellings, especially the distinction between choice and fate. Her stories reveal the ramifications of grief as she cares for her mother, who has Early-onset Alzheimer's in Virginia.

As a lover of the written word, she has been an editor for over eight years. She is a huge Austenite who collects beautiful copies of *Pride and Prejudice.*

Catriona's story continues in the pages of Eoin's book in this magical sequel.

Read on for a sneak peek of *The Enchanted Story*.

The house was quiet without Catriona. When Dad and I entered the sitting room after moving Cat into her flat in Edinburgh, we avoided voicing what we were both thinking: *how was this going to work?*

The sensation of losing Mum came over both of us, just as it was seven months ago—just me and him right after Mum's fatal car accident—Catriona still in Paris, blissfully unaware that our whole world had just ended.

Coming home from Catriona's new flat, knowing she would soon start her new life with Eoin, had an unsettling ring to *that* day—the day that we lost the very heart of our family. In the last year, healing came over us all, and we were able to start anew.

But unlike that dark day, this seemed to be the beginning of a fresh start that we all needed, and Catriona deserved it more than anyone—after sacrificing her life to take care of Dad and me in our debilitating grief that had diminished hers for so long.

I found myself just staring at the vacant spot that once held Mum's chair, a vibrant square of gray amongst the remaining faded carpet.

"We'll be all right, Son," Dad held my shoulder for a second but then naturally moved to his chair to focus on anything but the huge void that the women in our lives had left.

"Yeah, we will," I sat down on the couch and stretched out my legs. I focused on the game alongside Dad, not thinking about how anxious I felt about visiting Cat next week and finally meeting Eoin.

I ignored every preconception I ever had about what a fictional character would be like—look like, act like, and instead trusted my sister in whatever life she wanted to lead.

A week went by rather quickly—to my surprise. Dad and I moved around each other with very few words used, yet we both felt some contentment in our new routine.

It wasn't until Thursday morning, when Dad asked if I had heard from Catriona, that I felt a lurch in the pit of my stomach. I hadn't heard from her either, but I had pushed that fact far back into the cavities of my subconscious with rational excuses until Dad shattered my glass walls.

"Catriona? Yeah…she texted me. I'm meeting her at her flat tomorrow after she gets off work. I'll be back Sunday afternoon," I lied to stop him from worrying. *Since there is probably nothing to worry about*—that thought also stopped me from worrying.

Dad nodded, but his eyes brimmed with unshed tears as he shifted back to his morning paper, and I headed off to school. He was obviously disappointed that she had contacted me but hadn't bothered calling him—possibly fearing they had fallen back into their old, stalemate relationship.

I cursed Catriona in my head for putting me in that position, all for her new "boy toy," or whatever the hell he was.

As I neared the bus stop, something about that explanation just didn't add up. Catriona gave up her whole life to take care of us; she wouldn't just piss off because of a man, even if he was some fictional, ancient king.

The next day, as I grabbed my things to walk to the train station, the feeling in my stomach deepened. Without a second thought, I took Catriona's spare keys that she gave us "in case of emergencies" and sprinted out the door with one loud goodbye to Dad.

My knee shook the whole train ride, eliciting a sideways glance from an elderly woman with a small white hat attached atop her head and a Pekingese dog sitting perfectly poised on her lap across the aisle.

No doubt she thought I was some sort of druggie in the final stages of withdrawal—headed to Edinburgh for a score. Part of me wanted to feed into her bias more and start chattering my teeth and biting my fingernails, but I resisted the urge as the train pulled into Waverley Station.

I bolted as the doors opened—that certainly did it for the posh hat lady as I heard her say in a high-pitched voice, "Why, I never!" that harmonized with the squeak that came out of her little dog that I presumed was its bark. I couldn't stand on society's polite manners as I normally would with the uneasiness that squirmed within.

Others noticed my ill-kept manners as I dashed down Prince Street, bumping far too many shoulders and elbows with shouts aimed angrily in my fading direction.

I didn't stop until I reached the outside of her flat. With one hand resting on my knee, I rang the buzzer to Cat's flat with the other while wheezing a lungful of air.

When no answer came, I used the first key for the outside door and filled my lungs with enough air to run up four flights of narrow stairs.

Once I reached her door, I stopped short. *She could still be in there and simply not have heard the buzzer. She could be in the shower.* My mind still rationalized the most likely explanations, so I knocked. I knocked again. *But if that were true, Eoin would answer, wouldn't he?*

My heart raced, and my fingers shook as I put the second key in the lock, bracing myself for whatever I was about to find.

My eyes adjusted slowly to the darkness around me—unpacked boxes were left where Dad and I had left them when we moved Cat in. Mum's chair was still in the place Dad had set it down. It looked like it hadn't been used.

"Cat?" My voice cracked as it held back a hundred emotions. Her flat looked like she hadn't been here all week. No sign of life. I hesitantly flipped the light switch on in her bedroom and let out a lungful of air that I didn't realize I had been holding—the bedroom was empty. I searched the adjoining bathroom—nothing.

As I turned back, I saw it, on the bed—*the book.* Beside it lay a letter. Even from where I was standing, I could see it was in Catriona's handwriting.

I darted toward the bed and grabbed the letter, ignoring that blasted book altogether. Until I comprehended what she had written:

Dear Jeremy,

I know that in a week's time, you will have made it back to my flat. God knows what you and Dad will have gone through not hearing from me, but I hope that this letter will bring a small amount of comfort and explanation.

Eoin was meant to depart his book and join me in our world—with the help of Valez, the wizard of his story. But instead of honoring this agreement, Valez has taken Eoin. I don't know why, but Jer, I have to save him, I have to!

I know you'll understand, although I can imagine it won't be easy, and I know you'll be angry at first, but please take care of the book while I'm gone. Take care of me and Eoin, Jer. Keep us safe—don't let the book out of your sight. Its importance is far greater than you can ever imagine.

I'll do everything in my power to get us back…but I don't want you to be alone in this out there, so tell anyone you wish—anyone who will believe you and help, that is.

Let Dad and Gemma know I'm all right. Everything is going to be all right—I promise.

Love you,

Cat

"Son of a bitch!" I yelled into the practically empty space. I began to laugh despite myself, and tears escaped at the same time when I heard my own voice echo from the wall. *Cat was right. She knew I'd be angry as hell.*

Before my mind properly comprehended what this all meant, I saw movement out of the corner of my eye. I placed the letter back on the bed and hovered over the book.

What was once an empty page was now halfway full of words, and it continued to write itself until I saw her name—*Catriona Lamont.*

Made in the USA
Middletown, DE
13 August 2024

58604652R00285